D0340251

THE
COPELANDS

By Doug Bowman from Tom Doherty Associates

Gannon
Sam Curtin
The Three Lives of Littleton Blue
The H&R Cattle Company
Houston
The Guns of Billy Free
The Quest of Jubal Kane
The Copelands

THE COPELANDS

★

DOUG BOWMAN

A TOM DOHERTY ASSOCIATES BOOK

NEW YORK

This is a work of fiction. All the characters and events portrayed in this novel are either fictitious or are used fictitiously.

THE COPELANDS

Copyright © 1999 by Doug Bowman

All rights reserved, including the right to reproduce this book, or portions thereof, in any form.

This book is printed on acid-free paper.

A Forge Book
Published by Tom Doherty Associates, LLC
175 Fifth Avenue
New York, NY 10010

Forge® is a registered trademark of Tom Doherty Associates, LLC.

Library of Congress Cataloging-in-Publication Data

Bowman, Doug.
    The Copelands / Doug Bowman. — 1st ed.
      p. cm.
    "A Tom Doherty Associates book."
    ISBN 0-312-86547-3 (alk. paper)
    I. Title.
  PS3552.O875712C66   1999
  813'.54—dc21   99–26718
                                              CIP

First Edition: October 1999

Printed in the United States of America

0 9 8 7 6 5 4 3 2 1

To one of America's foremost guitarists, Mr. Tom Morrell, who has been my friend for most of my life.

PART ONE

★

I

★

Seth Copeland had known Emerald Jones since early childhood, and had proposed marriage on Christmas Day, 1855. The wedding had taken place the very next morning, after the parents of each of the young lovers voiced the opinion that the ceremony should be performed without delay. It was a known fact that the youngsters had on occasion spent time together when nobody was watching, some of the old folks were saying, and, "There just weren't no tellin' what young people might do with nobody keepin' an eye on 'em."

The suspicions of the elders had been vindicated seven months later, when Emerald Copeland gave birth to twin boys. Though not identical, the twins bore a strong resemblance to each other and weighed exactly six pounds apiece at birth. "Both ubb'm are the spit 'n' image o' their grandpa," one of the older male cousins had said, the same hour the boys were born. "I reckon they'll start lookin' a little more like Seth afore long, but right now, all red an' wrinkled up like 'at, they look jist like old Dan." All present agreed that the babies indeed favored their paternal grand-father, Daniel Copeland.

Having come into the world on the same day during the summer of 1840, Seth Copeland and Emerald Jones had still been a few months less than sixteen years old on their wedding day. Born ten miles apart in Caldwell County, Kentucky, they had met when they started school at the age of six. By the time they were seven, Seth had already told anyone who would listen that he intended to marry Emerald Jones someday.

Though still in his early teens when that day came, Seth Copeland stood almost six feet tall and weighed a hundred eighty pounds. He was as tough as nails, some of his kinfolk claimed, and knowledgeable beyond his years. Refusing help from everyone who offered it, he built a log cabin with his own hands, a three-room dwelling with two porches that had drawn comments of approval from every builder who saw it.

The cabin rested atop a grassy knoll on the west bank of Donaldson Creek, where Daniel Copeland had given his son twenty acres of land the day the boy was born. Seth had chosen the location of his cabin when he was still a small boy, and his plan never varied during his growing years. When the building was finally standing many years later, it was exactly the way he had envisioned it.

The only advice he sought during the construction of the cabin was from his mother's oldest brother, who gave him some pointers on the building of a good fireplace and a chimney that would draw properly. Seth had followed Uncle Buford's instructions to the letter, and was well pleased with the finished product. He moved his bride into her new home in May, and the twins, who were very quickly christened Mark and Matthew by their grandfather, were born there during the first week of August.

Emerald Copeland continued to have a baby every year till the outbreak of the Civil War, in 1861. Then, after his father had agreed to take care of Emerald and her six children, Seth had ridden away to join the Army of Northern Virginia. Nothing was heard from him during the next four years except an occasional few lines of hurried scribbling that passed for a letter.

Then, apparently among the few soldiers on either side who had been neither physically nor emotionally scarred by the fighting, Seth Copeland was back in Caldwell County in the spring of 1865, shortly after the war was over. He had come through the conflict without a scratch, he said, and was ready to take up right where he had left off.

His enthusiasm evaporated quickly, however, and the only thing he planted was another baby in his wife's belly. Neither the fields nor the cabin had a look of permanence, and during the last week of June, he rode his mule into the yard and made an announcement. "We're gonna be moving west, Em," he said, then dismounted and tied the animal to a post. "I've traded the cabin and the whole twenty acres to Uncle Buford. Got four big mules, two wagons, a good saddle horse, and a hundred dollars in gold.

"Now, putting that hundred with the money I already had, I believe I've got enough to set us up in Texas." He wiped sweat from his brow with his sleeve, then seated himself on the edge of the porch. "I don't know exactly why, Em, maybe it's because of all the other places I saw during the war, but I just don't want to live in Kentucky anymore."

Emerald was busy snapping green beans for the dinner pot. "It's just like I've been telling you ever since we were kids," she said. "I'll go wherever you go, and I'll do it without complaining."

He got to his feet. "All right, then," he said. "It's settled. Call all the kids together and tell them we're gonna be moving to Texas. As far as I know now, we'll be pulling out next Monday." He remounted and headed for his father's house at the top of the hill. "I'm gonna try to talk Pa and Ma into going with us," he said over his shoulder. "Pa's got enough money to buy a pretty big chunk of Texas if he wants it."

Daniel and Elsie Copeland listened enthusiastically as their son repeated one story after another that had been told to him during the war. Texas was beautiful, virgin country where a man with a thousand dollars could buy as much land as he could ride across in a day. The soil would grow almost anything, the stories went, and a man with a good rifle could truly live off the land. Millions of buffaloes roamed the plains, and deer, antelope, and many species of smaller game were there for the taking. "The men who told me all of these things were Texans, Pa," Seth said. "They were born and raised there, so they knew what they were talking about."

"I ain't doubting that for a minute, son," Dan Copeland said. "And this ain't the first time I've heard most of what you're saying. I've been hearing good things about Texas for close to twenty years, and I've got to admit that I'd like to own a little piece of it before it gets too high to buy." He looked toward his wife, who was sitting at the kitchen table nodding. Then he himself began to nod, saying, "I think you might have caught us at just the right time, son. Give us a little time to think on it and talk about it. I'll be letting you know something in a day or two."

Before the day was out the elder Copelands had decided to join their son and his growing family on their journey. A two-week delay in the date of departure was agreed to, for Daniel and Elsie needed extra time to dispose of certain things and to prepare for travel. Finally, after turning the farm over to his younger brother to sell, Daniel announced that he was ready to head for Texas.

In the middle of July, driving three covered wagons and trailing two saddle horses and two large dogs of indeterminate breeding, the Copelands crossed the Cumberland River and headed south. The lead wagon was driven by Dan Copeland, a six-footer who was now in his forty-sixth year. Elsie, who was a foot shorter and two years younger, sat on the seat beside him. Both were in good health, and neither of them had the slightest dread of starting over in a new place.

The decision that the grandfather should drive the lead wagon had been made by Dan Copeland himself, and though it was known to all that he had no more knowledge of the country between Kentucky and Texas than did his grandchildren, there were no dissenters. Besides, he had a pocket compass, a spyglass, and an up-to-date map, all he needed to show him the way west. And he would be going pretty far west. Only this morning he had made the announcement that he did not intend to slow down until he was halfway across Texas.

The second vehicle, referred to as the tool wagon because it was close to being overloaded with plows, hoes, saws, axes, and such, was alternately driven by the twins, Mark and Matthew, who would reach their tenth birthday in just three weeks. Sitting directly behind them on folded quilts were the three younger boys: Paul, Joseph, and Adam.

Seth and Emerald rode the third wagon, and their daughter, Rachel, who was thirteen months younger than the twins, sat on the seat between them. She was the only member of the small caravan who had been allowed to bring a trunk.

Aside from a Dutch oven and a wide assortment of pots, pans, and eating utensils, the wagon carried a month's supply of groceries. Added to the food the lead wagon carried, all agreed that they would have plenty to eat for at least two months, by which time they expected to be in Texas.

Two different men who had themselves made the journey west advised the Copelands to stay with the well-traveled roads whenever possible. "Every kind of thief and cutthroat you can imagine is out there waitin'," one of the men had said, "and they ain't all Indians. Now, I ain't sayin' th' Indians ain't dangerous, 'cause some of 'em are. But most of the red men you run into'll be beggars, not thieves and killers. It's th' damn white men that you'd better be leery of."

Both Seth and his father were heedful of the advice. They would at no time allow a distance of more than a few yards to accumulate between the wagons, and had worked out a set of signals to alert each other to the slightest hint of danger. And although they might not be able to hold off a large group of men intent upon taking their belongings, the Copelands would hardly be easy pickings.

Resting in its holster between Seth's feet was an 1860 model .44-caliber Army Colt revolver, a weapon with which he was adept. At arm's length behind him, and well hidden by the canvas, were three loaded rifles, all of them .44-caliber, twelve-shot Henrys. Dan Copeland also carried a Henry in the lead wagon, and a Colt six-shooter as well.

Though the twins could handle the Henrys, and were both fair marksmen, they were nonetheless ten-year-olds, and could not be expected to possess the judgment of a grown man. Therefore, Seth would keep all three of his rifles in his own wagon. If the time ever came when extra firepower was necessary, however, he would not hesitate to hand one of the weapons to each of the two youngsters.

They traveled in a southeasterly direction all morning, then pulled up at a roadside spring at midday. They allowed the animals to graze for an hour, while they themselves ate a cold meal of meat, bread, and apple jelly. Then they took to the road again, expecting to ford the Tennessee River before nightfall and make camp on the south bank. Three more days of travel would put them in Tennessee, where they would then turn west toward Arkansas.

There was more traffic on the road than either of the men had expected, most of it people on foot. What appeared to be entire families, many of them ragged, unkempt, and carrying large packs on their backs, were traveling in each direction. No doubt displaced by the war and now searching for any kind of gainful employment, most stepped aside and watched enviously as the Copelands passed in their well-built canvas-covered wagons. The Copeland women smiled and waved happily to the walkers, then dabbed at their own eyes and looked away.

They forded the Tennessee River an hour before sunset,

then pulled the three wagons side by side and set up camp on the south bank. As the two men and the twins set about unhitching the teams, Seth spoke to the three younger boys. "You boys look around till you find some dry leaves, twigs, and deadwood," he said, pointing. "Pile it all right over there beside the trunk of that big oak."

Emerald Copeland called after her youngest, "Don't you go wandering off by yourself now, Adam! You stay right with your brothers!"

The twins unhitched and unharnessed their mules. They allowed the traces, hames, harnesses, and collars to lie where they fell, for in the event of rain, water would not be harmful to any of them. When both of the men had completed the same chores with their own teams, all of the animals, having been watered when they forded the river, were led upstream and staked out on good grass.

Paul and Joseph, after striking a match and blowing on a pile of dead grass and leaves for a while, finally kindled a fire.

Mark, wanting nothing to do with a small chore like starting a cooking fire, motioned for Matthew to join him on the opposite side of the tree from their younger brothers. Paul, Joseph, and Adam were just kids, he said, while the two of them were almost grown. Hadn't Pa turned a team and wagon completely over to them this morning? Yes, and that by itself was enough to prove that they weren't children anymore. And hadn't he allowed them to harness and hitch up the team without even checking to see if they had done it right? Yes, and he had not looked it over later in the day, either. No doubt about it, Mark was thinking, he and his twin would be doing nothing but man's work from now on.

A short while later, Emerald set a big iron pot on the fire and poured in three half-gallon jars of venison stew she had cooked two days ago. She had six more in the wagon, and with the jars having been sealed with canning rubbers, the concoction would keep as long as was necessary. Nonetheless, she intended to serve the stew every day till it was gone, for it was a very nourishing meal, and warming it up took no more than ten minutes.

The Copelands would eat more dried beans than anything else during the trip. Aside from being the simplest things to cook, they were easy to transport and, when protected from moisture, would keep almost indefinitely.

A few minutes before sunset, Emerald began to dip bowlfuls of stew from the pot with a wooden ladle. "Come on, everybody," she said. "Get yourself a bowl of stew and a warmed-over biscuit." She pointed with the ladle to the twins. "Mark, Matthew, both of you get down to that river and wash your hands. You've been sitting there pulling ticks off them dogs ever since we got here."

"Aw, Ma," the boys said in unison, then headed for the river.

As the family sat eating their supper, neither of the dogs, named Booger and Beauregard, showed any interest in joining them, which was unusual. "They ain't got room for nothing else," Daniel said when one of the children pointed out the fact that both of the canines had refused part of a biscuit. "They've probably already eaten two or three rabbits apiece today."

"Four," Seth corrected, speaking around a mouthful of food. "They're big dogs."

When supper was over, the family sat around the campfire talking, with the men sipping coffee from tin cups. When the twins were told by their father that they could have half a cup apiece, Mark grabbed the pot and poured two cups almost full. Here was another sign that things were changing fast, the boy was thinking. He and Matthew were already being allowed to drink coffee right along with the men, and the day was not far off when they would be speaking with deep voices and shaving their faces. Yes, sir, Mark and Matthew Copeland were soon going to be big boys, probably even bigger than Pa and Grandpa.

Mark's thinking was correct on all counts. For quite

some time now it had been apparent to all that the twins, with their broad shoulders, long limbs, and wide, thick wrists, were indeed going to be big men. Even now, three weeks shy of their tenth birthday, each of them stood five six and weighed one-twenty. And despite the fact that they were not identical in appearance, they were exactly the same size. Seth had measured and weighed them a week ago, then stood them back to back and placed a book on top of their heads. The book had lain perfectly level.

As darkness closed in, Elsie reached for a cup and poured it half-full of coffee, which was a rare thing. "Might help to flush my kidneys," she explained, then seated herself on the ground and crossed her legs. She sat sipping the warm liquid slowly, while the flickering firelight played tricks with her silver-tinted hair and azure eyes. Staring into the fire, she appeared to be in deep thought.

She had been a dark-haired beauty in her younger days, with young men and old men alike calling her "the purtiest gal in Caldwell County." The fact that one Daniel Copeland had eventually won her heart and hand had nothing what-soever to do with his looks, most of the envious young men claimed, but was totally due to the fact that Dan's father, Rufus, was considered rich by poor people, and well-to-do by those who were well-to-do. Elsie had grabbed Dan Cope-land because she knew he would inherit all that money one of these days, they said, and then she would live a life of luxury.

The talkative young men who lost out to Dan Copeland had not even been half-right. While it was true that Elsie had known he would eventually come into at least half of his father's wealth, she had loved Dan since she was thirteen years old. Now, at age forty-four, she had been married to him for almost twenty-eight years, and though she had never had to wonder where her next meal was coming from, she had hardly lived a life of luxury. Dan Copeland did not be-lieve in luxuries.

When Elsie called it a day and crawled into her wagon,

the others were not far behind. Emerald and Rachel made themselves a bed in Seth's wagon, while the men and boys spread their bedrolls anywhere they could find a level spot. Once Paul, Joseph, and Adam had been ordered to quieten down and go to sleep, the only sound that could be heard in the dark camp was Seth Copeland's snoring.

2

★

Dan Copeland was up with a lighted lantern an hour before daybreak. After checking to see that the animals were all still on their picket ropes, he kindled a fire and put on the coffeepot.

Half an hour later, he sat sipping coffee alone, for none of the others had even turned over on their beds. Finally, maybe thinking that now was a good time to get some petting, the dogs walked over and lay down on either side of him. He patted their heads and rubbed their ears, then shooed them away.

Dan Copeland was a tall man, with brown eyes, a ruddy complexion, and dark hair that was now tinged with gray. And though he was well past middle age, he was still very close to the same weight he had been on his twenty-first birthday—about two hundred pounds. Any excess fat that had attempted to accumulate on his body had been discouraged by the fact that he was an incessant worker who was seldom still except when eating or sleeping. On several occasions his wife had accused him of laboring at pointless projects just for the sake of working.

Since reaching the decision to relocate in Texas, Dan had talked of little else. He had turned his twelve-hundred-acre farm, along with thirty head of livestock, over to his brother John, who was two years younger than himself. Instructed to sell the farm and send the proceeds to Dan, John had said that he just might deliver the money in person. "If things turn out good for you," he said, "I'm liable to put my own place on the market next year and bring my bunch to Texas."

Dan had assured his brother that nothing would please him more. "That'll be mighty good, John," he said. "I reckon we oughtta give our grandkids a chance to finish growing up together, anyhow. They all seem to get along a lot better'n you and I did when we were kids."

John chuckled, then nodded. "You just go on out there and see how things are, then let me know something by next spring. I'm sure liable to come knocking on your door, big brother." They shook hands, and a short time later, Dan led the wagons out of sight.

Now, as Dan poured his second cup of coffee, he saw Emerald step down from her wagon and head off into the woods. A few minutes later, she stepped into the glow of the campfire from the opposite direction. She had obviously circled down to the river after relieving herself, for she now stood drying her hands on the front of her ankle-length dress. "Good morning, Pa," she said. "Did you sleep well?"

He nodded. "Good as I could hope for, I reckon. Took me a long time to go to sleep, but I expect it to be like that till I finally know what lies ahead for us."

She patted his head and tousled his hair. "What lies ahead is a good life for all of us, Pa. You and Seth both have what it takes to make it anywhere, and the rest of us'll be right there to help." She poured herself half a cup of coffee. "You just quit worrying your head about it, 'cause everything is gonna work out fine." She patted her stomach. "Your next grandchild is gonna be born in Texas, you know."

He smiled, then nodded and winked.

Daybreak found Emerald squatted beside the fire frying Irish potatoes in an oversized iron skillet. When the hot grease began to pop, she reached for the lid, saying, "I guess I could have cooked these things a little bit drier, Pa, but they taste a lot better this way. Anyhow, we've got more lard than we can use up before it gets rancid."

Daniel nodded. "If the lard goes bad, we'll just stop somewhere and get some more," he said.

When the potatoes were done, Emerald poured them into a large baking pan to cool. Then, using the same skillet and a small amount of the same grease, she began to fry flour hoecakes. "We're just gonna have potatoes and hoecakes this morning, Pa," she said. "Ma's got five dozen eggs in her wagon, but I didn't want to wake her up." She stirred the fire with a stick for a moment, then placed the skillet back on the red-hot coals. "Tomorrow morning, I reckon, we'll have bacon and some of that good sorghum molasses you cooked up last year."

Daniel got to his feet. "That'll be fine, little girl." He headed for the woods to relieve himself. "Best I remember, last year's batch turned out pretty good," he added over his shoulder.

Emerald continued to fry one hoecake after another till her batter was gone. "This is a lot more bread than we'll eat for breakfast," she said to Daniel, who had now returned to the fire. "It sure won't go to waste, though. I imagine the kids'll be fighting over it by midafternoon." She checked the coffeepot. "More coffee there than anybody's gonna drink," she said.

Emerald Jones Copeland was a lady loved by all who knew her. And though she had given birth to six children, two of them ten-pounders, she was still an attractive woman.

She had turned twenty-six years old last month, and aside from the usual childhood ailments, had never been sick a day in her life.

Being an only child and growing up with only adults for company, she had early on begun to imitate their words and actions. So much so that her parents talked to her the same way they talked to each other, for neither of them believed that Emerald even thought like a child.

The young girl had few female playmates during her growing years, for even at school, where there were always several other girls her own age, she ignored them and spent as much time with her future husband as her teachers would allow. Although she learned her lessons well, she sat through many wintertime classes dreaming of summertime, and the many hours she would get to spend on Donaldson Creek with Seth Copeland.

And neither of her parents had objected to the time she spent with Seth. "You could do a whole lot worse than marrying a Copeland, young lady," her mother had said on a day when Emerald did not come home till almost dark.

"I don't know what all you and that boy do on that creek all day," her father had said, "but you'd better not go embarrassing me and your ma. You're twelve years old now, going on thirteen, and I reckon that's old enough for something to happen."

That "something" did happen, but neither of Emerald's parents lived to know about it. During the summer of 1855, they died only a few hours apart from some mysterious illness. An old doctor came out from Farmersville and visited them on their deathbeds, but after feeding them one spoonful after another of "medicine" that he had brewed himself, he said there was nothing more he could do. "Looks ta me like somebody's witched 'em," he told the relatives. "You know, put a spell or maybe some kinda curse on 'em. I don't b'lieve neither one of 'em is long fer this worl', neither."

Theodore Jones expired that same night, and his wife Dolly died the next day at noon. Emerald's aunt, Nora Cain, was quick to suggest that her niece vacate the Jones home immediately. "I don't believe a word of what that old doctor said about witches and curses," Aunt Nora had said, "but you'd better get out of this house right now, Emerald. Your ma and pa caught a real bad disease somewhere, and it's a thousand wonders that you ain't done got it yourself."

Nora waved her arm around for emphasis, then continued. "I'll bet you a pretty that whatever it was has even seeped into the walls of this kitchen; every other room in this house, too." She took Emerald by the arm and led her outside. "I want you to go home with me right now, honey. Don't take a single thing with you, nothing but the clothes on your back. Fact is, we'll burn them as soon as we find something of mine that'll fit you. Don't you worry about a thing now, I'm gonna buy you a whole closetful of new clothes."

Emerald lived with her aunt for the remainder of the year, right up till the day she married, and the "closetful" of new clothes turned out to be one coat, one dress, and one pair of shoes. Aunt Nora did give her several dresses, coats, and two pairs of shoes out of her own closet, however, and though they were not new, all were very nice, and much more expensive than anything Emerald had ever worn before. It was Nora Cain's own wedding dress that Emerald Jones had worn the day she married Seth Copeland.

Now, a few minutes after daybreak, she was still squatted on her haunches beside the cookfire. She brushed a wayward strand of hair out of her eyes and tucked it behind her ear, then spoke to her father-in-law again. "I guess you ought to get the rest of 'em out of bed now, Pa. This stuff'll be cool enough to eat before they can wake up and wash up."

A short time later, the Copelands sat around the dying campfire eating their breakfast in silence. Some of the youngsters still appeared to be half-asleep. "Wake up and empty your plates, boys," Seth said, addressing the two youngest. "I even slept a lot later myself this morning than I intended to, but we've all got to get used to hitting the ground early. It wouldn't hurt a thing in the world for us to start being on the road by daybreak."

Daniel nodded in agreement. "I'll try to get everybody up a little earlier from now on," he said. "We ought to be traveling every morning as soon as it gets light enough to see the road. It's cooler then, and it'll be a lot easier on the livestock and us, too."

"I'll put Ma's alarm clock in my wagon from now on, Pa," Seth said. "It's supposed to be my job to get my bunch moving in the morning anyway. From now on, I'll kindle Em's cookfire and get all the kids up in plenty of time to get an early start." Then he spoke to the twins. "Mark, I want you to drive the tool wagon today just like you did yesterday. Matt, you'll be driving your ma's wagon. Don't let the team fall behind, now. Stay up pretty close to your brother's tailgate."

"Yes, sir," Matt said, a hint of excitement in his voice. "You gonna be riding with Grandpa and Grandma?"

Seth shook his head. "I'm gonna put a saddle on that roan so I can scout up ahead of the wagons." He got to his feet and motioned upriver toward the grazing animals. "Let's get the mules and the saddlers into camp so we can hitch up and be on our way."

Half an hour later, they were ready to move out. Seth had allowed each of the twins to harness and hitch up his own team, but this time he did check to see that it had been done correctly. Mark and Matt stood by apprehensively as their father made his inspection. "You did good, boys," Seth said finally.

Each of the twins smiled broadly, but Matt was the only one to speak. "Grandpa showed us how to do all that while you were off at war, Pa. We've both been harnessing and hitching up teams for more'n two years now. Grandpa says that either one of us can plow a row just as straight as he can."

Seth placed a hand on Matt's shoulder. "Of course you

can," he said. He patted both boys on the back, then added, "I didn't look your work over because I doubted that you could do it right. It's just that I've always made it a habit to double-check everything. And I'd like to see both of you get into that same habit. Every morning when you hitch up your team and think you're ready to go, walk around everything one more time to make sure you didn't forget something. Even the slightest thing left undone can create a big problem."

The boys promised to be careful, then climbed aboard their wagons.

Seth placed his revolver in his saddlebag, then shoved his rifle in the boot. Both the Colt and the Henry actually belonged to his father, as did all of the weapons in the wagons. Seth himself owned no guns of any kind, for upon General Lee's surrender, General Grant had decreed that all Confederate soldiers must give up their guns and ammunition. Only the officers were allowed to keep their weapons.

Seth Copeland had walked out of Virginia with nothing but the shirt on his back, a few matches, and a rusty two-bladed pocketknife. And the old knife had come in handy more than once. On three separate nights when the moon shone brightly, he had climbed a tree and captured a possum. Without the knife, turning one of the small marsupials into a meal would have been difficult or impossible. He had also butchered bullfrogs, baby rabbits, and a large catfish that he had caught in a shallow stream with his bare hands. Although the knife had probably not saved his life, he had told several people that it had, and had put it away in a safe place as a keepsake.

Now he untied the roan's reins from a wagon wheel, then mounted. "Don't forget, Matt," he said as he rode around the wagon. "No slack."

"Yes, Pa. No slack."

Seth rode past the first wagon and motioned for his father to follow. A few moments later, the three wagons, with less than ten yards separating them, were strung out down the road. He expected to be in Tennessee within three days, and in Arkansas a week after that. Once there it would take at least another month to reach Texas, for they must travel northeast to southwest across Arkansas in order to enter the Lone Star State at its northeastern corner.

Even after crossing the Texas border, they would most likely continue their southwesterly course for several more weeks. Dan Copeland had said that he intended to keep traveling until he reached the Texas heartland, and Seth was certainly not going to argue the point. Pa was not only an excellent judge of farmland and livestock terrain; he was the man with the money, enough money to buy as much Texas real estate as the Copelands were likely to need. Those things considered, Seth was more than willing to let his father call the shots.

He continued to ride in front of the wagons all morning, sometimes getting as far as a mile ahead. Once, he stopped at a roadside spring and watered himself and his horse, then filled his canteen with the sweet-tasting water. The road was wider near the spring, with a level pullout, and he knew that the wagons behind him would also be stopping. He sat his saddle waiting for them for a short while, then changed his mind and rode on.

Though it was obvious that the prancing roan wanted to run this morning, he was kept on a tight rein. It had been different a week ago, however, when riding down the road Seth had suddenly decided to see how quick the animal could cover a mile. Giving him a loose rein, he kicked the horse in the ribs, then hung on. By the time he pulled up more than a mile down the road, he was more than a little impressed with the animal's speed. Then, seeing that the roan still had plenty of wind left, Seth whirled and headed him back up the road, still at a hard run.

When he slid to a halt at the corral, the horse was breathing hard, but not panting. Seth dismounted believing that the animal could easily have run twice as far. No doubt about it, he was thinking, as he loosed the horse into the corral and watched him gallop away bucking and kicking. The big roan had both the speed for a quick trip and the endurance for a long one.

Today Seth was happier than at any other time in his life. He had been thinking about going west for a long time, and now it was finally coming to pass. And the fact that his parents and every member of his family were sharing the experience with him added to his enjoyment. He also knew that if the country he was headed for was anything like he had been led to believe, he and his offspring had seen the Kentucky hills for the last time. He would finish raising his children in Texas, and the child Emerald was now carrying would be a native Texan.

Just as Seth Copeland had been bigger than most of the boys he had known while growing up, today he was bigger than most of the men he knew. He stood six foot three in his socks, and weighed two hundred twenty pounds. He had his mother's dark hair and complexion, with steel gray eyes and a small dimple in each cheek. Rawhide tough and more than a little handy with his fists, he had long been known throughout Caldwell County as an excellent scrapper.

Even during his school days the would-be bullies had given him a wide berth, and though he had been involved in hand-to-hand combat many times, both as a boy and as a man, none of his opponents had ever put him on the ground. He was also known to be a fine marksman with both the long and the short gun, and his experiences during the recent war had only served to sharpen his eye.

Although he had a sense of humor and sometimes laughed heartily, most of the time he was a serious man who tolerated little nonsense. He had no patience whatsoever with thieves or liars, and was a strong believer in the eye-for-an-eye principle. "Any man or woman convicted of will-ful murder should be put to death immediately," he had said many times. "And they should be executed by whatever means they used to bring about the death of their own vic-tim." He had become particularly upset one day when he read a story in the newspaper about a robber murdering a man with a knife. "If one man cuts the throat of another for personal gain, he should himself die from a severed jugular!" he emphatically said to his father, who had been visiting him in his home at the time. "No ifs, ands, or buts!"

Seth forded a shallow creek half an hour before noon, then dismounted under the canopy of a large oak. He loosened the cinch and staked the roan out to graze, then gathered deadwood for a fire. Once he had kindled a blaze, he took a seat on a stump to await the arrival of the wagons.

Ten minutes later, the drivers watered their teams at the creek, then followed Seth's instructions to pull off the road. "Take the mules out and let 'em graze for an hour," he said to the twins. "No need to take off their harness, just hang the traces on the hames, then take the bits out of their mouths and put 'em on the picket ropes." Both Mark and Matthew jumped to the ground and carried out their father's orders.

The women put the fire to use immediately, and a short time later there was enough hot stew and hoecakes for all. Over his second cup of coffee, Seth spoke to his father. "I'll keep on scouting ahead, Pa. If I happen to come upon something I don't like the looks of, I'll either stop and wait for you or come running back to meet you."

"You do that," Daniel said. "Don't you worry none about the wagons, either. The twins handle them teams just as good as it needs to be done."

When all had eaten their fill, Seth raked several handfuls of dirt over the fire. While the twins went to fetch the mules, Emerald poured the leftover stew back into the jars. She still had enough for at least two more meals.

When the hitching was done, Daniel piled the remainder of the deadwood Seth had gathered into the back of his own wagon, then climbed to the seat and led off. They would travel another ten miles before making camp for the night.

3

★

Ten days later, they were ferried across the Mississippi River at a place called Haley's Landing, the narrowest point on the big river for a hundred miles in either direction. Although the ferrymen had to make two trips, and charged an arm and a leg for their services, they had people, animals, and wagons on the west bank in less than an hour. The Copelands were now in Arkansas, where none of them had ever been before.

"One of the ferrymen told me that it's about seventy-five miles to Saint Francis County," Daniel was saying to his son. He thumped his map with a middle finger. "According to this thing, that's right on our way, so I don't reckon we'll have to change roads for at least three or four days." He was thoughtful for a moment, then added, "I'd like to stay south of Little Rock, 'cause I never have heard anything good about that place."

"I looked that map over real good last night, Pa," Seth said. "We don't have to go anywhere near Little Rock. We'll cross the Arkansas River at least forty miles south of there.

Then all we've got to do is stick with our southwesterly course till we reach the Texas border. I suppose there'll be times when there won't be a decent road heading southwest, but we'll be all right as long as we keep moving in that general direction." He mounted the roan, then led off toward Saint Francis County.

Still driving the lead wagon, Dan Copeland fell in behind his son. "We've been on the road for two weeks now, Elsie," he said to his wife. "Are you still happy about going to Texas?"

She finished tying the strings of her bonnet under her chin, then squeezed his arm. "Yes, Dan. I'm happy for you and me, but I'm even happier for Seth, Em, and the grand-kids." She patted his knee. "It's not that you and I are so terribly old, but Seth and Em are twenty years younger than us, and their children still have their whole lives ahead of them. They're all happy too, you can see it in their eyes and hear it in the way they're all the time laughing and carrying on. I expect us all to do well out there, but if Texas is like Mr. Speers told us, the grandsons'll probably be wealthy men long before they get to be our age."

"Maybe," Dan said. He was quiet for a while, then added, "Speers made Texas sound mighty good, all right, but sometimes I wonder why he didn't stay out there himself."

"Mr. Wiseman said it takes a certain type of man to make it in Texas. He said Mr. Speers didn't have what it takes."

"Maybe," Dan said again. He tapped the mules on their rumps with the reins, then added, "Wiseman didn't stay out there either."

A new conversation began when a large sow led a dozen small pigs across the road at a run. "Bacon on the hoof," Dan said, pointing his finger at the fleeing swine as if it were a pistol. "Bang," he added.

Elsie chuckled. "That reminds me, Dan. I told Seth to stop somewhere about three hours before dark, 'cause Em and I are gonna cook that big pot full of beans and bacon. We'll eat as many as we want for supper, then put the rest of 'em in them half-gallon jars. That'll be enough to last a week, so we can keep traveling till just about sunset every day. Don't take but a few minutes to warm up beans."

When they topped a long hill at midafternoon, they saw a small lake off to their right. Even from where he sat, Dan could see that the lake, which covered no more than three acres, was not stagnant. The creek that fed it was in plain view, and the runoff at the lower end created a short waterfall as it cascaded over a natural spillway. Elsie smiled when she saw Seth standing beside a fire at the water's edge. "Looks like he found the right place," she said, then pointed to the grazing roan. "Plenty of grass, too."

Dan nodded. "Plenty of grass, plenty of water, and plenty of mosquitoes." He guided the mules off the road and headed for the lake.

They parked the wagons thirty feet from the fire, then watered the animals and staked them out on picket ropes. As the women went to work around the cookfire, Emerald laid down the rules to her children: "Don't none of you kids go in that lake, now—it ain't to swim in. It's all right to cool off your feet or wash your face and hands, but I don't want to see a single one of you out in it."

"Probably got alligators in it fifteen feet long," Dan said. He was sitting on a toolbox beside his wagon rigging up fishing lines. He spoke to seven-year-old Paul: "See if you can find Grandpa some rocks about the size of hickory nuts, son. I need some weights for these lines." The boy scampered away.

A few minutes later, Dan gave each of four fishing lines an underhanded toss out into the lake. The rocks had been tied to the lines about a foot above the hooks, then the hooks baited, two with bacon, two with cheese. As soon as each line settled to the bottom, it was tied to a bush on the bank. Dan returned to the fire and poured himself a cup of coffee, then pointed to his handiwork. "Might be something good on the other end of them things when we wake up in the morning. This place looks awful fishy to me."

Elsie nodded, and stoked the fire. "I reckon it would break the monotony of eating beans all the time if you could catch enough for a meal."

"If I could catch enough?" Dan asked, chuckling. "If, you say? You just don't know what a good fisherman I am, woman. I expect to pull a whale out of that lake about day-break. Maybe two or three of 'em."

Elsie stirred the bean pot, then smiled at her husband. "I've seen the kind of whales you catch before, Dan," she said jokingly. "I've got no reason to think you won't get another one, either, 'cause there must be a million of 'em in this little lake."

Dan stuck out his lower lip as if pouting. "Just go ahead and have your fun," he said. "I'll bet you quit laughing when you see what I drag through them cattails and up onto this bank in the morning." He left the fire and joined his son, who was sitting on a wagon tongue going over the map again.

"I was just looking, Pa," Seth said. "This thing shows Gatesville to be about forty miles west and a little bit south of Waco. Ain't that where old man Wiseman said we ought to go? Didn't he say that the land was exceptionally good for farming or ranching either one, and that it could be bought cheap?"

Dan nodded. "That's what he said. I don't know how much he'd really know about what it costs, though, since he didn't buy any of it."

"Maybe he was broke, Pa. You know, even if something is cheap, it's still out of reach to a man that don't have any money at all."

Dan was thoughtful for a while. "I reckon that's about the size of it, son," he said finally. "I suppose Wiseman was exaggerating, but if even half of what he said is true, I'd sure like to have a look at some of that land in Coryell County. Hamilton County, too, for that matter. The map shows that the Leon River runs right through the middle of both counties. Wiseman says the terrain alternates between long, rolling hills and smooth, grassy plains. He says the soil will grow just about anything, and that there's plenty of rain if a man wants to farm. He claims that if a man decides to raise livestock for a living, all he's got to do is turn 'em loose and let 'em fend for themselves, 'cause Texas grass grows year-round."

"I think that's bullshit, Pa, I mean that part about the grass growing all year. I think it cures on the stalk just like hay, and I've been told that it holds on to its nutrients all winter long, even in freezing weather. The Texans I've talked to said that the cattle won't back away from eating it just because it turns brown, and that if they can get enough of it they'll make it through the winter in top shape."

"Sounds good," Dan said. He got to his feet and took a step toward the fire, then turned. "We'll drive right on by Waco and head straight for the Leon River."

Seth folded the map, then joined his father at the coffee-pot. "We'll probably find the traveling a little easier once we hit Texas," he said. "Wiseman said that right after joining the Union, the state started building a network of roads between the towns, and that most of the counties even have their own grading crews. If all that's true, Texas ought to have some good roads by now."

Dan poured coffee for both men. "I reckon there must be at least a little truth to it, 'cause Speers told us the same thing before we ever talked to Wiseman."

Seth blew on his coffee, then took a sip. "You might have something there," he said. "To the best of my calculations, we'll know in about two weeks."

Supper was done shortly before sunset, and the family seated themselves in a circle to eat. Once the beans, bacon, and cornmeal hoecakes had disappeared in large quantities, Emerald served each of them a fried, half-moon-shaped apple pie, what she herself correctly called fold-overs.

Seth refilled his cup, then turned his attention to the pie.

"I didn't even know you brought a jar of apples," he said to Emerald.

"I didn't," she said with a smile. "I brought four jars. We'll be having the pies again in a few days."

The children began to laugh and chase each other as soon as they finished eating. When they finally decided on a game of hide-and-seek and scattered in several different directions, Emerald called after them. "Y'all oughtta quit running around in them woods and all that tall grass!" she said. "The chiggers and the ticks are gonna eat every one of you alive!"

After Mark had tied the dogs to a wagon wheel in order to keep them from giving away the boys' hiding places, he decided that Rachel should be IT, and that she must close her eyes and count to a hundred before beginning her search for them. She went along with the game for several minutes, then announced that she was tired of doing all the searching, that one of the boys should take her place and allow her to hide a few times. The game ended at that point, for all of the boys refused to be IT.

The Copelands were already in bed by the time darkness closed in, and once the younger boys had had their nightly orders to stop talking and go to sleep, all was quiet. The men and boys had spread their bedrolls directly under a star-studded sky, for after staring at the heavens for a while, Dan had declared that there would be no rain this night.

It had rained on their camp more than once since they had been on the road, but the family had all slept warm and dry. A large tarpaulin was hung between the tops of two wagons on cloudy nights, and the bedrolls spread beneath it. A trench three inches deep was dug across the uphill side of the bedrolls, then on down along each side. Even during a downpour, no water ever reached the sleepers.

Seth was up long before daybreak next morning. He lighted a lantern and walked up the meadow to check on the livestock, then kindled a fire and put on a pot of coffee. As he waited for the pot to boil, he saw his father sit up on his bedroll, then slip on his boots and walk off into the darkness on the opposite side of his wagon.

A few moments later, Dan was at the fire. "Good morning, son," he said. "I reckon you meant it when you said you were gonna start getting up before I do."

"My eyes just popped open about an hour ago and I never could go back to sleep. I'm sure I got as much rest as I needed, though."

Dan poured himself a cup of coffee. "I don't sleep as much as I used to," he said, sipping from the cup noisily. "I've always heard that you don't need near as much after you get old."

Seth drained his cup and dashed the grounds behind him. "Hell, you ain't old, Pa. I'd bet a dollar that you're at least as strong as I am right now."

Dan shook his head back and forth several times. "No, no, son. That just ain't the way life works. Now, you might not be able to tell it by looking at me, but I'd venture to say that I ain't more'n half as strong as you are."

Seth said no more on the subject. He moved the coffeepot and began to stoke the fire, for he had just seen his wife step down from her wagon and walk off into the darkness.

Emerald stepped into the glow of the fire a few minutes later, slinging water from her hands. "I believe you might have been right about alligators being in that lake, Pa," she said to Dan. "While I was down there washing my hands I heard a whole lot of loud splashing going on, and it wasn't too far from the bank. I got myself away from there in a hurry."

Father and son looked at each other instantly. "The fishing lines!" they said in unison. Dan headed for the lake at a trot while Seth grabbed the lantern, raised the globe, and relighted the wick with a twig from the fire. Then he hurried after his father.

Dan was squatted on his haunches holding on to a fishing line. "It's this one right here, son, and that ain't no minnow on the other end of it. I've felt of him a coupla times already, and he didn't give much."

"You think he's big enough to break off?"

"No," Dan said. "That's a big hook tied on fifty-pound line. He ain't going nowhere." He jerked on the line lightly, then began to pull it in a few inches at a time. "He's lagging, but he's not really fighting," Dan added after a while. "After trying to throw that hook for several hours, he probably ain't got enough juice left to put up much of a battle."

While his father played the fish, Seth pulled in the remaining three lines and looked them over. "That monster you've got on your line bit the cheese, Pa." The bacon is still on two of these other hooks."

"I figured as much," Dan said.

The fish had moved into the glow of the lantern now. Floating on its side, it had obviously given up the fight, and a final pull brought it to the water's edge. Seth ran his hand into its gills very quickly, then held it at arm's length. "Channel cat," he said. "At least twelve pounds, maybe fifteen."

Dan nodded, then chuckled. "Make sure your ma sees it while it's still alive and flopping. Then maybe she won't think it's so funny next time she sees me baiting a hook."

"I certainly will," Seth said. "After that I'll gut it and skin it, then turn it over to her and Em. If they cook it up after breakfast, we can all eat on it for the rest of the day. Might even have some left for tomorrow." He headed up the slope to show the fish to his mother and his wife, who were both now standing at the fire drinking coffee.

4

★

It took the Copelands more than a month to travel across Arkansas, for it had sometimes rained for days on end, making travel difficult or impossible. Once, they had been forced to camp on a creek bank for three days waiting for the high water to recede, for it was too deep and much too swift to ford. On two other occasions they had simply grown tired of fighting the mud, and had parked their wagons on high ground and waited for the road to dry out.

Last night they had camped on the west bank of the Sulphur River and, after traveling for five hours this morning, reached the Texas border. Even as he read the sign informing him that he was now in Texas, Dan could see Seth standing beside his horse under the canopy of a large oak a hundred yards ahead. As the wagons pulled up at the tree, Seth pointed to a nearby spring. "Best-tasting water I've found since we left home," he said.

Every member of the family was soon on the ground testing the water. After slaking his own thirst, Daniel pointed off to his left, then spoke to the twins. "You boys take the

mules out and water 'em, then stake 'em out right over yonder. The grass looks good there. I decided a long time ago
that no matter what time of day we hit Texas, we'd set up
camp for the night right after we crossed the state line."

Within half an hour, all of the mules and both saddle
horses were on picket ropes. While the children played, and
the women sorted out the necessities for the preparation of
a meal, the men sat by the fire waiting for the coffee to boil.
"That ferryman back at the river said this road don't get any
better till it reaches Tyler," Dan was saying. "I would have
known that anyway as soon as I read that sign back there
at the state line. 'Now entering the Republic of Texas,' it
says. Hell, it's been more'n twenty years since Texas has even
been a republic, so the fact that nobody's bothered to change
the sign tells me that they're not too concerned about the
condition of this road."

Seth chuckled. "I'd have to agree with that," he said.
Then, with his voice taking on a more serious tone, he added,
"Of course, when you think about how big Texas is, and
how many roads it would take to make things convenient
for everybody, we're probably lucky to find one of any kind
that takes us where we want to go."

Dan was thoughtful for a moment, then reached for the
steaming coffeepot. "I reckon you said it a little better'n I
did, son. I didn't mean to be complaining, though. Just making talk." He poured two cups of coffee, then both men left
the fire and seated themselves on a wagon tongue. There they
remained until the women called them to eat an hour later.

After a dinner of warmed-over beans, cornmeal hoecakes, and fried sweet potatoes, the children and the dogs
scattered in every direction while the men and women continued to sit around the fire sipping coffee. Finally, Seth emptied his cup for the third time and set it on a rock. "I'm
gonna take my rifle and circle around that hill yonder," he
said, pointing. "If there's a creek on the other side, the deer'll
be coming down for water about sunset, and I might get a
shot at one." He got to his feet and shouldered the Henry.

"Don't let them dogs come sniffing after me, now," he said to no one in particular. "If they follow me, the hunt's over."

"I'll tie 'em to the wagon when they get back," Emerald said. She reached for a stick of deadwood, adding, "I reckon I'll keep this fire going, too, 'cause I can't remember you ever coming back from a hunt empty-handed."

"Some fresh meat would come in handy, all right," Elsie said as her son jacked a shell into the firing chamber of his rifle and headed for the woods. "That little bit of bacon we've got left sure ain't getting no younger."

Walking through the tall grass and sagebrush, Seth jumped several rabbits before he got to the hill, but held his fire each time. He needed bigger game. Not only did a running rabbit present a difficult target, but one of the small mammals would not even begin to fill the bellies of ten hungry people. Besides, a shot from the Henry could be heard for a mile, and would likely send any nearby deer into the next county.

The hillside was covered with a wide assortment of undergrowth, and a thick stand of hardwoods as well. Prime deer habitat. Seth climbed the steep slope slowly and quietly, his sharp eyes analyzing every clump of tall grass and short bushes. He was hoping to spot a deer in its bed, thereby making the hunt a short one. It was not to be.

Continuing to move slowly, taking one short step and waiting two, it took him almost an hour to climb the hill, the top of which was about two hundred feet above the valley floor. Once there, he took a seat on a log to study the opposite side. As he had suspected, a small stream ran in a southeasterly direction along the bottom of the hill. Although he could see the water in a few places, the overall view from his present position was less than promising. He got to his feet and began to creep down the hillside.

Halfway down the hill he halted beside a large oak, then seated himself on the ground behind a fallen log. He had an unobstructed view of the creek bank in several different places, and the log would serve as a rest for his rifle if a target presented itself. From where he sat he could see several narrow game trails that he knew were being used on a regular basis, for they were completely devoid of any kind of vegetation. About sixty yards below his position and twenty feet from the creek, all of the trails merged into one, which then disappeared beneath the leafy tree limbs as it led down to the water.

He had no doubt that he had discovered the main drinking place for most of the wildlife that lived in the vicinity. And although an animal would not be in his view as it drank, Seth knew that he would get his shot, for he had been through it all before. Back in Kentucky, when a deer had drunk its fill it would inevitably slink back up the bank and stand still for a few moments, taking stock of all its surroundings before moving off. He had no reason to believe that a Texas deer would behave differently.

The sun was low over the western horizon, and Seth had been behind the log for more than an hour when the deer came into view. First, three does and twice as many fawns meandered down a small path from the west. When they reached the intersection they took the main trail, which led directly beneath the trees that offered them cover while they drank. Within seconds, they were all out of sight.

As he sat behind the log with a cocked rifle, waiting for the deer to climb back up the bank and offer him a shot, he continued to look around him. It was then that he saw the cougar. Crouched as low to the ground as possible and moving stealthily through the tall grass, its bulging muscles rigid and ready to spring at any moment, the big cat was moving toward the opening in which it expected the deer to reappear.

Knowing that the mountain lion was stalking the same prey that he himself was, Seth lined his Henry on the opening and sighted down the barrel. He must beat his competition to the punch, for once the cat made its presence known, there would be no more deer in the vicinity this day.

Moments later, a large doe stepped out of the shadows

and raised her head to look about. Even as Seth put a bullet in the deer's chest, he saw the cougar spring. With the doe already lying on the ground kicking out her life, the big cat closed the distance and clamped its jaws around her throat. Seth kept his seat for a few moments, hardly able to believe his eyes.

Even after Seth got to his feet, the cougar, a big male, did not release its hold on the deer. Seth stood shaking his head, as he realized that the lion believed that the chokehold by its own jaws had brought the doe down. Had the big cat been so engrossed in the stalk that it had not even heard the gunshot? Was it even now unaware of the fact that a human was standing only a few yards away?

Those questions were answered when the lion let go of the doe's throat, then stood staring up the hill at Seth, who was by now waving an arm in an effort to shoo the animal away. When the cougar sat back on its haunches, indicating that it was prepared to do battle in defense of its kill, Seth put a bullet between its eyes. The big predator collapsed on its forepaws, and never moved again.

Seth was down the hill quickly. After checking both animals and finding no sign of life, he stood for a moment staring down at the beautiful cougar. "I sure didn't mean you no harm, old buddy," he said to the dead cat. "You brought it on yourself. If you'd gone on about your business when I gave you a chance, you'd still be alive." He dragged the lion's carcass out of his way, then took his knife to the deer.

It was past sunset when he arrived back in camp, and darkness was coming on fast. He spoke to Mark and Matthew. "You boys saddle my horse and catch up one of the mules for me. I've got a deer down on the other side of the hill." The twins went into action immediately.

"I heard two shots," Dan said. "Did you miss the first time?"

Seth shook his head. "Nope. A mountain lion tried to contest me for the deer's carcass, so I had to shoot him, too."

"Lion, huh?" Dan asked. "Big one?"

Seth nodded. "Biggest one I ever saw. This cat's at least five feet long, Pa."

"Five feet long," Dan repeated. "I'd like to see that. Do you mind if I saddle up and go with you?"

"Not in the least," Seth answered. "In fact, I can use your help. That doe's a big one, and lifting her carcass up on that mule's back would be a pretty big chore for one man." Seth went about lighting a lantern while his father headed for the meadow to catch up his horse.

An hour later, the men were back in camp with the doe hanging from one of the oak's big limbs. The children gathered around to watch the skinning process while the women waited by the fire, their pots and skillets ready for the fresh venison. "I thought you might bring the cougar into camp, Seth," Emerald said. "I don't reckon I've ever even seen one, or if I did I was too young to remember exactly what it looked like."

"I reckon a cougar is one of the prettiest animals on earth, Em," Seth said, expertly wielding the skinning knife while his father stripped the hide from the doe's carcass. He pointed toward the hill. "The one we left lying over yonder was no different, either."

"He was a pretty cat, all right," Dan said, "and he was a big one. I doubt that there's one in the whole state of Kentucky that's more'n half that size." He stripped the remainder of the hide from the doe and dropped it beside the trunk of the tree, then added, "It's like Seth said, though: we ain't got no use in the world for that cougar. The wolves, the coyotes, and the buzzards'll eat all its flesh and clean the area up completely, and Mother Nature'll most likely be happy to get the pretty hide back."

With the skinning job completed, Seth began to cut the venison into chunks that could more easily be managed by the women, who had already announced that they would spend the entire night cooking if necessary. They intended to fry as much of the meat as the family could eat before it spoiled, then boil the rest and seal it in the jars. That done, they would have plenty of venison on hand to last at least a week, maybe longer.

When all had been served a big supper, the women chased the children off to bed, then urged their husbands to do the same. There was plenty of deadwood to keep the fire going, Elsie said, and nothing more that the men could do. Far better that they get a good night's sleep, for tomorrow would be another long day of traveling.

After grumbling a little, both men took their rifles and spread their bedrolls well outside the circle of firelight, then lay down to guard their women. Within half an hour, both guards were asleep. The women continued their task till long past midnight.

5

★

They reached the town of Tyler ten days later. Although the time of day was barely past noon, Dan pulled over at a roadside spring and declared that the day's traveling was over. He added that he would be driving his own wagon into town. They were getting low on supplies, he said, and the women needed a few other things. Seth volunteered to stay in camp with the children while his father drove the women into town, which was less than a mile away. He helped his wife to the seat beside his mother, then stood watching till the wagon was out of sight.

The town had been chartered in 1847, and named for President John Tyler. The early settlers lived well right from the start, for an abundance of water, shade, perennial grasses, and soil that would grow almost anything made the area highly suitable for both ranching and farming. With the demand for beef usually ranging between low and nonexistent, most men tilled the land and planted crops.

Tyler's claim to fame, however, concerned neither ranching nor farming, but its proximity to Camp Ford, whose stockade at its zenith in 1864 held more than six thousand Union troops—the largest prisoner-of-war compound west of the Mississippi River. The town's merchants, many of whom had once prospered wildly from the pockets of the soldiers, were now dependent on the locals for business. With the Civil War over, the Confederate army no longer existed, and money was tight.

"Why, this town looks just like Farmersville, Kentucky," Elsie said as Dan drove down the wide street. "Every single building looks just like the ones back home." She pointed to a brick structure on the corner. "Look at that bank over there—it looks exactly like the First State Bank of Farmersville."

"You're right, Ma," Emerald said. "Wouldn't it be something if they were both built by the same man?"

Dan chuckled, then spoke to his daughter-in-law. "That possibility probably ain't nowhere near as remote as it sounds, my dear. I know that Texas was settled by southerners, for the most part, and a whole lot of 'em were Kentuckians. Only stands to reason that a few of 'em might have come from the same area we did."

He pulled over at a general store and tied the mules to the hitching rail. After helping both women to the ground, he laid some money in his wife's hand. "Take all the time you need," he said; "we've got the whole afternoon if we need it. I'll drive on down to the feed store and buy some oats and hay so I can surprise the livestock tonight." After only a few steps he brought the mules to a halt and looked over his shoulder, making eye contact with his daughter-in-law. "I'm sorry, Em," he said, "but my mind don't seem to be working right today. I forgot to ask if you need some money, too."

She smiled and shook her head. "No, thank you, Pa. Seth gave me at least as much as I'll need."

He nodded, then drove on down the street. The feed store was on the corner a few doors up from the livery stable, and Dan headed for its hitching rail. Once there, he jumped to the ground and tied the mules, then stepped inside the building. A muscular blond-haired man of about twenty appeared to be the store's only occupant. Hatless, with his shirtsleeves rolled up on oversized biceps, he walked from the back of the room and stopped behind the counter. "Thank you for choosing our place, sir. Can I get something for you?"

"I believe so," Dan said. "I need a bushel of oats and two bales of hay. If you'll drop 'em in the back of that wagon out front I'll appreciate it."

The young man nodded. "Yes, sir," he said, then headed for the back room. He soon pushed a dolly containing the hay and a gunnysack filled with oats past the counter to the porch, then down a wooden ramp to the wagon. A few moments later, he was back behind the counter. "Seventy cents for the oats and a quarter a bale for the hay. Dollar twenty all told."

Dan paid the man, then bade him good day. He turned his wagon around in the middle of the street, then returned to the general store, where he retied the team to the hitching rail and sat waiting for the women. The wait was not a short one. It was more than an hour later that Elsie and Emerald stepped through the doorway, followed by a middle-aged man carrying a large pasteboard box. He set the box on top of the hay in the rear of the wagon, then returned to the store. "There's more," Elsie said.

Dan helped the women to the seat, then stood watching as two additional boxes were delivered to the wagon. Then he untied the team and hoisted himself aboard. "Looks like we're gonna be eating a little better than usual tonight," he said.

She squeezed his arm. "Dan, you simply wouldn't believe that one store could stock so much merchandise. I mean, they've got everything you can think of in there."

He chuckled. "Sure, I would believe it," he said. "The building's nearly two hundred feet long and about half that wide. They've got enough room to stock everything you can think of."

Elsie was quiet till Dan had backed the mules away from the hitching rail and headed up the street. "Well, I certainly never have seen so much stuff under one roof before," she continued. "We didn't buy a single thing that can't be eaten, though. Got smoked ham, Bologna sausage, five dozen eggs, and several different kinds of tinned meat and fish. Even got four loaves of bread that the man said was baked yesterday, and I've got a good sharp knife to slice it with." She squeezed his arm again. "Oh, and they had some of that yellow cheddar cheese that you like so much. I bought five pounds."

Dan smiled. "Like I said, we're gonna be eating a little better than usual."

Not only did the Copelands eat better, so did their mules and saddle horses. As the boys led each of the animals into camp and tied it to a wagon wheel, a nose bag filled with oats was tied on its head. Two hours later, after each animal had emptied its bag and eaten two blocks of hay, they were all led back to the meadow and put on picket ropes.

Even though the family had already eaten supper once, darkness found them sitting around the ashes of the dead campfire eating ham-and-cheese sandwiches by the light of a coal-oil lantern. It was only after the children had finished eating for the second time that Emerald distributed the rock candy she had bought at the store. Then, with each of the youngsters sucking on one of the hard sugar crystals, they skipped off into the darkness to play.

Half an hour later, their mother called them in and ordered them to bed. The camp was soon dark, and once the children had quieted down, the only sound that could be heard was Seth's hoarse snoring, a sound that his wife said was always louder when he ate a big supper. Emerald also said that his snoring did not bother her in the least; that it sometimes seemed to be the very thing that helped her get to sleep at night. None of the kids ever complained, either. Few things bothered children enough to keep them awake.

Seth slept soundly, and was up a full hour before daybreak. After stepping off into the brush and relieving himself, he put a match to the wick of the lantern, then began to kindle a cookfire. The dead grass and leaves caught quickly, and the tongues of flame had just began to lick at the wood when his wife joined him. "As soon as that fire burns down a little I'll start breakfast," she said. "Pa says he wants to get an early start this morning, and I reckon we all do. The more time we spend on the road, the sooner we'll find us a place to light." She handed him the empty coffeepot and motioned toward the spring, adding, "That can't happen a bit too soon to suit me, either."

He filled the blackened pot with water, then watched Emerald measure and pour in the grounds. "I know the trip's been hard on you and the kids, Em," he said, seating himself cross-legged on the ground, "and we've got at least two more weeks of traveling ahead of us. But it's just like Pa said: if we settle on some place not to our liking just because we're tired, we'll regret it for the rest of our lives."

"I can certainly believe that," she said. She set the coffeepot on the fire. "I wasn't complaining, either. Just talking to my tired bones, I reckon."

Emerald fed the family in less than an hour, and just as Seth extinguished the fire, the twins came running from the meadow, where they had been sent to bring in the livestock. "Two of them mules ain't out there, Pa," Mark said breathlessly. "That big gray and the one named Nellie ain't nowhere to be seen."

Seth was on his feet instantly. "Did you look around good? Maybe they just pulled their picket pins and wandered farther down the meadow."

Mark shook his head. "They couldn't have done it, Pa. I drove them pins deep into hard clay with a heavy rock. The only way they'd come out of the ground is for somebody to pull straight up on 'em."

Seth stood quietly for a moment. Then, staring into the smoldering ashes of the cookfire, he spoke to the twins:

"You boys saddle my horse just as quick as you can. I want to have a look around." Mark ran to the meadow for the grazing animal while Matthew waited beside the wagon with the bridle in his hand and the saddle at his feet.

Less than five minutes later, Seth mounted the roan and left the campsite at a canter. When he reached the spot where the animals had been picketed, he dismounted and got on his knees to inspect the ground. It was just as Mark had said: the mules had not pulled the pickets. There was no loose dirt to indicate that they had been pulled out of the earth sideways. The ground around both of the holes was clean and smooth, which left no doubt that the pins had been lifted straight up by human hands.

He walked around for several minutes studying the tracks, finally reaching the conclusion that a mounted rider had led the mules away. He remounted and took up the trail. Following the tracks was easy in this particular area, for the ground was soft in most places. He decided very quickly that the mules were being led by a man on a big horse, for its tracks were half again as big as those of the mules. After a few hundred yards the meadow played out and the hardwoods began. There, Seth brought his roan to a halt and turned back toward the campsite.

As his family watched quietly, he dismounted and tied the animal to a wagon wheel. He filled both of his canteens with water, then tied two blankets behind the cantle of his saddle. He jacked a shell into the firing chamber of his Henry and shoved it into the boot. Then he added a sixth shell to the cylinder of his Colt and buckled the gunbelt around his waist.

Emerald had read his actions quickly and correctly. She stepped forward and handed him his saddlebags. "There's plenty of tinned meat, fish, and hoecakes in here," she said. "I put one of them new can openers in here, too. Bought it in Tyler yesterday." She handed him a handful of matches. "Put these in your pocket."

He laid the bags across the roan's back and pocketed the

matches, then took his wife in his arms and kissed her fore-head. "I'll keep following the mules till I come onto 'em, Em," he said. "Then I intend to take 'em back."

"I know," she said, pressing her face against his chest. "Please be careful."

He mounted, then spoke to his father: "Keep everybody together right here at this spring, Pa. You might ought to go back up to Tyler and buy some more feed so you can keep the animals in camp at night. Otherwise, the next thief might take all of 'em."

Dan nodded. "I'll do that, son, and we'll all be waiting right here when you get back."

Seth whirled the roan and headed across the meadow. Five minutes later, he disappeared into the woods. Though he had no problem seeing the tracks, following them was not so easy. The thief had done everything he could to make tracking the animals difficult, such as leading them right throught the middle of clumps of bushes and briers rather than going around.

Then, using one of the oldest diversionary tactics in the book, he had on two separate occasions led the mules along the bottom of a shallow creek for several hundred yards. Seth had simply crossed the creek and ridden north till he reached the point where the animals had left the creek, then continued to follow them in an easterly direction.

As was the case with all trackers who knew what they were doing, Seth was not fooled for a moment by the old creek-wading trick. If he had failed to encounter the tracks by riding north, he would merely have reversed his direction, for the thief could not stay in the water indefinitely.

When Seth pulled up and dismounted to relieve himself, he looked at his watch and was surprised to see that it was almost noon. He had obviously been so engrossed in the business at hand that he had lost track of time. He opened a tin of sardines and ate them while standing beside his horse. When he had thrown the empty container into the brush and remounted, he sat his saddle for a while, thinking.

He was now convinced that he was following a local man, or at least one who knew the area intimately. Last night had been overcast and dark as pitch, and only a man who was totally familiar with the area could have maneuvered three animals well enough to lay down the trail Seth had been following all morning.

Nor was Seth surprised when later in the afternoon the tracks turned south, crossed the road, then just before sunset, turned west. The horseshoe-shaped trail, which Seth had been following for at least twenty miles, was now headed back in the direction of Tyler. He followed the tracks till he reached a shallow branch, then guided the roan off the trail. He unsaddled and picketed the animal on good grass, then made himself a bed of leaves and spread his blankets on top.

Then he took a seat on a log and opened a can of meat. Even after he had eaten it all he still did not know exactly what kind it was, and when he consulted the label he found that the print was too small to read in the twilight. The hell with it, he said to himself, then threw the empty tin over his shoulder. Meat was meat.

He stretched out on his bed of leaves in the gathering darkness and, though it made him uncomfortably warm, spread one of his blankets over his body in an effort to partially shield himself from the mosquitoes that had already begun to buzz around his head. With both of his guns within easy reach, he lay on his back thinking of the thief he had been tracking all day. What kind of man was he? Did he have a family?

Surely the answer to the latter question was no, for a family man would never lay his life on the line in order to steal two mules that could so easily be identified by their owner. And lay his life on the line was exactly what the thief had done, for Seth could not even imagine a man who would not use deadly force against anyone he caught leading off his livestock. Even back in Kentucky, horse stealing could get a man ten years in the penitentiary, and Seth had read that the penalty in Texas was often much more severe: hanging at the end of a rope. And when one man happened to catch another right in the act of stealing an animal, the thief was quite likely to die on the spot. Justifiable homicide.

He slept fitfully, and at daybreak was sitting on the log eating another tin of meat. He had saddled his horse in the dark, and was now waiting for enough light to see the tracks. He estimated that he was at least ten miles east and about five miles south of Tyler, so he ruled out the possibility that the mules were being taken to town. Nor did Seth believe that the man he had been following was a farmer who needed the animals for the plow. He was more likely a full-time thief with a ready buyer for anything he could steal.

As daylight began to filter through the treetops, Seth stepped into the saddle. Even from where he sat he could see the animals' tracks leading up the opposite bank, and he was relieved to see that the thief had discarded the old creek-wading trick. About three hundred yards up the slope and in the middle of an open field, the tracks for no apparent reason veered sharply to the southwest. No doubt about it, the man knew exactly where he was going, and it would probably turn out to be a long way from Tyler.

Although he was well aware of the fact that he might ride into an ambush at any moment, Seth stayed doggedly with the trail. There was simply no other way, for he had no idea which direction the thief might turn next. And trying to guess correctly, then riding ahead to cut him off, could prove to be even more dangerous than the tracking.

He stayed in the saddle all morning. Every hundred yards or so he would stop and follow the trail with his eyes as far as he could see it, then move up to that point and repeat the process. Not an effective maneuver against a rifle, but much of the time it kept him out of pistol range.

By the time the sun was directly overhead, Seth had decided that his quarry was no more than an hour ahead of him, for the animal droppings he was passing were fresh. After another mile or so, when he crossed a shallow creek and came upon a pile of dung that was still steaming, he knew that the thief was taking his time, and that his lead had now been cut to no more than a few minutes.

Seth halted to look over the terrain ahead. The open plain that was directly in front of him became a wooded hillside about two hundred yards farther on, and he could see nothing past the tree line. However, he could see that the tracks led straight to the trees; so, wanting to reach the protection of the timber quickly, he bent low over the roan's neck and kicked the animal to a canter.

Once inside the tree line he saw that the vegetation was nowhere near as dense as it had appeared from the other side of the plain. In fact, it was so sparse that even from his position under a big oak he could see the animals' tracks leading up the hillside. He unholstered his Colt and, with his thumb on the hammer ready for a quick shot, kneed the roan up the steep slope.

When he reached the summit he saw that the search for his mules was over. The south side of the hill was largely treeless due to a recent logging operation, and Seth had an unhampered view of the area below. A large white farmhouse stood no more than twenty yards from the base of the hill, with large barns and corrals nearby. On the front side of the house, two men were carrying on a conversation over a picket fence, and the man outside the fence was holding Seth's mules.

Try as he might, Seth could hear none of their words, but he could read their gesticulations very well. It was easy to see that the man holding the mules was trying to sell them, pointing to one, then to the other, no doubt extolling the many excellent qualities each animal possessed.

It was just as easy to see that the man in the yard was in no hurry to buy. Even now he stood shaking his head emphatically, waving his arm back and forth as if refusing to further discuss whatever deal he was being offered. When he turned toward the house, the man with the mules called him back. He stood listening for a while longer, then spun on his heel and headed for the house again. This time he stepped inside and closed the door. He did not return.

The thief continued to stand outside the fence for several minutes. No doubt now willing to offer the farmer a better deal, he cupped his hands around his mouth and called out to the house repeatedly. All of his calls were ignored. Then, appearing to have finally accepted the fact that the farmer had lost interest, he led the mules across the road, where his horse was tied at the hitching rail.

Once mounted, he held his bay on a tight rein while he looked toward the horizon in several different directions, as if having a problem deciding where he should go next. Then he began to look down the narrow road that came up from the southwest and ended in the farmer's yard. When he finally put his heels to the bay, he guided the animal onto the road and headed southwest at a fast walk.

Seth had no way of knowing where the road led, but supposed that, after winding around and serving several other farms and ranches, it most likely turned northwest and wound its way to Tyler. He stood watching only long enough to determine that the thief actually intended to follow the road; then he stepped back into the timber and mounted the roan.

The farmer's house, his barn, and most of his cultivated land were located in a large bowl, with timbered ridges on all four sides. The ridge to the southwest was a long distance away, however, and the thief would have to travel for close to an hour before he reached any kind of cover. It appeared that after three or four miles of relatively level and open country, the road either went over or around the southwestern ridge. Seth expected to be on the opposite side of that ridge when the thief arrived, and he had less than an hour to get there.

He looked at his watch, then whirled his mount back down the hillside at a fast trot, dodging the limbs and saplings that would truly hurt, and ignoring the briers and bushes that would only scratch. Once off the hill and on the treeless plain, he kicked the roan again and headed around the southeast corner of the ridge at a hard run, intent upon being at the southwest corner ahead of his quarry.

At what he believed was roughly the halfway point, he looked at his watch again. Seeing that he had been in the saddle for less than fifteen minutes, he pulled the roan down to a canter, for the animal was already beginning to show signs of tiring. He held the same pace for the next twenty minutes, then saw that the ridge between himself and the road was about to play out.

He kicked his mount to a run once again, and was soon sitting his saddle among the trees. He was almost at the bottom of the ridge now, and was pleased to see that the road did not go over the hill, but turned south around it, coming even closer to his present position than he had hoped. From where he sat he could see that the road was no more than a hundred feet away. He jumped to the ground and tied his mount to a sapling, then unholstered his Colt. He dropped his hat on the ground beside the horse and then, bending over as low as possible, trotted to the road.

A bulky cedar about ten feet tall grew hard by the roadside, and Seth was behind it quickly. He bent a few of the short limbs so he could see up the road to the northeast, then hunkered down on his haunches to wait. After a while, when his knees began to feel uncomfortable, he pulled one leg under his body and sat on it for what seemed like hours. With his eyes on the road and his ears listening for the slightest sound, he had begun to think that maybe the thief had decided to leave the road and ride in another direction, when the man suddenly topped the hill a hundred yards away.

With a short length of rope connecting the mules' bridles together, he was leading them down the hill at a fast walk. Shorter than the average man, he sat low in the saddle, and was at the moment puffing on a cigarette and blowing a big cloud of smoke to the wind. With almost half of his head poked into a high-crowned hat, his facial features were indiscernible at this range.

Copeland cocked his Colt and drew both legs under his body so that he could move quickly. The thief was much closer now, and Seth could read his face quite clearly: beady eyes, ruddy complexion, lantern jaw, and long hooknose. And though no weapon was visible from this angle, Seth could see that the man wore a gunbelt around his waist.

On he came, looking as if he did not have a care in the world. Almost as if he were afraid someone might take it away from him, he took three quick drags from the cigarette, then flipped the butt into the road ahead of him. When he was forty feet away, he turned his head to the right to look back at the mules. At that moment, Seth stepped into the road, now able to see that the man indeed had a side arm on his right hip. "Pull up, fellow!" Copeland commanded. "This is as far as you go!"

The man jerked his bay to a halt. "Wha . . . wha—"

"I'm here to repossess my mules!" Seth interrupted. "I want you to use your thumb and one finger to toss that gun over your shoulder. Then dismount on this side of your horse." He made a quick motion with his six-gun, adding, "Now!"

The thief obeyed neither command. He began to move his right hand toward his hip slowly, as if intending to comply with the order, then suddenly snatched his weapon from its holster with unbelievable quickness. Even as he took a shot in the face, he got off a round in Seth's general direction.

Copeland's big .44 had snuffed out the thief's life instantly, turning his face into an unsightly mess and knocking him completely out of the saddle. He slid over his horse's rump and never moved again. Seth stood watching for a few moments to make sure it was all over, then holstered his weapon and went into action.

Thankful that none of the animals had bolted at the sound of gunfire, he picked up the mules' lead rope and tied it to the cedar. He stripped the saddle from the thief's bay and dropped it beside the road, then pulled off the bridle and gave the animal a hard whack across the rump. As the horse whirled and headed back down the road toward the farmer's house, Seth walked into the trees and retrieved the roan. Moments later, riding the big horse and leading the mules, he crossed the dusty road and headed north. The main road was probably no more than five miles away. Once there, he would turn west and ride straight to his camp.

He took one last look over his shoulder. The first person to come upon the scene he was leaving behind would have no problem reading the picture, he was thinking. The fact that the dead man's weapon was lying only a few inches from his hand with a spent shell in the chamber would make it obvious that he had died in a gunfight. Seth kicked the roan in the ribs and rode into the woods at a trot.

6

★

It was past midnight when he reached his camp. Knowing that riding in unannounced could be dangerous, especially since the recent visit by the thief, Seth sang out: "Wake up, Pa! It's me, Seth!"

"I ain't asleep, son," the elder Copeland answered. "Ain't slept much since you left. Come on in."

By the time Seth dismounted and tied the roan to a wagon wheel, his father was standing beside him. "Did you have to do any shooting?" Dan asked softly.

"Didn't have any other choice, Pa," Seth answered just as softly. "He tried to kill me when I caught up with him."

"I see," Dan said. "You done right." He turned his back to Seth and cupped his hands around his mouth. "All right, gang!" he shouted loudly. "Everybody up! We need to put some miles behind us before daylight!" There was an immediate stirring in the wagons and bedrolls.

Within minutes, the entire family was gathered around Seth. "Did you kill 'em, Pa?" Mark asked excitedly.

Emerald spoke quickly: "You know very well that I told all of you kids not to ask your pa no questions, Mark. Now take that lantern and start hitching up the teams. You heard your grandpa say that we need to be on the road." Both Mark and his twin were soon busy rattling harnesses and chains.

Seth lighted a second lantern, then jerked his thumb toward his saddler and the mules he had just led into camp. "I want to wait long enough for them to eat a bag of oats apiece, Pa. Truth is, I hate to work 'em without some rest, but like you say, we need to put some miles behind us." He dug the nose bags and a sack of oats out of his father's wagon and fed the tired animals.

"We'll skip breakfast this morning and try to fix an early dinner somewhere," Emerald said to no one in particular, then began to load boxes of cooking and eating utensils into her wagon. "I don't expect us to travel too many miles before the men start wanting some coffee."

Seth unsaddled the roan and dropped his saddle in the wagon. When the mules had finished eating, he harnessed and hitched them to the wagon. Half an hour later, with the roan tied to the tailgate, he blew out the lantern and climbed to the seat. The Copelands were soon headed down the dark road. This time, Seth himself drove the lead wagon.

They traveled nonstop throughout the morning and made more than twenty miles. Seth forded a shallow stream at midday, then led the small caravan off the road. He jumped to the ground. "This is as far as we go today," he announced to the others. "I've got to feed and rest these mules."

Dan was soon standing beside him. "They're bound to be awful tired, son, and you're smart to rest 'em before they balk. You know, a horse will let you work him to death, but a mule will quit when he decides he's being overworked. And once he learns how to balk, he ain't worth a shit for nothing from then on."

Seth nodded. "We'll let 'em graze till about sundown, then bring 'em into camp for the night. No use giving another thief a chance at 'em when we don't have to."

The twins put the animals on picket ropes without being told, for they had by now learned exactly what was expected of them. Rachel, the least vocal member of the family, sat leaning against the trunk of a nearby oak staring off into space. She was concerned about Booger and Beauregard, for it had been almost a week since any of the Copelands had seen the dogs.

Though the animals were hardly members of the family, Rachel was a dog lover, and for the first few nights had spent several minutes walking around the camp calling for them. Now, seeming to have finally accepted the fact that they might be gone forever, she sat by the tree with a mournful look on her face.

Though he felt a twinge of sorrow for his daughter, Seth himself would not miss the dogs in the least. Being a hunter, he considered them to be absolutely worthless, for neither of them had ever been known to chase anything it could not eat on the spot. They had trotted up to the cabin while Seth was at war, and made themselves at home after somebody fed them. Dan Copeland had named one of them after a hound he had owned many years before, and the other after a Confederate general.

Rachel believed that someone had stolen the dogs, for never had they stayed away so long, and never had they failed to come when she called. Seth agreed, for both of the animals were very colorful, and it was easy to imagine that a man might think he was stealing something special. All the thief would have to do was tie them up and feed them extra good for a while. They would soon forget about the Copelands and settle into their new home. Seth smiled at the thought, for he knew that the thief was going to be mighty disappointed when he became a little more familiar with the good-looking mongrels.

When they reached Corsicana several days later, Dan left

the others camped at the side of the road while he drove his own wagon into town to buy grain. He bought no hay this time, for since the theft of the mules, the Copelands had adopted a new traveling schedule that allowed the animals a few hours of grazing time each afternoon. Nowadays, the wagons were on the road every morning at daybreak, traveled almost nonstop till midafternoon, then made an early camp. The animals were put on picket ropes till sunset, then brought into camp, where each of them was fed a hefty portion of grain. All of the mules and both saddle horses then spent the remainder of the night standing only a few feet from their sleeping masters, both of whom were armed to the teeth.

With several sacks of shelled corn in his wagon, Dan left the feed store and stood at the hitching rail for a few moments. He had attempted to gain some information from the storekeeper, but the man was untalkative, supplying the shortest possible answers to every question he was asked. Dan was just about to untie the mules and head back to camp when a deep voice spoke to him from only a few feet away: "Good afternoon, sir."

Dan turned to see a tall middle-aged man with a salt-and-pepper beard standing on the boardwalk behind him. Dressed in jeans, flannel shirt, Mexican short jacket, and high-crowned hat, he wore a low-hanging Colt on his hip and had a marshal's badge pinned to his chest. "I reckon I know everybody who lives in this town," he continued, "so you must be just passing through."

Dan nodded. "Just stopped to buy some grain for my animals," he said. "My name is Dan Copeland, and I'm on my way to Coryell County." He offered a handshake.

The lawman grasped the hand. "I'm Clifford Rountree," he said, gripping the hand firmly, "and I've been Corsicana's town marshal for the past seven years." He stood thoughtful for a while, scratching his bearded jaw on both sides. "You ain't more'n a week shy of your destination," he said finally. "Have you come very far?"

"Came from Caldwell County, Kentucky," Dan answered. "Looking back on it, it seems like I've traveled about halfway around the world. Of course, I've got my wife, my son, and all of his family with me, so that breaks up some of the monotony." He pointed toward the road. "They're all camped back yonder at the spring waiting for me."

The marshal nodded, then pointed to a bench on the boardwalk. "If you ain't in too big a hurry, let's get out of the sun and have a seat over there. I like to talk with people from Kentucky, 'cause I came from western Tennessee myself."

Dan followed the marshal to the bench and seated himself. "Do you know anything about Coryell County?" he asked. "It might help my feelings a little if I knew what to expect when I get there."

Rountree chuckled. "I was coming to that," he said. "The fact is, I know a lot about it 'cause I lived there for years. Of course, it wasn't called Coryell County back then. That county's only twelve years old, organized and named in fifty-four. I took this job in fifty-nine, so I've been gone from there since then."

Dan sat quietly for a while. "Well, I reckon you'd know something about the country I'm headed for," he said finally. "Coupla fellows back home told me that a man could buy property along the Leon River in Coryell and Hamilton Counties at a reasonable price; that he could run cattle year-round without feeding 'em, and that the soil was rich enough to grow just about anything. Did they tell me right?"

Rountree nodded. "I reckon that part of what they told you was right, but they probably didn't tell you that the Comanches would pick you clean unless you plant twice as much of everything as you really need. It's the same with your cattle. The Indians'll take a steer occasionally, but they'll pretty much leave your brood cows alone.

"You'll probably do well along the Leon if you don't start making war on the Comanches every time they gather some of your corn for you or one of your calves comes up missing. You ain't gonna build anything along that river without them knowing exactly what it is and where it's at. Of course, that don't mean that they're gonna tear down everything you put up or harm you and your family. They're more likely to sit back and wait till they see how you act.

"I doubt that you have anything to fear from the Indians if you don't push 'em, Mr. Copeland." He broke into laughter. "Hell, even the Comanches ain't dumb enough to hurt somebody who's supplying them with plenty of beef and vegetables every year."

Dan found little humor in the lawman's remark, and changed the subject. "Is there a place around Gatesville where I can buy building material?" he asked.

"Should be. Like I said, I've been up here for the past seven years, and I've pretty well lost track of what goes on down there." He pointed up the street. "If you'll stop by my office, I'll give you a note to my brother who lives in Gatesville. I'd say that he can give you whatever information you're gonna need—he's sheriff of Coryell County."

"The hell you say!"

Rountree nodded. "He's halfway through his second term now, and I'm sure he'll do everything he can to help you get settled. His area's biggest need right now is people, especially people with lots of children who'll probably one day start their own families right there in Coryell County. When you get to Gatesville, you take my note by the sheriff's office. You'll get help." He got to his feet and pointed to his office again. "Follow me," he said, then began to walk in that direction.

Dan untied his mules and drove up the street, then halted again at the marshal's hitching rail. He climbed to the ground, crossed the boardwalk, and stepped inside the office door.

The marshal, who was already seated behind his desk with pencil and paper in his hands, motioned him to a chair. "Make yourself comfortable, sir. This'll take me a few minutes."

Dan seated himself and sat waiting for almost half an hour. A deputy came into the office and deposited something in a desk drawer, then returned to the street. He nodded to Copeland as he passed the chair, but did not speak. Dan also nodded a greeting, but remained quiet.

Finally, the marshal got to his feet. "Sorry I took so long writing this," he said, handing Dan a sealed envelope, "but it turned out to be a letter instead of a note. Just give it to Sheriff Wilson Rountree, then you're gonna have a friend in Gatesville. His office is right in the middle of town."

Dan accepted the letter. "I'll do that, Marshal, and I certainly appreciate your help."

"Think nothing of it," Rountree said. "I would have liked to have you and your family settle here, but since you already knew where you wanted to go, turning you over to my brother seemed like the next best thing. You folks be careful now." He stepped through the doorway and headed down the street toward the feed store.

Dan folded the letter and shoved it into his pocket, then moved out to the hitching rail and untied the mules. He climbed to the seat and drove out of town at a fast trot. He could hardly wait to tell Seth and his family that they had a friend waiting in Coryell County.

7

★

Eight days later, they made a late-afternoon camp at a boarded-up spring where a roadside sign informed them that the town of Gatesville was only two miles ahead. The twins took care of the animals, and the smaller children went hunting for deadwood; Dan, Seth, and the women gathered around the spot they had chosen for their cookfire. "If things go like I'm hoping, our journey is about over," Dan said. "First thing in the morning, Seth and I will ride into town and talk to some people.

"I need to set up an account at the bank right off. Then I'll take this letter to Sheriff Rountree. Like his brother said, it stands to reason that he'd know what's for sale in the county, and about what it's worth. If he's an honest man, he not only could steer us to some good property, but he might save us some money to boot."

"You don't need anybody to tell you what a piece of property is worth, Dan Copeland," his wife said quickly. "Just 'cause a man lives in Texas don't mean he knows any more about land than you do. You just look it over and use your own judgment, 'cause you're as good at that as anybody else is."

Dan smiled and winked at his wife. "I appreciate the compliment, little lady, but there's more to it than that. You see, we ain't looking to settle just any old place; we want property on the Leon River. Of course, land along that river is gonna cost more, and I'm willing to pay for it, but I don't intend to let some shyster take advantage of me."

The children had found plenty of wood, and Elsie was now busy kindling the cookfire. "Ain't nobody gonna take advantage of you on a land deal, Dan. It's like I said before: you'll know just as much about what you're looking at as they do; probably more."

"Well, I reckon we'll find out about all that soon enough," Dan said. Then, as the women began to select their cooking utensils for the preparation of the night meal, he changed the subject. "Venison and potatoes again?" he asked.

"We'll call it potatoes and venison tonight," Elsie answered.

They ate their supper by lanternlight, and just as had more than fifty others since they left Kentucky, the night passed uneventfully. All had agreed that there was no longer a compelling reason for them to rise before daybreak, and it was well past sunup when Seth threw off his blanket and got to his feet. Even after he had gone to the woods to relieve himself, then returned to the ashes of the dead campfire, it still appeared that he was the only one awake. He kindled a fire as quietly as possible, then walked to the spring and filled the coffeepot.

When he returned to the fire, Emerald was there. He kissed her on the nose and handed her the potful of water. "Here," he said. "You make better coffee than I do."

"I know," she said. She poured a measure of grounds into the pot, then set it on the fire. "No use to wake them boys up till it's about time to eat breakfast," she added. "They ain't getting nowhere near as much sleep as the rest of us. I reckon it must have been way past midnight when I woke up the second time, and I could still hear 'em whispering back and forth. That's why they moved their bedrolls on the other side of the wagon from you, so they could stay awake and talk all night."

Seth chuckled softly. "I knew that, but I don't reckon a fellow oughtta keep getting after his kids about every little thing. Anyway, if they're losing sleep at night it sure ain't been showing on 'em in the daytime. Won't make no difference now, though; Pa says we've just about reached our destination."

Emerald stoked the fire. Then, keeping her voice almost to a whisper, she asked, "Are you gonna let Pa choose the land and make all the decisions, or are you gonna speak up and do some looking of your own?"

"Of course I'll do some looking, and if I see something that I think Pa has overlooked, I'll certainly point it out to him. You've got to remember, though, that most of what I know about land I learned from him, so it ain't likely that I could tell him much." He pulled the coffeepot off the fire and filled his cup. "Remember too," he continued, "that it's Pa's money. He says there ain't no use in buying but one piece of property, 'cause it'll fall to us and the kids one of these days, anyway. Common sense tells me that he's right, so when buying time comes, I'll probably just sit back and learn a few new tricks while I listen to him negotiate a deal. Anything that pleases him is gonna suit me fine."

"Me, too," Emerald said, then busied herself with preparing breakfast.

Located on the Leon River, Gatesville, whose name derived from nearby Fort Gates, became the county seat when Coryell County was organized in 1854. Surrounded by perennial grasslands and some of the richest soil in America, the town began to prosper immediately, and soon became a major shipping and supply point for area farmers and ranchers.

The town's one claim to fame, however, had nothing to do with its location, but with its unusual double-wall log jail, which boasted an underground dungeon. The jail had been built in 1855, and though the town marshal, a man named Henry Gray, claimed never to have kept any man in the dungeon for more than a few hours at a time, several of the locals were quick to give him the lie. More than one man claimed to have spent weeks or even months there without ever seeing the light of day. However, the former prisoners' claims of harsh treatment elicited little sympathy, for the citizens of the town not only approved of the unusual hoosegow, but had quite willingly paid for its construction.

When Dan and Seth Copeland rode into Gatesville shortly after nine o'clock in the morning, they saw immediately that the town was wide-awake. The main street was crowded with wagons and men on horseback, and the boardwalks on either side were congested with foot traffic. Men appeared to be moving from one place to another with unnecessary haste, while a few women went about their business at a slower pace.

"I already see the Bank of Texas down at the end of this block," Dan said, pointing.

"I see it, too," Seth said, "and there's the sheriff's office up there on the right-hand side of the street."

Dan nodded. "Uh-huh. We'll stop there and give him this letter after I have a talk with the banker. You coming into the bank with me?"

Seth shook his head. "I don't see any use in it," he said. "I left what money I had with Em 'cause I know we're gonna be needing it all when we start setting up housekeeping. I reckon you're gonna be doing the banking for all of us, so you just go ahead and take all the time you need. I'll make it a point to stay where I can see the front door, so I'll know when you're done."

When Dan tied up at the hitching rail and disappeared into the bank, Seth rode on. For the next half hour, he continued to ride up one side of the street and down the other till he had familiarized himself with most of the commercial buildings in town. Finally, he dismounted at the bank's hitching rail and began to saunter along the sidewalk, idly gazing into one display window after another.

He walked the entire length of the town on both sides of the street, then returned to the bank. As he stood leaning against the hitching rail, he decided that Gatesville must be a friendly town, for every man who walked by either spoke or nodded a greeting. And they were not all dressed like farmers. At least half of them wore jeans, boots, and wide-brimmed hats, and more than one man who had a Colt on his hip also had a rifle cradled in the crook of his arm. Seth attributed the heavy armament to the fact that Comanches still roamed the area at will, and many of them were down-right hostile.

Dan spent more than an hour inside the bank. When he returned to the hitching rail he stood staring quietly off into space.

"Did you have a problem with the banker, Pa?" Seth asked.

"No," Dan said, untying his horse. "No problem," he repeated. "The man just acted like that bill of exchange was the biggest one he'd ever seen or heard of."

"You mean he didn't want to accept it?"

"No, not that either. He jumped on the check right away 'cause it was signed by the cashier at the Bank of Farmers-ville. It's just that he took a lot more time with it than was necessary, passing it around from one employee to another so they could all get a good look at it. He finally did his bookwork, then set up two different accounts and gave me a receipt. Said I could start drawing on either account any time I need to." He threw a leg over his saddle, adding, "The man's name is Horace Biddle."

They had ridden only a few steps in the direction of the sheriff's office when Dan mentioned the banker again. "I wish now that I hadn't put that check in the bank till after I made a deal for some property," he said. "After seeing how impressed Biddle was with the size of it, it occurred to me that he might pass the word on to some of his friends in the real estate business. Now, I'm sure I don't have to tell you that negotiating a deal with a man who already thinks you're rich can get to be mighty tricky."

Seth nodded and rode on.

They dismounted and tied their horses in the center of town, then stepped up on the boardwalk in front of the sheriff's office. They lingered there for only a moment, for the thick oaken door was not only closed, but padlocked. They turned away and were about to untie their horses when a middle-aged man trotted his animal up to the hitching rail and dismounted. A badge on his vest identified him as the county sheriff.

"I'm Sheriff Rountree," he said, wrapping his horse's reins around the rail several times. "Is there something I can do for you?"

Dan stepped forward, his right hand extended. "I'm Dan Copeland," he said, "lately from Kentucky." He pumped the lawman's hand a few times, then jerked his head to indicate his son. "This man with me is my son Seth, and we've been thinking mighty strongly about settling in this area."

Smiling broadly, the sheriff gripped Seth's hand firmly, then spoke to both men. "Well, you'd have to look long and hard to find another place as good as Coryell County, so you've already made one good decision just by coming here. If you think I can do something to help you, all you gotta do is ask."

"Glad to hear that, Sheriff," Dan said, " 'cause I reckon we're about to ask." He took the folded envelope from his vest pocket and laid it in the lawman's hand. "I had a talk with your brother last week when we passed through Corsicana, and he suggested that we look you up as soon as we got here. He asked me to give you this letter, so I guess it'll tell you what he was thinking a lot better than I can."

Rountree nodded, then pointed to his office. "Let's go inside where we can sit down. Sounds like we've got some talking to do." He fumbled in his pocket for the key, then unlocked the door and pushed it open. "Just seat yourselves there at the desk," he said, pointing to two cane-bottomed chairs. He walked on to a small cookstove in the far corner of the room. "I'll stoke up this fire and put on a pot of coffee, then be right with you."

Though he was a six-footer, Rountree was not a big man. With round, narrow shoulders and a small waist, he appeared to weigh no more than a hundred fifty pounds. Nonetheless, his countenance fitted his occupation perfectly. With his leathery complexion, graying temples, and confident look of self-control, he indeed looked like a man who should have a sheriff's badge pinned to his vest.

Once he had a fire going in the stove and his coffeepot over the firebox, the lawman joined them at his desk, seating himself in an upholstered chair on the far side. He tore open the envelope. "So you had a talk with my brother Clifford, huh? Is that hacking cough still bothering him?"

Dan shrugged. "I talked with him for close to an hour," he said. "I didn't hear no cough."

"Good," Rountree said. "Glad to hear that. There's an old army doctor living in Corsicana that everybody says is mighty good with lung ailments. Last I heard, Clifford was going to see him about twice a week. You say he ain't coughing now, so the old doc must be doing him some good." He unfolded the letter. "Now," he said, "let me see what my dear brother has to say."

Father and son sat quietly while the sheriff read the two-page letter. When he had finished, he refolded it and dropped it in a desk drawer, then spoke to Dan: "Clifford says you might be interested in buying some land, Mr. Copeland. How much land are we talking about?"

"Don't have no way of knowing till we see the property and hear the price. If we see some land we like and the price is right, we might buy a few acres or we might buy a few sections."

"A . . . a few sections, you say?"

Dan nodded. "We're gonna need plenty of room. We might grow crops for the first year or two, but we'll eventually go into the cattle business."

"I see," Rountree said. He sat thoughtfully for a while, scratching his jaw and staring through the window. "A man could put a herd of longhorns together pretty cheap right now," he said finally. "And this might be exactly the right time to do it. Every smart man I know thinks the railroad'll be coming west within a year or two, and that sure oughtta create a market for cattle. Hell, they could haul 'em back east alive, and not even butcher 'em till after they get to market.

"As I said, you can buy cows mighty cheap right now, but you can get 'em for nothing if you want to take a bunch of men into the Big Thicket after 'em. All you gotta do is drag 'em out of the brush and put your brand on 'em. Then they belong to you. The way I hear it, you can hire good ropers for a dollar a day down in southeast Texas." He thought on the matter a little longer, then added, "Now, them cows can hide in the brakes and brush so well that most folks would need a hound to sniff 'em out, but I hear that them Mexican vaqueros can ride straight to 'em."

The sheriff got to his feet and walked to the stove. A few moments later, he placed three cups of steaming coffee on the desk, then reseated himself and continued the conversation. "If I was wanting to put a herd of longhorns together myself," he said, "I'd hire the Mexicans. They know exactly what they're doing, and they're known to be the best ropers in the world. Now, there are men all over Texas who are out of work, and you could probably round up a crew most anywhere, but they wouldn't be nowhere near as good as the vaqueros. Putting a rope around the neck of a wild longhorn is not something a man learns overnight."

"No," Dan said. "I would think not." He was quiet for a few moments, then added, "We'll remember all the things you've said, Sheriff, but we won't do much thinking about a herd of cows till we've got somewhere to put 'em. Have you got a particular place in mind that you think we should look at?"

Rountree shook his head. "None in particular," he said, "but there's sure a lot of good cattle country between here and the Hamilton County line." He sat biting his lower lip for a moment, then suddenly snapped his fingers. "Bud Shumaker!" he said loudly, then quickly lowered his voice. "Bud Shumaker would know if there's anything for sale in the county that would fit your needs. He actually sells insurance for a living, but he dabbles in real estate a little bit, too. He may or may not be able to find what you're looking for, but I can promise you one thing: if you do any business with him you can count on a square deal, 'cause he's as honest as the day is long."

Dan nodded, and drank the last of his coffee. "That's the only kind of people we care about meeting," he said. "Does this Shumaker fellow live here in town?"

The sheriff was on his feet quickly. "His office is right down the street," he said. "Let's go have a talk with him."

A few minutes later, they entered Shumaker's office, which was adjacent to a hardware store. Though little more than a hole in the wall, the room was neat, with everything appearing to be in exactly the right place. A medium-sized man with a ruddy complexion and a thick shock of yellow hair sat behind a small desk. Rising from his chair, he spoke to the sheriff: "Good morning, Will. Something I can do for you?"

Rountree nodded, then made the introductions. "Bud Shumaker, meet Dan Copeland and his son Seth." When the handshaking was about over, the lawman continued. "They're thinking about buying some property and settling in Coryell County, Bud. They talked with Clifford up in Corsicana and he sent 'em on to me, so now I'm turning 'em over to you. I'll consider it a personal favor if you'll help 'em find what they need at a decent price. They're the kind of people we need in this county, and they've brought their women and children with them."

That said, the sheriff turned to leave the office. He stood with his hand on the doorknob for a moment, then spoke to the Copelands again. "I'm leaving you two in good hands," he said. "Bud'll work hard for you, and like I told you earlier, I'd swear by his honesty." He stepped outside and closed the door behind him.

With the sheriff gone, Bud Shumaker motioned the Copelands to chairs, then seated himself behind his desk. "Now," he said. "If you men will tell me what sort of place you're looking for, I'll try to put my lazy brain to work."

Dan slid his chair closer to the desk. "We want a place on the river," he said. "Like I told the sheriff, we expect to go into the cattle business, so we'll need plenty of good grass and a year-round source of water."

Shumaker smiled. "Plenty of good grass is just anywhere you look in this area, Mr. Copeland, and the Leon River sure ain't likely to run dry." He pulled out a desk drawer and continued to speak as he thumbed through some papers. "Let me look through these listings and see if I can find something that might interest you." He read from a particular sheet of paper for a while, then spoke again, almost as if talking to himself. "That wouldn't be it," he said softly, moving the paper to the bottom of the stack. "Not much demand for twelve-section tracts of land."

Dan spoke quickly. "Twelve sections sounds about right to me," he said. "Of course, the price would have to be right."

Clearly surprised, Shumaker raised his eyes and leaned back in his chair. "Well," he said, "I had no idea that you wanted to purchase twelve square miles of the county, Mr. Copeland." He retrieved the paper and tapped it with a finger. "This is what folks around here call the old Rainwater place. Nobody ever called it a ranch, 'cause they never ran any cattle. It's been in the Rainwater family since long before statehood, and after all the older ones died off, it fell to Newt. He's crippled up so he can hardly walk now, and lives with his daughter and son-in-law a few miles out of town.

The three of them came in here a week after the war ended and authorized me to sell the place, lock, stock, and barrel."

Seth, who had spoken few words since their meeting, leaned closer. "How much did they authorize you to sell it for, and where is it located?"

"It's up in the northern part of the county—reaches almost to the county line. I don't know exactly how many, but I'll guarantee you that at least five miles of it borders the west bank of the Leon River. No water problems, ever." He studied the paper a few moments longer, then spoke again. "The Rainwater place is one of the largest single tracts of land in the county, and the terrain varies from level, grassy plains to low, rolling slopes. With its perennial grasses, shade trees, and never-ending water supply, its about as good as cattle country ever gets.

"As to the price, Newt's asking a dollar and a quarter an acre, the going rate for grazing land throughout this area." He picked up a pencil and began to write figures on a tablet. "Twelve sections amounts to seven thousand six hundred eighty acres," he said after a while. "At a dollar and a quarter an acre, the price comes to nine thousand six hundred dollars. My four-percent commission on that figure comes to three hundred eighty-four dollars, but it will be paid by Mr. Rainwater." He returned the papers to the drawer and got to his feet. "It's possible that Newt might lower the price a little if you dicker with him yourself. I'd be glad to give you directions to his house if you want to give it a try."

The Copelands were both on their feet now. Dan shook his head. "That won't be necessary," he said, "at least not till after we've looked at the property. I'd like to do that as soon as possible."

Shumaker's smile broadened. "Yes, sir," he said. "If you fellows'll meet me out there at the hitching rail about sunup in the morning, we'll get an early start on it. All you need to bring is your canteens and your bedrolls. I'll be leading a packhorse loaded with everything else we'll need, including plenty of grub. Be prepared to be gone for a while, 'cause a proper showing will take at least three days."

"That figures," Dan said. "We'll be here."

After another round of handshaking, the Copelands departed. As they rode out of town, Seth spoke to his father: "I heard you tell Shumaker that we'd both be back here in the morning, Pa. I'm gonna let you go with him to look at the land by yourself, 'cause I ain't about to leave Ma, Em, and the kids out there at that spring with no man around. Things ain't like they used to be. Every kind of scoundrel you could possibly imagine is prowling up and down the roads nowadays."

Dan nodded, and rode on quietly for several minutes. "We could just flip a coin to see who goes with Shumaker and who stays in camp," he said finally.

Seth chuckled loudly. "Not a chance, Pa. I'd still want you up on that river even if I won the toss, 'cause it's your eyes I want looking at that property, not mine. You just go ahead and take all the time you need. If you like what you see, you sure won't need any help dickering with Rainwater."

Dan mumbled something and rode a few steps farther, then added, "I guess you're right, son. I'll get an early start in the morning and see what comes of it."

8

★

Dan Copeland rode out at daybreak next morning, and was not seen again for almost a week. When he returned to the spring at midafternoon on the sixth day, the broad smile on his face made it obvious that he had good news. The family gathered around his horse as he rode into camp, all wanting answers, but none asking questions. Still smiling, he dismounted and handed the reins to one of his grandsons. "We've got us a ranch!" he announced loudly.

Both of the women threw their arms around his neck and kissed his cheek. "I'm so proud of you, Dan," Elsie said. "We're all proud, and it's gonna be so good to finally get out of these wagons."

Seth stood in the background till his father joined him; then both men seated themselves on a wagon tongue. "Did you have any problems with Rainwater?" Seth asked.

Dan shook his head. "None at all. I just made him an offer, then he asked me to leave the room while him and his daughter talked it over. After a while they called me back and said they'd decided to sell the place to me at my price. I got all twelve sections for eight thousand dollars, son."

"Eight thousand dollars," Seth repeated. He sat quietly for a few moments, then added, "That sounds mighty good, Pa, almost too good to be true. You've been up there long enough to look it over mighty well. Is it anywhere near as good as we hoped it would be?"

Dan nodded. "I don't know how it could be any better, son. At least seven miles of it lies right on the river, and I counted five springs and two creeks. What Shumaker didn't tell us when we first talked with him, and didn't tell me till we were halfway up there, was that there's a livable house on the property. Barn, shed, and a pole corral, too. He said he just forgot to mention them things.

"Now, the house ain't nothing we'd want to call home permanently, but it'll sure take care of us till we can build something else. It's a big building with two sections under one roof, and there's an open dog run in the middle with five rooms and a fireplace on each end. We can winter in it, then build a big house for you and Em wherever you decide. I know your ma wants something smaller, so I'll let her be the boss on what we eventually put up." He accepted a cup of coffee from Emerald, then added, "I'd say we've got one of the finest ranches in central Texas, son. It's duly registered at the Coryell County Courthouse, and your name is on the deed right along with mine."

Seth swallowed hard, and said nothing more on the subject.

When Dan took Elsie's hand and led her across the meadow, Emerald joined Seth on the wagon tongue. He put his arm around her shoulder. "I reckon Pa made a good deal on the ranch, Em, and he talks like it's the prettiest place he's ever seen. He mentioned building a big house for us and the kids next spring, but we might not want to wait that long." He motioned toward his father and mother, who were now disappearing into the woods. "Nope," he added, "we won't wait nowhere near that long."

She snuggled against his shoulder. "First chance they've had to be together since we left Kentucky."

Seth got to his feet and reached for her hand. "Us, too," he said, pointing to the woods in the opposite direction.

After eating an early supper, the family sat around the campfire talking till long after dark. "If all goes well, we'll be sitting around the fireplace in our own house tomorrow night," Dan said finally.

"I'll sure be glad," Rachel said, speaking for the first time tonight. "I'll be glad to get out of that cramped wagon, and I just can't wait to see that big ranch."

Mark snickered. "Don't matter how big it is," he said. "Ain't gonna be nothing on it that a girl can do."

Seth placed a hand on his son's shoulder and squeezed . . . hard. "There'll be plenty of things for her to do, Mark. You apologize to your sister right now."

Mark sat looking off into the night. "I'm sorry," he mumbled.

Seth squeezed harder. "Speak clearly, boy," he said. "Look her in the eye and call her name."

Mark sought out his sister's eyes on the opposite side of the campfire. "I . . . I'm sorry, Rachel," he said. Then, as soon as his father released his shoulder, the boy headed for his bedroll without another word.

Within the next few minutes, all of the Copelands called it a night. Seth lay awake on his bedroll for what seemed like hours, thinking of the ranch. Though he had never seen it with his own eyes, he knew that his father's assessment had been accurate, for few things, good or bad, ever escaped Dan Copeland's scrutiny. He had called the old Rainwater Place one of the best ranches in central Texas, and Seth had accepted that proclamation as gospel.

Seth had lost all interest in farming, and nowadays spent most of his waking hours thinking about the cattle business. With twelve sections of good grass and water, he and his father could run a sizable herd, and with no mortgage to worry about, they could grow at their own pace. And he believed that right now was the time to get into the business, while it could still be done relatively cheaply.

Most of the men who were expected to know had said that with the railroad coming west, it was only a matter of time till there would be a thriving market for beef. There was also a logical answer to the question of why those same men did not buy up all the cattle and make a killing for themselves when the rails did come: they simply did not have the money.

The Civil War had left most Texas men broke, and as it was for those living in other Southern states, just scratching enough food out of the ground to sustain their families was a full-time job. Though unmarked and unbranded longhorns ran wild throughout the Texas thickets, few men made an effort to round them up and lay claim to them. The market for cows was practically nonexistent, for even when a beef was needed for the table, it was a rare man who would pay money for it knowing that all he really had to do was load his rifle and hunt up a young heifer.

Things were going to change drastically in the not too distant future, Seth was thinking as he lay on his bed recalling the things his father had said around the campfire tonight. "I talked to more'n a dozen men up in Gatesville yesterday and today," Dan had said, "and every one of 'em told me he thought we'd be smart to load the old Rainwater Place up with longhorns. One fellow said the only reason he hadn't bought it and stocked it himself was 'cause the bank wouldn't lend him the money. He said he believed that two years from now a man with a herd of fat steers could just about set his own price." On that thought, Seth smiled, turned over, and went to sleep.

He slept soundly, and was wide-awake again long before daybreak. After lying on his back staring at the stars for a while, he rose to his knees, struck a match, and looked at his watch. Four o'clock. He got to his feet and walked behind the big oak to relieve himself, then lit a lantern and began to kindle a fire. He was not alone for long. No doubt as anxious to see the ranch as he was, the entire family was at his side by the time the flames took hold. Adam, who was just two months away from his sixth birthday, leaned against his father's knee. "Is it morning yet, Pa?" he asked.

"Not yet, son," Seth answered, giving his youngest a big hug. "Won't be long, though."

The women cooked and served breakfast by lanternlight, and the family was ready to be off at daybreak. The animals had all been fed and watered, and the mules stood in their traces at the heads of the wagons. Dan climbed to his seat and released the brake. "Just follow me and stop when I do," he said to the twins, each of whom was driving a wagon. Then to Seth he said, "I'll stop at the hardware store in town 'cause I want Elsie and Em to look at some of the cookstoves they've got in stock. I checked 'em out yesterday, and they looked mighty good to me." He sat quietly for a moment, then added, "There's a furniture store on the west side of town, too, and your ma and your wife are probably both gonna squeal when they see all that stuff in there."

Seth smiled. "I'll follow you," he said, "but I sure ain't gonna go inside the stores. I don't have the money for store-bought stuff, Pa."

"It don't cost nothing to look, Seth, and that's all we're gonna be doing. We couldn't buy nothing today even if we wanted to, 'cause there ain't no room for it in these wagons. We can come back another day and get what the women need. Just let 'em look, then by God I'll see that they get whatever they decide on."

"I'm sure you will, Pa."

With his saddle horse tethered behind his wagon, Dan led off, and the twins quickly fell in behind. Their father brought up the rear aboard the big roan.

Seth helped Emerald to the ground when the wagons pulled up in Gatesville, and knowing that each of the women was about to be given a houseful of store-bought furnishings, he seated himself on a boardwalk bench and watched them follow Dan up the street.

Whatever they wanted they would get, Seth was think-ing, and Pa would be more than happy to pay the bill. It had always been that way. He had not only taken care of his daughter-in-law and his grandchildren during the war years, but had been there with a helping hand on many ear-lier occasions when Seth's crops fell below the needs of his growing family. And his generosity was hardly limited to his own offspring. He was known throughout Caldwell County as a man quick to part with a dollar if a neighbor was down-and-out.

Continuing to sit on the bench, Seth watched his wife and his parents till they left the boardwalk to enter a store. Deep inside, he was happy that Emerald was going to get some pretty new things, but the fact that he was unable to pay for them himself bothered him greatly. He believed that situation would change within the next few years, however, for Pa had made him a full partner in the ranch. If the ranch made money, he would make money. Then he could buy his wife whatever she wanted.

He got to his feet and spoke to his children, all of whom were sitting quietly on the wagon seats. "You kids stay where you are, now." He pointed behind him. "I'm going into that store, and I'll be right back."

Five minutes later, he was back at the wagons handing out treats. "Every piece of this candy is exactly alike," he said, "and you've all got the same amount. I don't want to hear any fussing or arguing about it."

"Oh, Pa," Rachel said, hugging his neck. "You bought chocolate."

All of the boys began to eat their candy without a word of thanks.

Seth returned to his seat on the bench and was still sitting there an hour later, when he saw his wife and his parents coming toward him. Elsie carried a broom in one hand and a mop in the other. Bud Shumaker walked beside them, ges-ticulating with one hand and then the other as he carried on a conversation with Dan.

"Good morning, Seth," Shumaker said when he reached the bench. "I ran into your folks up at the hardware store and decided to walk down here with 'em so I could shake your hand again." He thrust his right hand forward, and Seth grasped it with his own. "Like I was telling your pa," Shumaker continued, "I'll be out to the ranch about the middle of next week to check on you folks, and if there's anything I can do for you, don't hesitate to call on me." He turned to Elsie. "Of course, I'll be bringing your new cookstove and six joints of pipe with me, Mrs. Copeland."

"I'll appreciate that, sir. I reckon we all will. I'm already looking forward to trying out that newfangled oven and that big hot-water tank."

Dan helped his wife to the seat and climbed up beside her. "I thought it was mighty nice of you volunteering to bring the stove out to us in the first place, Bud, and I won't forget it." He unwrapped the lines, released the brake, and slapped the mules on their rumps. "We've got to roll these wagons. Even now we'll have to stay at it all day in order to get to the house before dark."

Shumaker stepped to the boardwalk and stood watching the receding wagons for a few moments, then spun on his heel and disappeared inside a dry goods store.

Sheriff Rountree and a deputy stood on the porch as the wagons passed their office, and both waved. The sheriff cupped his hands around his mouth and called loudly: "Thank you nice folks for coming to our county! I'll be out there to see you after you've had enough time to get settled in!"

Father and son nodded to the lawmen, and the women and children waved.

They were soon traveling northwest on River Road, which, according to Bud Shumaker, ran parallel to the Leon River for more than a hundred miles. Like most river roads, it was good in places and barely passable in others, for the winter rains sometimes brought high water that washed out whole sections. At those times, the heavy wagons simply took out across the open plain. Their wide-rimmed wheels and the hooves of the draft animals would pound out a new road in short order, and other travelers would quickly accept it as the correct way to go.

They stopped at noon to eat their beans and feed the animals, then traveled steadily throughout the afternoon. Then, with the sun no more than an hour high, Dan topped a rise and brought the team to a halt. "That's our new home, Elsie," he said, pointing up the grassy slope.

She took a deep breath and squeezed his arm. "I love it, Dan," she said. "From the way you were talking last night, I thought it was gonna look real bad. Why, after I get through sweeping and mopping the house and trimming up that yard, it's all gonna look real pretty."

"Well, maybe so," Dan said. "Now that I'm seeing it for the second time, I reckon it even looks better to me." He patted his wife's knee. "I'll leave it entirely up to you, little lady. If you're pleased with it, we'll live in it. If not, we'll build something else."

She smiled broadly. "I'm pleased," she said. "I've always liked old houses. If we find something wrong with it, we'll just fix it. No need to build another one." She pointed to the wooden wellcurb in the yard, less than a dozen steps from the front porch. "And look how close the water well is to the house, Dan. I believe the windlass is still there, too."

"It is," Dan said. "Needs a new rope, though. There's a big spring on the hill behind the house, so we'll get our drinking water up there till after we clean out the well." He slapped the mules with the reins and drove on up the slope. He tied the team to a hitching rail twenty yards from the house, then helped his wife to the ground.

"Thank you for not driving the mules into the yard," she said. "I'm gonna have enough work to do without having to clean up after them."

He pressed his finger against her lips. "No reason to thank me, 'cause I didn't even think about that. I just stopped out here because this is where the hitching rails are."

All six of the children had by now scampered noisily up the steps and disappeared inside the house. While the women followed after the children, the men stood in the yard talking. Pointing down the western slope toward the barn, shed, and corral, Dan was saying, "I looked that barn over pretty good the other day, son, and I sure didn't see any sign that it leaks. About as much room in it as we're likely to ever need, too. Wide hall with four stables on each side, and them big timbers supporting that loft'll hold up as much hay as you can stack in it. Big corncrib and harness room, and somebody even left us two metal grain bins."

"It looks mighty good from here," Seth said. "You say the corral's in good shape, too?"

Dan nodded. "I walked all the way around it. It's gonna be there for a while."

"Well, I reckon we need to get these animals in it," Seth said. He called the twins from the house and reminded them that the teams must be unharnessed, fed, and turned into the corral. Then he led his saddler to the shed and stripped the saddle. When he slipped off the bridle inside the corral, the horse whirled and ran completely around the inside of the enclosure, bucking and kicking wildly with every jump. Seth smiled, and stood watching for a while. He knew that he would take some of the vinegar out of the big animal within the next few days, for he had a twelve-section ranch to look over.

He instructed his sons to feed both of the saddle horses along with the mules, then took an ax to a dead tree lying a few yards from the house. When he had chopped up a few limbs, he called to his wife: "Where do you want this wood, Em? Are you gonna cook supper outside, or in there in the fireplace?"

She stepped through the doorway and onto the front porch. "Build a fire right there where the wood is," she answered. "We'll do our cooking the same way we've been doing it till Mr. Shumaker brings that stove out."

After sending Matthew to the spring for a bucket of water, Seth raked up several handfuls of bark, twigs, and dead grass, then put a match to the pile. A few minutes later, he turned the cookfire over to the women and got out of their way.

Darkness had already closed in when supper was served. They extinguished the fire and ate their beans, potatoes, and hoecakes by lanternlight, then continued to sit beside the woodpile talking. "That spring up there puts out some of the best water I've ever tasted," Elsie said to no one in particular.

"It is good," Dan agreed. "I drank some of it the other day. I reckon the water in that well might be just as good, but we need to clean it out before anybody drinks out of it." He was quiet for a few moments, then spoke to his son: "We'll unload the wagons first thing in the morning, Seth. Then I want to take all three of 'em back to Gatesville. I'm gonna buy furnishings for this house, and I won't wait for Shumaker to bring out the stove. I'll haul it home myself.

"Your ma will be going along with me so she can pick out the things she wants. I'll drive one of the wagons, and the twins can drive the other two. I reckon you should stay here with Em and the rest of the kids, 'cause if we all go to town, there won't be enough room left in the wagons to haul anything." He pointed to the plain on the west side of the house. "As soon as I get back I'm gonna plow up about an acre of that land over there so we can get some turnips in the ground. If we're lucky, we might get a few messes of greens before frost comes along and wipes 'em out."

"It's worth a try," Seth said. "Won't cost us anything but some seed to find out. Let's plant some mustard greens while we're at it. I like them better, anyway."

"Me, too," Dan said. "We'll plant several rows of each."

9

★

Dan, Elsie, and the twins left for Gatesville an hour after sunup next morning, leaving Seth, Emerald, and the other four children behind. Emerald immediately put eight-year-old Paul and seven-year-old Joseph to work carrying bucketfuls of water down from the spring. She and Rachel intended to scrub and mop every room in the house, she said, and the dog run and both porches as well. The first place they would clean was the room on the northeast corner, which Emerald had already designated the schoolroom. That was where she would teach her children, and their grandfather had volunteered to bring them a long table and some chairs when he returned from Gatesville.

With his gunbelt buckled around his waist, Seth spent an hour inspecting the barn, shed, and corral, then roped the roan and cinched down the saddle. He shoved his Henry in the boot, then mounted and rode to the top of the hill, where he sat his saddle unmoving for the next half hour. His present position was two or three hundred feet above the valley floor, and offered an unobstructed view of the area for miles around.

With the exception of the tall pecans that grew wherever excessive moisture accumulated, the rolling plains to the west were practically treeless, with only an occasional cluster of mesquites, junipers, or cedars scattered about. Casting his eyes to the northwest, he could determine the path of the crooked Leon River for many miles. All the way past the Hamilton County line, he was thinking.

To the south was relatively level pastureland, with lush perennial grasses that stayed green for about half of the year, then cured on the stem much like hay. Seth sat shaking his head at the wonderment of it all. At no time in his life had he ever expected to be a partner in such a layout.

He took one last look at the terrain in every direction, then guided the roan back down the hill. He would turn the horse into the corral, then find out if there was something he could do to help his wife. When he reached the spring he watered his mount from the runoff, then continued on down the slope.

He pulled up sharply after only a few steps, for he had detected motion across the river. It was the white horse that had first caught his eye, but now he could see the darker form of its rider. He sat his saddle watching, gauging the snowy animal's progress by comparing it to stationary objects. More than a mile away, he finally decided, and headed directly toward the river, which was shallow enough to ford just below the house.

He kicked the roan down the hill and dismounted when he reached the yard. He tied up at the hitching rail, then walked to the porch and took a seat. He was convinced that he was about to have company, for the big white horse had by now cut the distance in half. When the rider splashed across the river and headed up the slope a few minutes later, Seth slid off the porch and walked to the hitching rail to meet him.

"Howdy," he said when the man had brought his animal to a halt. "Get down and tie up."

The man stepped from the saddle and offered a handshake. "My name's Tom Tipton," he said, pumping Seth's arm. Seth returned the firm grip and introduced himself, then dropped his hand to his side.

"I own three sections across the river," Tipton continued, wrapping his horse's reins around the hitching rail. "Me and my boys do a little truck farming and run a few head of cattle. I ran into Bud Shumaker in town yesterday, and he told me he'd just sold this place. Then I saw your fire early last night, and decided I'd come over and meet you this morning." Though he appeared to be at least fifty years old, and stood no taller than five six, Tipton was nonetheless a powerfully built man. Broad shouldered, with long, muscular arms and scarred hands, he had the look of a man who was no stranger to hard work. He stepped away from the rail and raised his bushy eyebrows, his leathery face breaking into a smile. "You folks about to get settled in?"

Seth shook his head. "Not even close," he said. "My parents and my two oldest boys are gone to Gatesville right now to pick up some furnishings. We traveled awful light coming from Kentucky. Didn't even bring a cookstove."

Tipton chuckled. "Even a little stove's too heavy to haul that far. We didn't bring one when we came out here, either."

Seth stood thoughtfully for a moment, then asked, "How long ago was that?"

"Be fifteen years next February. We starved out trying to make a living in Alabama, so me and my wife and two sons just piled what little we could in a one-horse wagon and pulled out in the dead of winter. It was a long, cold trip, but I don't reckon none of us has ever regretted it." He pointed across the river. "Fellow sold me that west section on credit back in fifty-two, and over the years I've bought the rest of what I own a few hundred acres at a time."

Seth nodded, then motioned toward the house. "Let's move up there out of the sun," he said. "I can't offer you a chair, but that wide plank on the edge of the porch makes a pretty good seat." They walked to the porch and seated themselves. "I reckon you must have been here before Gatesville or Coryell County either one," Seth said.

Tipton smiled. "Aw, there were a few people over there where Gatesville is now, on account of old Fort Gates," he said, "but I don't remember ever hearing anybody call it a town. Weren't nothing up at Hamilton then, either. Everything we needed that we couldn't build ourselves had to be hauled out of Waco.

"As for Coryell County, I reckon we'd already been here a couple years by the time they got it surveyed and named. Comanches killed the first two surveyors who tried to lay it out. That not only brought the army down on the Indians, but it put close to a hundred armed civilians in the saddle as well.

"The killing of the surveyors was the Comanches' undoing in this area, 'cause every settler within fifty miles was soon on their trail and breathing fire. When they found 'em they didn't treat 'em nowhere near as nice as the army did, either. No sir, when a civilian came onto a Comanche, he left him lying right where he found him. After that went on for a while, there didn't seem to be none left to find."

"You mean they never did come back?"

Tipton shrugged. "Maybe a few of 'em did, but I sure ain't seen 'em. Don't reckon I've seen a Comanche in four or five years. Now, I've been told that there's still a few up around Hamilton, and a whole lot of 'em north and west of there."

"Well, I don't have no score to settle with the Comanches," Seth said. "Don't want no truck with 'em one way or the other."

Tipton shook his head. "You ain't likely to ever see one around here, but I certainly wouldn't recommend riding about the country unarmed."

"I wouldn't dream of it," Seth said. "I didn't even do that back home. I intend to have a short gun and a Henry both with me every time I step out the door." He sat quietly for a moment, then pointed to the blackened coffeepot beside the ashes of their morning cookfire. "Plenty of coffee left in that pot. If you'd have a cup with me, I can warm it up mighty quick."

Tipton smiled. "I don't recall ever turning down a cup of hot coffee."

Seth kindled a small fire and placed the coffeepot on some rocks above it, then stepped inside the house for some cups. Ten minutes later, with the men back on the edge of the porch sipping the hot liquid, Seth continued to question his visitor: "You say you run a few head of cattle, Mr. Tipton, and I was just wondering how many cows that amounts to. Do you have a market for beef?"

Tipton chuckled. "I've got about two hundred head, and no, I don't have a market for beef. I reckon I sell enough tallow and hides to break even, but that's only 'cause it don't cost much to run the cattle. Fact is, I just leave 'em alone and let 'em look after themselves, and the only real money I ever spend on 'em is to get 'em rounded up and processed.

"The day's coming when longhorns are gonna be worth something, though. The way I hear it, the railroad is gonna split Kansas wide open, and a whole lot of people think that'll bring about a market for live cattle. If that actually happens, it's gonna make a lot of ordinary men mighty rich, 'cause Texas has got enough cows to feed the rest of the world. There won't be no shortage of young boys who'll jump at the chance to make some money rounding 'em up and delivering 'em to the rails, either."

"No," Seth said, "I guess not." He walked to the pot and refilled their cups, then reseated himself. "Pa and I intend to start a herd of longhorns next year, and I suppose we'll be asking you for a little advice now and then."

"Be glad to help you any way I can," Tipton said. "If you go to southeast Texas and hire up a bunch of Mexican ropers, you can get your cattle for nothing. Several million head of unbranded stuff in the Big Thicket, and they belong to any man who can drag 'em out of there and put his mark on 'em."

"We've been told about that before," Seth said, "and we've already decided to look into it. We'll try to hire the Mexicans, too, 'cause neither one of us knows anything about putting a herd of wild longhorns together."

Tipton was on his feet now. "The vaqueros know everything there is to know about it, so you'd be smart to pay 'em some decent wages and then just turn the job over to 'em. They'll put a herd together for you in short order." He dashed his coffee grounds into the yard and set the cup on the porch, then offered a parting handshake. "I've got to be getting on back home, Mr. Copeland. I've enjoyed meeting and talking with you, and I hope you'll tell your pa that I'm sorry I missed him. I'll probably run into him somewhere later on."

"I'm sure you will," Seth said, gripping the man's hand. "Thank you for coming by, and I suppose we'll be talking again before long. I appreciate the information, and I'll pass it all on to Pa."

Tipton nodded, then walked to the hitching rail and mounted the big white gelding. He kneed the animal down the slope at a trot, then splashed across the river. Once on the other side, he turned in the saddle and waved good-bye. Then he was gone.

PART TWO

★

10

★

In the fall of 1872, Dan Copeland sat on his porch watching the soft blue haze of smoke drifting upward from the smokehouse, the small log building below the cookshack. The cook's helper had been assigned the task of smoking a winter's supply of beef and pork, and the fire had been burning constantly for the past several days. When the process was over, hams, pork loins, and several sides of beef and bacon would be properly cured, and would keep almost indefinitely.

That none of the meat would go to waste was a certainty, for in addition to the Copeland family, the ranch employed fourteen hired hands nowadays. And every man on the payroll was needed most of the time, for six years of hard work and careful management had turned the Copeland spread into the largest ranch in Coryell County. As a result of having the ready cash when many other men fell on hard times, Dan and Seth Copeland now owned thirty sections of land, with about an equal amount of acreage on each side of the river. Their property reached as far north as the Hamilton County line, and three thousand head of longhorns now wore the 2C brand.

Never one to take advantage of another man's misfortune, Dan Copeland himself had initiated none of the land deals. On each occasion, the owner had simply come to him with an offer to sell. Tom Tipton had been the first. During the spring of '67, he had ridden his white horse into the Copeland yard and offered to part with his three sections across the river for two thousand dollars in cash. Being a man with both money and foresight, Dan Copeland had added the Tipton place to his own holdings before the day was out.

As soon as word got around that Copeland had been buying property for cash money, one landowner after another visited him on the Leon. He bought only one additional tract during the summer, however, for he had early on decided not to buy anything that did not join property he already owned. Later in the year, when he told one man that he would not buy a particular piece of property because it did not join his own holdings, the man was back two days later with the owner of the property that lay between them in tow. Copeland bought both men out, then spread the word that he was no longer in the market for acreage. The sprawling 2C already covered thirty square miles.

Five years ago the Copelands had hired a crew of Hardin County vaqueros to drag a thousand head of cows and fifty bulls out of the Big Thicket. Though none of the Mexicans missed a day's work during the roundup, all refused to take part in the delivery of the cattle to central Texas. Indeed, a young vaquero who would voluntarily give up the ladies and the fiesta for such a long period of time was a rarity. The Copelands had known this beforehand, however, and had recruited a crew of eight men from the Gatesville area for the job. Five of the eight had signed on as regular ranch hands, and still lived and worked on the 2C to this day.

In both 1870 and 1871 the Copelands had contributed a small herd to a community drive up the Chisholm Trail to

Kansas, and had been well pleased with the price they had received for the steers. This year, however, they had hired their own trail boss, who in turn hired his own drovers, then delivered a herd of two thousand longhorns to the rails, losing only fourteen head on the trip.

The trail boss, Bill Penny, had returned from Kansas with some advice for Dan and Seth Copeland: they should consider upgrading their herd, he said, for the Kansas buyers all claimed that their customers in the East were complaining about the low quality of beef produced by the longhorns. Too lean, too tough, and too stringy, they said. "The buyers are begging for any of the shorthorn breeds," Penny said, "and they're willing to pay more money for them. Now, if I owned a big ranch like this, I'd be switching to Herefords. I wouldn't be long about it, either."

Though the Copelands did not immediately act on Penny's advice, it was nonetheless enough to send Seth to a stock growers' meeting in Fort Worth, where he spent three days in conversations with successful ranchers. To a man, they had either already upgraded their own herds or were in the process of doing so. The clamor for quality beef was getting louder every year, they said, and though the longhorn had brought the state of Texas back from the brink of bankruptcy, the animal had served its purpose, and its days were numbered.

Though it would initially create a financial burden for Texas ranchers, the fact that the customers in the East were beginning to demand a higher quality of beef was actually a blessing in disguise: the Herefords were not only decidedly better table fare, but a single animal might weigh twice as much at maturity as would one of its longhorned cousins. And a Hereford could be brought to market in only two years, as opposed to four years for a longhorn. "The long and the short of it," one of the ranchers had said to Seth, "is that a man can grow twice as much beef in half the time on the same amount of grass. Hell, that oughtta be enough to convince just about anybody."

It was more than enough to convince Seth Copeland, who immediately headed for the 2C Ranch to pass the things he had learned on to his father.

"Did you talk to anybody up there about buying some Hereford bulls?" Dan asked after listening to his son's report.

Seth nodded. "I discussed it with several men," he said. "The best offer I got was from a man named Joe Simpson, who lives up on the Bosque River. His place ain't more'n fifty miles from here, and he says he'll deliver seventy-five head of purebred Hereford bulls to us for four thousand dollars. I talked to several other men who had the bulls, but they all wanted more money. One man priced seventy-five head at six thousand dollars."

Dan Copeland scratched his chin and sat thinking for only a moment before saying, "I reckon we'd be smart to do business with Simpson, then."

"Are you saying you think we ought to buy the bulls and breed the longhorn strain out of our herd?" Seth asked.

"Of course that's what I'm saying, son. Otherwise, there wasn't no use in you going to that stock growers' meeting. If we ain't gonna act on the things you learned up there, you might just as well have stayed at home." He sat quietly for a moment, then asked, "You think you can find this Simpson fellow's place?"

"Don't see how I could miss it," Seth answered. "According to his directions, all I gotta do is ride to Meridian and follow the Bosque River northwest."

"Well, you do that. Tell Simpson we'll buy the bulls just as soon as he can get 'em here."

Seth was on his feet and about to head for his own house, which was located three hundred yards across the hill to the west. "I'll leave for Simpson's ranch early in the morning, then," he said. "I'll have a talk with Lefty tonight, and have him put a castration crew together. I want the nuts cut out of every longhorn bull on these premises before the Herefords get here."

That conversation had taken place in the middle of September, and the bulls had been delivered on the first day of November. They had first been driven to the center of the ranch, then allowed to wander wherever their instincts dictated. They had taken to the longhorn cows immediately, and even now, two weeks later, Dan Copeland had never seen a single one of them.

Nor was he likely to see one unless it wandered close to the house, for he seldom walked farther than a hundred yards, and almost never took to the saddle. He had lost his right foot and several inches of his leg to a mowing machine in the summer of 1867, and for the past five years had spent a large portion of his time sitting at a table on the west end of his front porch. Although he owned three peg legs, one made by himself and the others bought from a doctor in Gatesville, he preferred to do his limited amount of walking with crutches, complaining that none of the legs fitted his stump and all were too painful to wear.

He took part in only the most important decisions concerning the day-to-day operation of the ranch nowadays, leaving most 2C matters in the hands of Seth and his foreman, Lefty Ingalls. Dan himself had been spending almost as much time in town as he spent at home during the past several months, for he had discovered a new pastime. On Friday mornings, he would usually order that his favorite mare be hitched to his buggy, then head for Gatesville, seldom returning before Monday or Tuesday. Once in town, he spent his days playing dominoes at Runt Bailey's billiard parlor, and his nights at the Durant Hotel.

Aside from good-naturedly accusing her husband of being addicted to the game, Elsie had accepted his long absences passively, and spent much of her time across the hill with her daughter-in-law and her grandchildren, the youngest of which was a boy named Abel, born on the 2C Ranch in January of 1867.

Even as Dan sat on the porch reminiscing, Seth rode around the corner of the house on the big gray he had recently acquired. "Good morning, Pa," he said, remaining in the saddle. "Today being Friday, I figured you'd already be gone to the domino parlor."

Dan chuckled softly. "I've been sitting here thinking about it ever since breakfast, and the day ain't over yet. Fact is, if you'll have one of the men hitch up my buggy, I'll be heading down the road to Gatesville right away."

"I don't need to ask anybody else," Seth said, turning his horse toward the corral. "I'll hitch up your buggy myself and deliver it to you right here at the steps."

Half an hour later, with his wife and son standing on the steps waving good-bye, Dan drove the buggy out of the yard and down the road. "Your pa won more'n a hundred dollars playing dominoes last weekend," Elsie said, staring after the vehicle.

"He told me," Seth said. "I can't see that he has a pressing need for a hundred dollars, but if playing dominoes takes his mind off the fact that he can't get around well enough to do anything else, I don't reckon there's anything wrong with it. I keep hoping that he'll finally get bored with the game and start staying home with you, though."

Continuing to stare after the buggy, Elsie put her hand on Seth's shoulder. "Your pa's a good man, son, and I know for a fact that he never done nothing to deserve all this bad stuff that's come on him with that leg. I don't care how much time he spends in town, either, not if it puts his mind at ease. I tell you, it just breaks my heart to see him standing on the edge of that porch watching everybody else walking around." She squeezed his shoulder. "I've known him most of my life, Seth, and last week was the first time I've ever seen a tear on his cheek." She pointed to the west end of the porch. "He was standing over there watching Joseph and Adam race each other to the top of the hill, and all at once he just started crying."

Seth turned to his mother and hugged her tightly. "I reckon understanding exactly how he feels is impossible for the rest of us, but I believe he'd start acting like a different man if he could walk around without hurting."

"Why, I'm convinced of that," Elsie said, "but I sure don't know of anything we can do to stop that leg from hurting him."

They seated themselves on the top step. "I've been seeing men walking on peg legs for most of my life," Seth said. "I don't recall ever seeing one who looked like he was hurting, so there must be somebody somewhere who knows how to make 'em fit." He stepped into the yard, then turned back to his mother. "I've been thinking about riding over to Waco, Ma. A town that size oughtta have more'n one man with a peg leg, and it seems to me that they'd be the right folks to talk to. Maybe one of 'em could put me in touch with a man who knows what he's doing."

Smiling broadly, Elsie got to her feet and leaned against a post. "I think that's the best idea any of us has had, Seth. Maybe you oughtta leave today, while your pa's not here to argue with you."

Seth nodded and looked toward the corral, where his saddler stood tied to a fence post. "I'll be on my way within the hour," he said, then walked away at a fast clip.

He stopped at the cookshack and instructed the cook to prepare enough smoked meat and biscuits for two meals, then rode on to his own house to inform his wife of his decision. Half an hour later, he buckled on his gunbelt and shoved his Henry in the boot, then rode to the bunkhouse to pick up a bedroll. It was not that he intended to spend the night on the trail, for he expected to be in Waco before dark, but he had always been one to prepare for unforeseen circumstances whenever possible.

He put the food and two canteens filled with water in his saddlebags, then headed down the hill toward the river, waving good-bye to his mother as he rode through the yard. Moments later, he splashed across the shallow ford and headed cross-country, knowing that he could save ten miles or more by disregarding the roads. He turned the gray's head in an easterly direction and kicked the big beast to a lively canter, intending to eat his supper in Waco.

With the exception of the few times he dismounted to relieve himself, Seth stayed in the saddle all day, and the trip was uneventful. He arrived in Waco with daylight to spare, and stabled his mount on the west side of town a few minutes before dark. "I reckon the Palace Hotel is the best place to stay," the liveryman said in response to a question from Seth. "And the Texas Saloon must have the best vittles, 'cause that's where just about everybody eats." He stood in the wide doorway pointing. "The Palace is on the left-hand corner two blocks east, and the Texas is a few doors down on the same side of the street."

"Thank you," Seth said. Then, with his saddlebags across his shoulder and his Henry cradled in the crook of his arm, he crossed the street and headed for the hotel. A few minutes later, he stepped inside the establishment just as the desk clerk touched a burning match to the wick of a coal-oil lamp.

"I guess you'd be wanting a room," the scrawny old man said in a weak, raspy voice. He placed the globe back on the lamp, then turned to face his prospective customer. "The price of rooms went up two days ago. They cost ninety cents a night now."

Seth nodded, and began to fish around in his pocket.

"You don't need no money yet," the man said, spinning the register around on the counter. "At least not till you sign your name right there. That's another thing that's new around here. The town marshal says that every man who sleeps in this hotel has got to have his name in that book."

"Sounds reasonable to me," Seth said. He wrote his name in the register, then laid ninety cents on the counter.

The old-timer picked up the money and handed over the key to room 210. "It's right at the top of the stairway," he said. "Now, we ain't responsible if you let somebody steal your stuff, 'cause that key was made to lock that room. If you don't use it, and a thief cleans you out, it'll be nobody's fault but your own."

Seth smiled at the old-timer. "Yes, sir," he said, then climbed the stairs and turned his key in the lock. Once inside, he lit the lamp and raised the room's only window, then sat on the edge of the bed for a while, thinking. It had been a long time since he had been inside a watering hole, but the hostler had said the best food in town was served at the Texas Saloon. Aside from being hungry, Seth also needed to talk to some of the local men, and the largest gathering of local men could almost always be found in a saloon.

His decision made, he got to his feet and poured water in the washpan, then washed his face and hands. He brushed most of the dust from his new felt hat with a corner of the bedspread, then shoved his rifle and his saddlebags under the bed. He turned the wick low on the lamp and left it burning, then stepped through the doorway and locked the room. Moments later, he was out on the street.

He stood on the boardwalk in front of the hotel for a while. Looking east, one could easily spot the Texas Saloon, for not only did it boast a large sign, but the nearby hitching rails were all filled to capacity, including those across the street in front of businesses that had closed for the day. Finally, he nodded a greeting to a passerby, then headed for the saloon. He would eat a big supper there, then have a drink at the bar, the first one he had taken since the day he came home from the war.

He stepped through the batwing doors, then moved to the side, waiting for his eyes to adjust. The lamps on the east side of the establishment as well as those behind the bar were all turned low, for it was a well-known fact that most drinkers preferred dim lighting. On the opposite side of the bar, however, back in the northwest corner of the building, there was a roped-off area where the lighting was much brighter. One glance told Seth that this was the dining room. Moments later, he selected a table and pulled out a chair, then doffed his hat and seated himself. A young waiter of Mexican descent was there quickly. "You look like a man who already knows what he wants," he said in perfect English, "but I'll leave this for you, anyway." He laid a bill of fare on the table, then backed away to await Seth's decision.

Seth looked at the menu for only a moment, then motioned the waiter back to the table and ordered his supper. Half an hour later, he was enjoying the best meal he had ever eaten in a restaurant. The T-bone steak was tender enough to cut with a fork, and the mashed potatoes were creamed and seasoned to perfection. There was a bowl of lima beans on the side, and the light, fluffy biscuits were still hot enough to melt butter. Dessert was a dish of fruit cobbler, and the coffee was second to none. Even after Seth was done eating, he held up his cup and asked the waiter for a refill.

He complimented the lady on the quality of the food when he paid his bill, then left a coin on the table for the waiter. A moment later, he slid onto a stool on the west side of the bar. A husky blond-haired bartender who appeared to be in his late thirties was there quickly. Though he said nothing, his raised eyebrows asked the obvious question. "I'll have whiskey and water," Seth said.

The man nodded, and a few moments later set the drink before him. "I saw you over there in the dining area a while ago," he said. "Did you enjoy your supper?"

Seth had been tasting his drink. "I certainly did," he said, then set the glass on the bar. "Best food I've ever eaten in a restaurant."

The bartender smiled. "I've heard that before," he said. "Maggie's reputation for dishing up good vittles is known all over Texas, and one fellow told me that he'd even heard about it out in New Mexico Territory. There ain't no doubt that she's the best cook in this town, and she's hired herself some helpers who do it about the same way she does."

Seth nodded, then pointed to his glass. "How much for the drink?"

"One dime," the man said. "That's regular bar whiskey you're drinking; the better stuff costs fifteen cents."

Seth upended his glass, then dropped a quarter on the bar. "Let me see what the better stuff tastes like," he said.

The bartender pulled a bottle from underneath the counter and poured two fingers of brown liquid in the glass, then topped it off with water. "This is slow-sipping whiskey," he said, placing the glass at Seth's elbow. "According to the label, it's seven years old, and was distilled in Bourbon County, Kentucky."

Seth took a small sip, then ran his tongue over his lips. "Good," he said. "Reminds me of home."

"Home?" the barkeep asked. "You from Kentucky?"

Seth nodded. "Caldwell County. I'm a partner in a ranch over on the Leon River nowadays. The 2C is our brand."

The bartender chuckled. "The 2C?" he asked. "Hell, I've heard men talking about that spread plenty of times. They say a man named Dan Copeland and his son put it together, so you must be the son."

Seth nodded, then pushed his right hand across the bar for a shake. "I'm Seth Copeland," he said.

"I'm Hardy Stillson," the bartender said, grasping the hand with a firm grip. "I used to think that I might eventually own a ranch myself, but I decided a long time ago that it's not ever gonna happen. Costs too damn much money to get into it nowadays."

"I reckon it does cost a lot more now than it used to," Seth said, taking a sip of his whiskey. He sat staring into the glass for a moment, then added, "I sure didn't do anything special to deserve a partnership in the 2C. I just happened to be born in Dan Copeland's house, and Dan Copeland had money."

"I reckon it must be nice," Stillson said. "My folks were as poor as church mice when I was born. Still are, for that matter." Then, turning quickly, he hustled off to the end of the bar to check on the drinkers seated there. It was then that Seth noticed a slight limp in the man's gait. He slid off his stool and raised himself to his full height so he could see the bartender's feet. The man's legs appeared to be perfectly normal, and he wore brown leather boots that were about the same size as Seth's own.

Suppressing a chuckle, Seth reseated himself. The limp he thought he saw had obviously been a figment of his imagination, for there was certainly nothing wrong with Hardy Stillson's feet. Anyway, the man had probably walked several miles behind the bar today, and if his gait had appeared to falter momentarily, it had no doubt been because he was tired. Seth dismissed the matter from his mind and sat sipping at his drink.

Twenty minutes later, the bartender was back. He replenished Seth's drink, then refused payment. "So, Mr. Copeland," he said, leaning halfway across the bar. "What brings you to Waco?"

"It's a long story," Seth began. "You see, my pa's been dragging around on crutches for more'n five years 'cause he can't wear none of his peg legs. He—"

"I had already heard that he lost a leg," Stillson interrupted. "I just kept quiet about it because you didn't mention it yourself."

Seth began again: "Anyway, I came to Waco hoping to find somebody who can build my pa a leg that he can walk on. A doctor in Gatesville had two peg legs made up for him, and Pa built another one himself, but he finally threw all three of 'em in the closet and sat down on the porch. He just sits there all day long looking across the hillside. Feeling sorry for himself, I reckon."

"Sitting around feeling sorry for yourself is a habit that's mighty easy to fall into," Stillson said with conviction. "I know I whined about my peg leg hurting for years before I finally let my wife talk me into going to see old Doc Beeson."

Seth got to his feet and leaned across the bar, craning his neck so he could see the floor. "What do you mean?" he asked. "You ain't got no peg leg."

"I've got something better now," Stillson said, then raised his left leg up even with the bar. He rapped his knuckles against the bar, then against the leg, getting the same sound from each. "It used to be an old pine tree," he said, chuckling.

Clearly impressed, Seth spoke quickly: "That beats anything I ever saw, Hardy. Does it hurt you to walk on it?"

The bartender shook his head. "Not since my stump got toughened up to it. The harness I have to wear to hold it on is a little bit aggravating sometimes, but as far as the leg goes, I hardly ever even think about it anymore."

"Beats anything I ever saw," Seth repeated. "Do you have any problems getting on and off of a horse?"

"Nope. I just put my good leg in the stirrup and pull myself up, then use my left hand to lift the wooden leg over the saddle. I use the same hand to put the artificial foot in the other stirrup, then I ride about as good as I ever did. When I dismount, all I have to do is reverse the process." That said, he turned and walked away to check on some of the other drinkers.

Seth sat thinking for a while, his elbows on the bar and his chin resting in his hands. The limp he had thought he noticed in the bartender's gait had been real, all right, but it had been slight. And judging from the way the man talked, he could do about anything he wanted on his wooden leg. The mere fact that he could hold down a job as a bartender meant that he could stay on his feet and walk around all day.

Would a stubborn man like Dan Copeland be willing to try one of those things? Seth had no way of knowing, but he intended to find out. He put another question to the bartender when the man came back to check on his drink. "Is there a place around here where a man can buy a wooden leg like you've got, Hardy?"

Stillson nodded. "Doc Beeson made mine," he said. "Well, I don't reckon I oughtta say that he made it, but he did all the measuring. He drew the leg up on paper just like he wanted it, then hired somebody else to take it from there. I've heard that a fellow up in Corsicana does the actual carving."

Seth had heard enough. "I'd like to buy one of 'em for my pa," he said. "I'm not sure he'd wear it, but I reckon he's got a little more room left in his closet."

Stillson chuckled. "I think he'll wear it. Ain't no one-legged man gonna be content to sit on his ass once he knows he can get up and prowl around without hurting. Especially a man who loves the outdoors."

The bartender excused himself and made his rounds, then stopped in front of Seth again. "I'll tell you what," he said. "I don't have to come in to work tomorrow till two o'clock in the afternoon. If you'll meet me here in front of the saloon at ten o'clock in the morning, I'll take you over to Doc Beeson's office and introduce you."

Seth was on his feet now. "I'll be here," he said. He pushed his change across the counter for the bartender, then added, "I've already rented a bed for the night. I'm gonna take my butt up there right now and crawl in it."

II

★

The sun was already shining through Seth's window when he opened his eyes next morning, and a glance at his watch told him that it was past seven o'clock. After a few moments of stretching and yawning, he fluffed up his pillow and lay back down, for he was trying to recall some of the details of the dream he had just had. He had dreamed that his uncle John Copeland was dead, accidentally shot by a hunting partner who had mistaken him for a deer.

Although Seth knew that some people believed that dreams amounted to the foretelling of coming events, and others claimed that they sometimes delivered a picture of true simultaneous happenings to a sleeper's mind, Seth put no stock whatsoever in them. Hadn't he dreamed more than once in his lifetime that he himself was dead or dying? Yes, and here he sat very much alive. Nor had he ever been sick.

Nonetheless, the dream had left him with an eerie feeling, for Uncle John had always been one of his favorite people. When Seth and his father had left Kentucky more than six years ago, they had both felt that John Copeland and his family would be joining them in Texas the following year. Uncle John himself had almost said as much, but it had never happened. He had used several different excuses in his letters during the first few years, then finally informed his brother Dan that he had decided to live out the remainder of his days in Caldwell County, Kentucky.

When it became clear to Seth that he was not going to be able to reconstruct the dream, he pushed it out of his mind and dressed himself, then washed his face and hands. A short time later, he was down the stairs and out on the boardwalk.

The town was already beginning to come alive. Several men on horseback and a few wagons were traveling up and down the street, and a considerable amount of foot traffic moved along the sidewalks. He could see that the small restaurant across the street from the hotel was open for business, so he pointed his footsteps in that direction.

Just as he opened the door, a beautiful dark-haired woman who appeared to be about twenty-one years old stepped from the building, fluttering her eyelashes and smiling flirtatiously. "Thank you, sir," she said softly as Seth held the door open. Once she had passed through the doorway, he withdrew his hand and allowed the door to close on its own. Then he stood watching as she crossed the street and headed north, her shapely hips cutting a wide swath. The type of woman that even a happily married man could hardly keep from noticing, Seth was thinking, and his was not the only pair of eyes taking in her movements at the moment. Two men had brought their horses to a halt in the middle of the street, and now sat their saddles gazing northward. When the young woman finally left the boardwalk to enter a store, the men smiled at each other and rode on.

Seth opened the door a second time and stepped inside the restaurant. He selected a table and was just about to pull out a chair when the lady behind the counter spoke: "It would be a big help to me if you'd settle for one of these stools up here," she said. "Our waiter didn't come in this morning."

He nodded, then walked to the counter and seated himself.

A few moments later, she placed a cup of steaming coffee at his elbow, then continued to talk: "You can't depend on these schoolboys nowadays," she said. "They ain't about to get out of the bed and go to work this early in the morning. At least not as long as their daddies keep giving 'em all the spending money they want for doing nothing."

Seth smiled, then changed the subject. "I'll have ham and eggs," he said.

The lady called out the order to the cook, then disappeared into a small room adjacent to the kitchen. She remained there for several minutes, returning just as the cook delivered Seth's breakfast to the service window. "Nice and hot," she said as she set the plate on the counter. "Sing out if you need anything else." Then she pushed a cane-bottomed chair against the kitchen wall and sat down.

Although four of the five men at the counter were on the opposite side from Seth, a bearded middle-aged man dressed in faded overalls sat only two stools away. He had nodded a greeting when Seth first sat down, but had said nothing. He spoke now: "You live around here?" he asked.

Seth shook his head. "I've got a spread over on the Leon River. I rode into Waco on business yesterday, and I expect to be gone tomorrow."

The man nodded, and said nothing more. A moment later, with his curiosity apparently settled, he got to his feet and paid for his meal, then left the building without looking back.

Seth finished his breakfast in silence, then left the restaurant and walked to the livery stable. "I'll be needing my gray for a few hours," he said to the hostler, who had met him in the wide doorway.

The old-timer nodded. "Yes, sir," he said. He took a coil

of rope from a peg on the wall, then disappeared down the hall toward the corral. In a surprisingly short period of time, he led the big horse to the front of the barn. "You want me to put your saddle on him, or do you prefer to do that yourself?"

Seth shook his head. "Don't bother," he said. "I'll take care of it."

A few minutes later, he rode the gray out into the street and turned east. Once past the Texas Saloon, he turned south and rode along the west bank of the Brazos River. The Brazos separated Waco east from west, and was spanned by the largest suspension bridge in America, completed just two years before.

The farther south Seth rode, the more he realized that he was now down where the poor people lived. One crudely built shanty after another lined both sides of the street, with dilapidated bars or saloons occupying most of the corner lots. The street traffic consisted mostly of two-wheeled carts pulled by bony mules or burros, and the hitching rails were barren of saddle horses. Most of the people along the sidewalks, the majority of whom were of Mexican descent, were dressed shabbily, and naked children who appeared to be almost of school age played in some of the yards. Shaking his head at what appeared to be a hopeless situation, Seth guided the gray west for a while, then turned north.

Once he had ridden in a half circle, he could easily see that the men with the money preferred living on the north side of town. Expensive homes that were nothing short of showplaces appeared to be the rule rather than the exception. At one point, Seth brought his animal to a halt in front of two stone mansions facing each other from opposite sides of the street.

He sat his saddle looking from one of the stately buildings to the other, either of which he believed had cost more money than had the 2C Ranch. What were the men like who lived in them? he asked himself. And how could a rational man ever convince himself that he needed such splendor?

The truth of the matter, Seth believed, was that none of them actually did think he needed it. It was simply a way for a man to flaunt his wealth, to perpetuate the false impression that he was exceptionally brilliant because of his ability to accumulate large sums of money.

Seth smiled at his thoughts, then kneed his animal on down the street. The men who lived in those mansions were undoubtedly the same type of men who paid thousands of dollars for flashy diamond rings, he was thinking.

At ten o'clock Seth was back at the Texas Saloon, where Hardy Stillson stood at the hitching rail holding the reins of a tall chestnut. "Good morning," Stillson said as he stepped into the stirrup and threw his leg over the saddle. "You're right on time."

Seth nodded a greeting. "Have you been waiting long?"

Stillson shook his head. "No more'n three minutes." He motioned toward the river. "We'll have to ride across the bridge. Old Doc Beeson's office is on the east side of town, where the rent's cheaper." He led off down the street, and Seth was beside him quickly.

Once across the river, they turned south along a row of small houses. As they neared the corner, Stillson pointed to a medium-sized clapboard building with a sagging roof and peeling brown paint. "That's Doc Beeson's office," he said. "Well, that ain't all it is; he lives there, too."

They tied their animals at the hitching rail, then walked across the porch. Hearing their footfalls, the doctor himself opened the door. Appearing to be about sixty years old, he was a gray-haired, stoop-shouldered man who stood about five six and probably weighed a hundred thirty pounds. "Good morning, Mr. Stillson," he said in a high-pitched voice. "Come right in."

Inside the large room, the doctor pointed to a long, high-backed sofa. "You men have a seat there," he said. "Don't neither one of you look sick, so you must have something else on your minds."

Both men remained standing. "This is my friend Seth

Copeland," Stillson said, "and he's got a problem I think you can help him with." As Seth shook the doctor's hand, Stillson continued to talk: "His pa lost a leg a few years ago and all he wants to do now is sit around feeling sorry for himself. Got three peg legs and won't wear none of 'em." He motioned to Seth. "I reckon he can tell you about it a lot better'n I can."

The doctor nodded, then directed Seth to a chair on the near side of a large desk, seating himself on the opposite side. "Now," he said, "tell me about your pa. I'd especially like to know what he does for a living, what he used to do for pleasure, and how long it's been since he lost the leg."

Seth pulled his chair closer to the desk and spoke for several minutes, laying out most of Dan Copeland's life history.

Beeson listened attentively and never interrupted once. "Has your father ever tried an artificial leg?" he asked when Seth had finished talking.

"No. I don't know that he's ever even seen one."

The doctor was quiet for a moment, then asked, "How tall is he?"

"He's just a little shorter than me," Seth answered. "I remember hearing him say more'n once that he measured exactly six feet."

Beeson sat scratching his jaw for a few moments, then smiled. "Six feet, huh?" He walked across the room and opened a closet door. When he returned he was carrying a contrivance whose very appearance left no doubt as to its intended function: a wooden leg about fifteen inches long with a foot that looked almost human. "The fellow who wore this was a six-footer," he said. "Reckon he's dead and buried now, though." He handed the device to Seth, then reseated himself behind his desk.

Seth examined it closely. Complete with an adjustable harness that buckled around the waist, thigh, and calf, it appeared to be about the right length for his pa.

"It came all the way from France," Beeson said. "They're way ahead of us on stuff like that. The same Frenchman who made that leg invented an artificial arm with a hand and fingers that will actually pick up things and hold on to 'em." He scratched his jaw again, then added, "I'd like to see your father strap that thing on and give it a try."

"So would I," Seth said, continuing to look the contraption over. "It might be that he could walk on it without hurting so much."

"Shouldn't hurt him at all," the old doctor said quickly. "At least not after he gets his stump toughened up a little bit." He walked around the desk and took the leg in his hand. "This concave here, where the stump rests, is about four inches deep. That not only keeps it from slipping off when a man raises it off the ground to take another step, but it makes it adjustable. If the leg's too long a fellow can dig the concave a little deeper, and if it's too short, you just pack something in there to build it up. Cotton is all right, but you need something firm underneath it. Felt works best." He fingered the leather harness. "Now, all these straps are adjustable too, so your pa shouldn't have no problem finding the right length." He laid the device back in Seth's lap, then returned to his seat behind the desk.

Seth sat quietly for a moment, then asked, "How much does this thing cost?"

Beeson answered quickly. "I'll let you have it for twenty dollars," he said. "Just take it with you and make sure your pa likes it. If he does, you can bring the money to me first chance you get."

"Why can't I just pay you for it now?" Seth asked. "Then if it turns out that Pa wants to keep it, I won't have to come back over here."

Beeson chuckled. "Well, of course that'll work. The reason I didn't suggest it myself is 'cause I don't know anybody who carries that kind of money around with 'em."

Seth fished an eagle and two half eagles from his pocket

and laid them on the desk. "I don't have any way of knowing what Pa's gonna think of it, but I kinda believe he might wear it."

"So do I," Beeson said, getting to his feet. "Now, I'm gonna ask you to do something that might be a little hard for you, but it's got to be done. You've got to be firm with your pa, 'cause it's quite possible that at least a little bit of his problem is in his head. You're gonna have to order him to put that leg on every morning and keep it on. Once he gets used to it and his stump gets toughened up real good, you might just have a little trouble keeping up with him."

Smiling broadly, Seth got to his feet. "I'll be looking forward to that day," he said. He laid the artificial leg over his shoulder and, with Hardy Stillson close on his heels, headed for the doorway. Once at the hitching rail, he rolled the device up in a blanket and tied it behind his saddle. He mounted the gray, then spoke to Stillson: "I sure appreciate all this, Hardy; maybe I'll get a chance to return the favor someday." He patted the bundle behind his saddle. "After I looked that thing over a little better, I got to thinking that Pa might actually be pleased with it."

"He'll be pleased," Stillson said. "Doc Beeson told you right, though: if your pa don't take to it right away, you've got to ride the hell out of him just like my wife rode me. He'll thank you once he gets used to it." He reached down and tapped his own wooden leg. "I thought I'd never get used to this thing, but now I tend bar on it five days a week. Sometimes I work all day long without even thinking about it."

Seth smiled, and kneed the gray toward the river bridge. "I'll tell that to Pa," he said.

Half an hour before sunset next day, Seth rode into his father's yard. Dan Copeland occupied his usual seat at the west end of the porch, the stump of his right leg dangling from his chair. Seth spoke a greeting, then rode to the corner of the porch and dismounted. He untied the blanket, then hoisted Doc Beeson's contraption over the railing to his father. "This is your new leg!" he said with authority. "It was built to help you walk, and I don't want to see you again without it!" Then, without another word, he spun on his heel and led the gray to the barn.

12

★

When the Copelands had decided to stock the ranch with longhorns in the spring of 1867, Lefty Ingalls, a thirty-year-old native of the Gatesville area, had been the first man hired. Since he was well acquainted with most of the capable cowhands in the county, his first assignment had been to put together a crew to drive the cattle from the Big Thicket to their new home on 2C range.

During the first week of April, the Copelands and their newly hired eight-man crew had ridden southeast to Hardin County. Once there, Dan Copeland had hired a crew of Mexican vaqueros to drag more than a thousand head of longhorns out of the Big Thicket, an endeavor that had taken almost a month. As the vaqueros captured one animal after another, it had been the job of Ingalls and his seven hand-picked men to brand and hold them together. Not an easy task, with the Mexicans adding twenty to fifty new cows to the herd every day, each bunch seeming to be a little wilder than those delivered the day before.

The fact that Ingalls was an excellent cowhand was evident right from the start, and every man he had chosen for his crew soon proved to be of the same caliber. He had demonstrated his vast knowledge of cattle on many occasions by the time the herd reached central Texas, and his ability to handle men had long since become obvious. Two days before the drive was over, Seth offered Ingalls a permanent job as ranch foreman, and the offer had been accepted.

That same night, with everyone present except the two night herders, Seth spoke a few words around the campfire. "Starting tonight," he said, "Lefty Ingalls is foreman of the 2C Ranch. I don't know what kind of plans you men have for the future, but anybody who's interested in a full-time job can take it up with Lefty. From now on, he's the boss." That said, he headed for his bedroll beside his father, who was already snoring loudly.

Seth had made that little speech almost five years ago, and Lefty Ingalls had been calling the shots for the 2C Ranch ever since. Though he rigidly insisted on hard work and self-discipline, and had dismissed more than one man for slacking, Ingalls was considered to be fair-minded by most, and the fact that he knew his business was questioned by none. Not only did he always seem to know exactly what needed doing, he knew the best way to do it, and not a single one of his decisions had ever been overruled by either of the Copelands.

As knowledgeable as the 2C foreman had been, however, his decision-making days were over. Today Lefty Ingalls lay on a cot in the bunkhouse with nickels on his eyelids, shot through the heart with a .44-caliber Colt.

The killing had taken place in the horse corral, and both Dan Copeland and his wife had heard the shot. Dan, who was getting around well on his artificial leg these days, was out of the house and down the slope quickly. The body of Lefty Ingalls lay just inside the corral gate, and Jim Bundy, a dark-haired twenty-two-year-old six-footer who had been working on the ranch for about six months, stood leaning against the barn wall, his Colt riding low on his leg in a tied-down holster.

"He's been treating me like a dog for weeks, Mr. Copeland," Bundy said, pointing to the body. "When I finally told him that I'd had enough of it, he called me a dirty name and drew on me. It turned out that I was just a little bit faster'n him, but you can plainly see that he tried to kill me. See his gun lying there on the ground where he dropped it?"

Dan stood looking down at the corpse for a moment longer, then said softly, "I see the gun."

"Well, I just wanted to make sure you knew exactly what happened here," Bundy said. "Now that you know I shot Ingalls in self-defense, I reckon I'll get my bedroll and hit the road. I damn sure don't want all his buddies looking down their noses at me day and night." He headed for the bunkhouse, where his saddled horse stood waiting at the hitching rail. "Yesterday was payday," he said over his shoulder, "so I don't reckon the 2C owes me any money."

Dan was still standing beside the body when he heard Bundy ride down the hill and take the Gatesville road, making no effort to spare his mount. A moment later, twelve-year-old Adam stepped through the corral gate, saying, "I was afraid of that man, Grandpa; that's why I've been hiding over there behind the chicken house. I watched him shoot Mr. Ingalls, and I was scared he'd shoot me too if he saw me."

Dan turned to the boy quickly. "You saw Bundy shoot Lefty down?"

"Yes, sir," Adam answered. He pointed to a medium-sized oak a few feet from the west side of the corral fence. "I was standing right there by that tree when he walked out of the stable and called Mr. Ingalls's name. He was already holding his gun out like he was aiming at something, and when Mr. Ingalls turned around, well . . . that's when Mr. Bundy shot him."

"Lefty didn't go for his gun?"

"No, sir, he didn't have time. He went down mighty quick after he got shot."

Dan pointed to the Colt lying beside the body. "Then how come—"

"Mr. Bundy done that, Grandpa," Adam interrupted. "After Mr. Ingalls fell, Mr. Bundy walked over and jerked his gun out of its holster, then threw it on the ground. I reckon the gun didn't land just right to suit him, 'cause after he looked it over for a little bit, he went back and moved it up closer to the fence, where it's at now. I hid behind that tree, and just as soon as he moved back against the barn, where he couldn't see me, I eased back down the hill, then snuck up behind the chicken house."

Dan stood staring off into space for a moment, then spoke to his grandson again: "Are you absolutely sure it happened just like you said, Adam? Is there even the slightest chance that you could be mistaken?"

The boy shook his head. "No, sir. I told you exactly what I saw, Grandpa, and I sure ain't made no mistake."

Dan put his hand on the boy's shoulder. "I believe you, son." He pointed to a particular animal in the corral, then added, "Put a saddle on that bay, then hunt up your pa and tell him to come to the house. Tell him to bring at least two men with him if they're handy."

Adam took a coil of rope off the barn wall and shook out a loop. "I already know where he's working at, but it'll take me about an hour to get there. He took three men with him and went to finish filling in that old well up by the northeast line shack. One of the hands said a calf fell in it last week."

"Well, you hurry on up there, son," Dan said. "Tell your pa to get here as quick as he can." He glanced at the body again, then limped off to the house, where he stood on the porch watching till Adam had ridden over the hill.

When Seth Copeland pulled his lathered team to a halt in the barnyard three hours later, it was obvious that he was an angry man. He handed the reins to one of the men in the wagon with him, then jumped to the ground. "Adam says that no-good Jim Bundy shot Lefty down in cold blood!" he said to his father, who stood leaning against a fence post.

Without a word, Dan swung the corral gate open and pointed to the body.

Seth was through the gate quickly, bending over to shoo a green fly out of his departed friend's open mouth. He stared at the corpse for a while longer, then pointed to the shed and spoke to one of his three helpers, all of whom were now standing beside him. "Bring that old discarded door over here, Rusty. We'll put Lefty on it, then take him to the bunkhouse and put him on his own bed."

Once the body had been moved to the bunkhouse, Seth called Rusty Walker aside. "I want you to saddle that big roan gelding and head for Gatesville, Rusty. The horse can travel the whole distance at a good canter, so don't waste any time getting there. Tell Sheriff Rountree we need him out here immediately. Tell him a murder has been committed on the 2C."

"I'm on my way," Walker said, heading for the corral.

By late afternoon, the only members of the 2C crew who were unaware of the shooting were the four men at the line shacks. All of the others had drifted in from their jobs, and now stood around in clusters of two or three discussing the untimely death of their foreman. The ranch cook, an old-timer who answered to the name of Pappy Wade, had cried like a baby at the news, for he had known Lefty since the foreman was a schoolboy. In fact, it had been Ingalls who had hired Wade and put him in charge of the cookshack. And though Pappy had stood over the stove with tears in his eyes for most of this afternoon, he had been quick to inform those who asked that supper would be on time tonight.

Though young Adam had seen the body early on, neither of the women nor any of the other children had viewed Lefty Ingalls's remains. Elsie had crossed the hill to the home of her daughter-in-law when Dan first gave her the news, and had been there all day. Emerald had ordered the younger children not to even walk down the hill, and the twins, now sixteen and a half years old and over six feet tall, refused to look at the dead man, saying they wanted to remember him the way he looked when he was alive.

When the sun was only a few minutes above the treetops, Seth and his father sat on the west end of the porch. "Don't you think the sheriff has had plenty of time to be here?" Dan asked.

"I believe so," Seth answered. "Rusty took the fastest horse on the premises, so he probably got into Gatesville around dinnertime. That don't mean he found the sheriff right away, though. Rountree ain't always where you'd expect him to be."

They sat quietly for a while. Then Dan leaned over the railing and pointed up the road. "Looks like three riders coming yonder," he said. "I reckon one of 'em would be Sheriff Rountree."

"Most likely," Seth said.

Nothing else was said till after the riders left the road and turned up the hill toward the house. "It's the sheriff, all right," Dan said. "Got Deputy Winters with him, too."

"I see Rusty's riding a different horse," Seth said. "He probably used the roan up on the way into Gatesville and dropped him off at the livery stable." He put a hand on the railing and pulled himself out of the chair. "Come on, Pa. Let's go talk to these lawmen about a cold-blooded murderer named Jim Bundy."

13

★

While Rusty Walker rode his borrowed horse on to the barn, the sheriff and his deputy dismounted just outside the yard, where both of the Copelands stood waiting. "Thank you for coming out here," Seth said, nodding a greeting to each of the lawmen. "Get down and tie up."

After the four men shook hands all around, Dan pointed to the corral. "The shooting took place just inside the gate," he said.

Rountree nodded. "I'll look the corral over later," he said, "but I'd like to see the body first. Rusty said it had already been moved to the bunkhouse. I wish it had been left lying where it fell, but what's done is done."

"I'm the one who told the men to move it, Sheriff," Seth said. "I just couldn't stand the thought of them damn blow-flies laying their eggs in his mouth."

"I understand," Rountree said, patting Seth's arm. "I doubt that I could have stood it either. I've known Lefty for more'n twenty years."

When the men entered the bunkhouse a few moments later, Seth stopped at the first cot and pulled back the sheet. After the lawmen had stood for a long time looking down at the chalky, swollen face of the departed 2C foreman, the sheriff turned to his deputy. "Did you ever know of Lefty drawing a gun on anybody, Jeff?" he asked.

"No," the deputy answered. "Never."

The four men stepped outside and put their hats back on. "I understand that one of your sons actually witnessed the shooting, Seth," Rountree said. "How old is the boy?"

"Twelve years and two months," Seth answered.

The lawman nodded, and scratched his chin. "I'd like to talk with him if you don't mind," he said. "I'd like for him to stand in the corral and point out exactly what he saw, and show me where he was standing when he saw it."

"That'll be fine with me," Seth said. He turned to Walker, who was standing close by. "Go up to the house and tell Adam I want to see him at the corral, Rusty. Tell him to come running; it's gonna be dark before long."

Walker nodded, then trotted off up the hillside.

A short while later, young Adam, along with Sheriff Rountree and Deputy Winters, stood beside the oak that had concealed the boy's presence as he watched the shooting. "I saw Mr. Bundy step out of that first stable there with his gun in his hand," Adam was saying as he pointed between the corral poles to the backside of the barn. "He called out Mr. Ingalls's name, and—"

"Let's get closer," the sheriff interrupted. "I think I can follow what you're saying better if we move into the corral."

Inside the corral, Adam spent the next ten minutes drawing the lawmen a vivid picture of the shooting, with every word and every description being written down in a notebook by the deputy. Adam motioned to the dead man's revolver, which had deliberately been left lying where it was found. Then he pointed to a different spot several feet closer to the fence. "The first time Mr. Bundy threw that gun on the ground, it landed right there," he said. "Then after he backed off and looked at it a little bit, he walked over and moved it to where it is now."

Rountree stepped forward and picked up the Colt. "No shell in the chamber," he said after a moment, "but the cylinder's full. Five live shells." He sniffed the barrel, then tucked the weapon behind his waistband, adding, "This gun ain't been fired since God knows when."

Once the sheriff had thanked Adam and said he had no more questions, Seth dismissed his son and sent him back up the hill. As soon as the youngster was out of earshot, the lawman turned to Seth. "I believe it happened exactly like that boy told it," he said, "and there ain't no doubt in my mind that a jury would believe it, too.

"I'd like to go back to town and charge Jim Bundy with murder, but it ain't quite that simple. I'd have to know that young Adam is gonna tell a jury the same things he told me before I go asking the judge for a murder warrant. You see, with the kid being just twelve years old, the prosecutor can't subpoena him to testify in a court of law, and without his testimony, one of them Waco lawyers could come over here and make me the laughingstock of the county."

Seth nodded and smiled, then turned serious. "Did you ask Adam if he was willing to tell a jury what he saw?" he asked.

"No, no," the sheriff said. "A slick lawyer could have used something like that against me. You're the one with the say-so. You're his pa, so it's up to you whether he appears in a courtroom or not." He scratched his chin, then added, "Of course, even if you do decide to let him testify, it'll still have to be agreeable with him."

Seth nodded, then walked to the front of the barn and cupped his hands around his mouth. "Adam!" he called at the top of his lungs. "Adam! Come back down here a minute!"

Two minutes later, the youngster trotted around the corner of the barn. He came to a halt beside his father, then looked up at him questioningly. "Yes, sir?"

"We just thought of a few more things that we need to talk about, son," Seth began. "Do you think what you saw here in the corral this morning was murder?"

"Yes, sir," the boy answered quickly.

"Well, the sheriff's thinking about getting a murder warrant for Jim Bundy, but he'd need your testimony to make the charges stand up in court. Are you willing to tell a jury exactly what you saw? Remember, now, Bundy'll be sitting right there in the courtroom looking at you."

"I don't care how much he looks at me," Adam said. "I'll just look right back at him, 'cause I won't be afraid of him like I was this morning. He knows what he did, and I ain't scared to look him in the eye and tell him that I saw him do it."

Seth tousled his son's hair, then spoke to Rountree: "Is that enough, Sheriff?"

"Guess so," the lawman said. He patted the youngster on the back. "Just tell me one more time, Adam. Exactly what did you see Jim Bundy do?"

Adam pointed first to the stable on the southeast corner, then to a particular spot inside the corral, about ten feet away from the barn. "I saw him sneak out of that stable and step into the corral with his gun aimed at Mr. Ingalls's back. He called Mr. Ingalls's name, then shot him when he turned around."

Rountree nodded. "One more thing, Adam. You say you heard Bundy call Mr. Ingalls's name. Is that what he called him? Mr. Ingalls?"

The boy shook his head. "No, sir. He called him Lefty."

The sheriff smiled. "Thank you, son," he said. "I have no further questions."

When Adam had been dismissed and sent back up the hill a second time, the sheriff announced his decision. "Jeff and I will be heading on back to town now, Seth," he said.

"I don't want to give Bundy any more time to think about it than I have to. I know he was in town when we left, 'cause Rusty saw his horse in the corral at the livery stable."

"His horse was there, all right," Walker said. "Only ring-eyed piebald in the county, that I know of."

Seth pointed to the cookshack. "You men come along and stuff yourselves with some of Pappy's vittles. You ain't about to leave here without being fed."

Each of the lawmen nodded, then began to follow Seth up the hill. "I reckon we'll take you up on that offer," Rountree said. "Then we'll light out right after we eat. Traveling after dark ain't gonna be no problem, 'cause the horses know the way a whole lot better'n we do."

Though the lawmen ate their supper quickly, the sun had already dropped behind the trees when they walked back to the hitching rail. Before untying his animal, the sheriff paused and pulled Seth aside. "I kept quiet in that cookshack on purpose," he said. "Now, I don't mind telling you what I'm gonna do, but I'm asking you to keep it under your hat. I intend to arrest Jim Bundy and charge him with murder, and I expect to have him in jail before daybreak. He should be easy enough to find—he'll most likely be at the hotel sleeping off a quart of whiskey."

The sheriff's deputy was already in the saddle. "I hope we do catch him asleep," he said. "I don't want to have to kill him." A muscular sandy-haired thirty-year-old who stood about five ten, Winters had been Rountree's deputy for the past four years, and was reputed to be extremely fast with a six-gun. "I don't know Bundy very well," Winters continued, "but I've heard that he'll fight at the drop of a hat."

"I've heard that, too," the sheriff said, throwing a leg over his saddle, "but I don't intend to drop no hat. He'll be looking down my gun barrel when he opens his eyes." The lawmen rode down the hill and never looked back, striking a slow canter once they reached the road.

Seth walked to the house and took a seat beside his father, who sat in his usual place on the west end of the porch. Dan Copeland was mourning more than the loss of a foreman. He was having a difficult time coming to grips with the fact that his brother John had been killed in a hunting accident two months ago.

Seth himself had not only mourned the death of his uncle, but had walked around in confusion for many days after the information was received. According to his aunt's letter, the accident had happened exactly the way he had dreamed it more than a month earlier: four friends had been deer hunting on Christmas Day, and John Copeland, who had been wearing a yellowish coat with a gray collar, had been mistaken for a buck by one of the hunters. Buel Fry, Copeland's closest neighbor, had fired into the brush and killed Copeland instantly.

Seth had not only been surprised that his uncle would be foolish enough to wear such colors on a deer hunt with other gunners, but had been appalled by the accuracy of the dream he had had in a Waco hotel room. So much so that he had begun to wonder if it was possible that he had been singled out by some higher power to be apprised of coming events. Without telling anyone else of his actions, he had discussed the matter with both a preacher and a doctor in Gatesville.

"I've always known that dreams were the Lord's way of putting people on notice," the preacher had said. "I know my aunt Bessie used to dream a whole lot of what happened to us long before it came about. Now, that ain't saying that everybody's dreams are gonna come true. The good Lord don't let but a scarce few people know what's gonna come about in the future."

"A dream don't mean a goddamn thing!" Deford Brimley, an old retired army doctor, informed Seth loudly. "Your brain don't go to sleep just because you do; it keeps right on working just like it does when you're awake. The difference is that when you're awake you've got control of it. When you're sleeping, though, you're really unconscious, and you ain't got no control of nothing. Once you go to sleep your mind can just ramble around any old way it wants to, and a good bit of the time it's gonna latch on to the most innocent little thought it can find and blow it all outta proportion."

The conversations with the preacher and the doctor had taken place several weeks ago, and though Seth had continued to think on it for the next few days, he had finally accepted the old doctor's definition of dreams, and had closed his own mind on the matter.

Now, sitting on the porch in the gathering darkness, he spoke to his father more to make conversation than for any other reason. "The sheriff said he sent a man to tell Lefty's sister Sadie about the killing," he said. "I suppose she'll send a wagon after the body tomorrow."

"That's what I expect to happen," Dan said. "You never can tell about folks, though. We ain't got no way of knowing how thick him and his sister were, but if it turns out that nobody comes after him, we'll bury him up yonder on the hill beside that Rainwater baby's grave." He got to his feet and took a few steps toward the door, then added, "We'll wait till noon the day after tomorrow, and if they ain't come after Lefty by then, we'll put him in the ground ourselves." He stepped inside the house and closed the door.

Seth stepped into the yard and, using the lantern hanging over the door as a beacon, walked down the dark path to the cookshack. Inside, he helped himself to a cup of coffee and took a seat at the end of the table. "Have all the men already eaten, Pappy?"

The cook nodded. "They've all been in here," he answered. "Didn't take half as much food to feed 'em as it usually does; most of 'em are pretty well tore up about Lefty, I reckon." He motioned to several large bowls stacked on a shelf along the wall. "This stew's still warm," he said. "You want me to dip you up a bowl?"

Seth shook his head. "No, thank you, Pappy. After I finish off this coffee I'm gonna talk to the men for a minute, then get on up the hill to my own supper table. Emerald complains about me eating down here at the cookshack so often. She says she believes I like your cooking better than hers."

The cook rolled his eyes upward and smiled. "Well?"

A few minutes later, Seth set his empty cup on the table, then walked to the bunkhouse. The nine occupants were all seated in the center of the building near the cast-iron stove, most of them holding their hands out to its warmth. This was the last week of February, and though it usually warmed up during the daytime, most of the nights were downright cold. Seth walked to the stove and addressed the men as a group. "What do you fellows think about us moving the body into the corncrib?"

Simpson Bain was on his feet quickly. "I don't mean no disrespect to Lefty, now," he began, "but I think he shoulda been put in the crib to start with. Even though he was one of the best men I've ever known, I don't reckon me nor nobody else wants to sleep in the same room with a corpse." He pointed to a stack of extra bedding in the corner. "We could wrap him up in one of them thick quilts and put him out there in the shed, for that matter. The shed's a better place for him anyway. Rats might get to him, but hell, we got rats right here in the bunkhouse."

Seth stood quietly for a moment, then asked, "Anybody disagree?" When he received no answer, he turned to Walker. "I guess you ought to get that old door again, Rusty. It'll be a lot easier to move him on that."

Ten minutes later, the body was lying under the shed in the bed of a wagon, wrapped in one of the extra quilts and covered with another.

When all of the hands had returned to the bunkhouse and seated themselves around the stove again, Seth remained standing. "There's a little matter that needs to be cleared up before anybody goes to bed," he said. "We all know that Lefty knew his business and that he left some big shoes to fill, but none of that changes the fact that the 2C needs a foreman." He turned to face Walker. "How about you, Rusty? Do you want the job?"

"I knew that was coming," one of the men said under his breath.

Walker, who appeared to have been taken completely by surprise, did not answer right away. He stood for several seconds with a blank expression, then slowly began to smile. "I don't see how it could amount to any more work than I'm doing now," he said. "I could certainly use the raise in pay, so I reckon I'm the new foreman."

"I'm sure all of you heard the man!" Seth said with authority. "It's like Rusty Walker just said, he's the new foreman of the 2C Ranch. As of right now, he's completely in charge, and I'll be expecting every man here to follow his orders." He spun on his heel and walked to the front of the building. "One more thing," he said as he reached the door. "I reckon somebody ought to ride to all four of the line shacks tomorrow. The line riders ain't got no way of knowing about Lefty, and they all need to be told. Unless some of his folks come and get the body, we'll bury him up yonder on the hill. If that turns out to be the case, I want the line riders to be given the day off so they can come in and pay their last respects."

"Consider it done," Walker said quickly. "I'll send word to Boone and Williams on the west boundary first thing in the morning. Barnes and Drury are riding line on the east side, so I'll visit their shacks myself."

Obviously pleased, Seth nodded and smiled. "Good night, everybody," he said, then closed the door and stepped out into the night.

An hour before sunset next day, when no wagon had come to pick up the body, Walker called a hand named Jud Welty aside, saying, "Ain't nobody coming after Lefty, Jud. Do you feel up to building a coffin for him?"

Welty nodded. "Nothing I ain't done before," he said, then pointed toward the corncrib. "Plenty of good dry lumber under that crib. Are you saying you want it done to-night?"

"No, no," Walker said. "You'll have plenty of time for that in the morning."

Lefty Ingalls was laid to rest at two o'clock the next afternoon. The entire Copeland clan and all of the 2C riders were present, bringing the number of mourners to twenty-four. Though Elsie, Emerald, and all of her children were dressed in their Sunday best, none of the men had departed from the jeans, flannel shirts, and short jackets that they wore every day.

The coffin had been placed in the wagon at a quarter past twelve, then driven up the hill to the grave that two men had finished digging only an hour before. At precisely two o'clock, Dan Copeland nodded to the four men standing beside the wagon, who quickly placed the coffin beside the grave.

The elder Copeland wasted no time. He doffed his hat and held it against his chest, then began to speak slowly: "Lord, we ain't got no preacher, so I reckon I'll have to do. We're about to give You back the remains of our friend Lefty Ingalls, and it just seemed to me like somebody oughtta say a few words. Now, everyone of us standing here has always been taught that You take care of Your own, so I reckon You'll be looking out for Lefty. He was a good, honest man, and we're asking you to take him to that special place you've got for folks like him." He lifted his eyes skyward, then added, "Thank you, Lord."

As most of the mourners began to amble down the hill-side, and the four men prepared to lower the pine box into the grave with ropes, fifteen-year-old Rachel was suddenly standing behind the wagon screaming and sobbing uncon-trollably. Even with the loving embraces and comforting words of her mother and her grandmother, her raving con-tinued for several minutes.

When her sobs had finally given way to an occasional whimper, she laid her head on her mother's shoulder, saying,

"This was all so unnecessary, Ma, and Mr. Ingalls was such a nice man. He used to get me to read his mail to him and write letters for him, and he was all the time telling me how smart I was. He told me more than once that I ought to be enrolled in that big girls' school in Dallas."

Dan Copeland, who had been standing by listening, took his granddaughter in his arms and squeezed her tightly. "Now, you just hurry up and dry your eyes, little girl. There's not a thing in the world any of us can do about what happened, so we've got to live with it." He backed away and held her at arm's length, one hand on each of her shoulders. "You were right about Lefty being a nice man, and Lefty was probably right when he said you oughtta be in that school of higher learning." He released her and took a few steps toward the house, then stopped and turned halfway around. "I'll tell you something else, little girl: if you decide you want to go to that school, I'll see that you get the chance." He walked on down the hill and never looked back.

14

★

Jim Bundy had been in the Gatesville jail for more than two weeks now, charged with the murder of Lefty Ingalls. Just as Sheriff Rountree had predicted, he and his deputy had taken the man into custody in a hotel room, where he had been sleeping off a night of hard drinking. The arrest had been accomplished without incident. Using a spare key supplied by the desk clerk, the lawmen had let themselves into Bundy's room without knocking, and even the fact that the deputy held a lighted lamp in his hand had failed to rouse the sleeping man. The sheriff had shaken him awake with a gun barrel six inches from his nose.

The prisoner had ranted and raved every waking minute for the first few days he was in jail, cursing the law and proclaiming his innocence at the top of his lungs. He was being charged with a murder that had never even been committed, he shouted to anyone within earshot. Even when talking face-to-face with Sheriff Rountree, he swore that he was innocent, that he had fired his gun only after Ingalls had reached for his own weapon.

At the beginning of the second week, however, Bundy had become strangely quiet. His silence had begun shortly after a conversation with a young jailer named Wally Newhouse, who had been hired only two days before. "You're looking at an innocent man," Bundy had said to the twenty-one-year-old apprentice lawman, who was busy sweeping the floor in front of his cell. "Lefty Ingalls tried to kill me, and I had to shoot him in self-defense." When the young man said nothing, Bundy continued. "Anyway, the jury's gonna laugh the sheriff right outta the courtroom, 'cause he ain't got a damn lick of evidence."

"No evidence?" the young jailer asked, leaning his broom against the wall. "What do you call evidence? Twelve-year-old AdamCopeland was an eyewitness to the whole thing. He was standing less than fifty feet away when you shot Lefty Ingalls down in cold blood, and he'll be testifying to that in court." He chuckled, then retrieved his broom and walked on down the hall. "I'd call that pretty strong evidence, mister," he said over his shoulder.

Bundy's ranting had ceased after that conversation, and when he did say something he spoke in lower tones. He spent most of the daylight hours standing on his cot looking through the double-barred outside window. When he asked the sheriff when the trial was set to take place, he actually appeared to be relieved when Rountree told him it would most likely be at least a month before the circuit judge would be in town. "You in a hurry?" the lawman asked.

Bundy did not answer, and turned his face to the wall.

The prisoner's demeanor had changed considerably after he had a couple visitors, and he had even begun to laugh and joke a little with whichever jailer was on duty at the time. The two male visitors, appearing to be about Bundy's own age, had informed the young deputy that they were friends from out of the county, and after turning over their guns and submitting to being frisked for other weapons, they had been allowed to stand outside the cell and talk with Bundy. After several minutes of muted conversation, they had thanked the jailer and departed.

Though the visitors had told the unsuspecting jailer that their names were Tom Ripley and Buddy Banks, from Mills County, they were actually Eldridge Boone and Clint Williams, the line riders on the 2C Ranch's western boundary. Neither man had liked Lefty Ingalls, but both were enamored of Jim Bundy. They had witnessed his awe-inspiring fast draw, and had been equally impressed with his long-winded tales of gunfights in Kansas cattle towns. His claims that he had outdrawn and killed several well-known gunmen, that he had run a Kansas marshal out of town, and that he had once backed down two Texas Rangers in Austin were all it had taken to gain the admiration of the gullible line riders, each of whom had himself recently taken up practicing the fast draw.

Neither Boone nor Williams had asked Rusty Walker's permission to take time off from work, and their absence from the ranch had gone undetected. They had ridden almost to Gatesville in the dark of night, then stopped and slept on the ground for a few hours. Shortly after sunup, they chose a hitching rail at the edge of town so the jailer would not see the brands on their animals, then walked to the jail. Once the visit was over they had almost ruined two good horses getting back to the west boundary unseen.

Bundy's trial was finally set for the third week in March, and the prosecuting attorney sent a rider to the ranch with a notice advising the Copelands of the date. Seth would first have to stand before the court and verbally give his permission for his young son to testify, the note read; then Adam would be expected to describe to the jury exactly what he had seen in the corral.

Five days before the trial date, Adam left the house before daylight and eased off into the woods on foot. Bundled up against the cold morning, with his rifle over his shoulder, his intent was to harvest an old turkey gobbler that he had seen on several occasions back in the fall. And Adam believed he knew the exact tree in which the flock roosted, for he had bagged two gobblers there last year. He had called the first one to his rifle at midmorning, and had shot the other off a limb shortly after sunup a week later. For some reason the bird had remained in the tree much later than usual, which had been its downfall.

When Adam had not returned from the hunt by noon, his mother expressed her concern at the dinner table. "It ain't like Adam to stay in the woods this late," Emerald said to her husband, who had been down below the barn all morning building a new hogpen. "He's always been home by nine or ten o'clock, no matter whether he got a turkey or not."

"Ain't nothing to be concerned about," Seth said, sopping his gravy with a biscuit. "If he didn't get a shot at a gobbler, he's probably off hunting something else. He likes to hunt more'n he likes to eat, and he's mighty proud of that new rifle he got for Christmas." He got to his feet and headed for the door. "Don't you worry about Adam no more, now, Em; he'll come dragging in here after a while. I bet he'll have something for you to put in the pot, too." He stepped through the doorway and headed back down the hill.

The sun was no more than two hours high and Seth was still hammering nails when he turned to see Emerald standing beside him, the anxiety she was feeling plainly written on her face. "I sent Mark and Matthew to look for Adam," she said. "I'm worried to death about him."

Seth laid his hammer aside and pulled her to him, holding her tightly and caressing the back of her neck. "Of course you are," he said. "I guess I figured he was already back, but since you say he ain't, I reckon I oughtta be getting a little bit concerned about him myself." He released her and kissed her eyes, then stood thoughtfully for several seconds. "Come to think of it, that rifle of his can be heard for two or three miles, and I don't think he'd walk any farther than that on a turkey hunt.

"Since there ain't none of us heard the rifle, maybe he's hurt himself and ain't in no shape to fire it." He untied the carpenter's apron from his waist and let it fall to the ground. "I'll saddle up and go looking for him myself." He headed for the corral, adding, "You just go on back to the house, now, and quit your worrying."

It was as dark as pitch when Seth and the twins returned to the house, each of them riding in from a different direction. The two lanterns hanging from the porch railing cast a faint glow all the way to the hitching rails outside the yard, where the twins stood waiting for their father to dismount. "Either one of you boys see or hear anything of Adam?" Seth asked, remaining in the saddle.

The twins shook their heads in unison. "No, sir," Mark answered, with his words being echoed by Matthew.

"Where all did you two go?" Seth asked.

In turn, the boys recounted their activities of the afternoon: Mark had ridden west while Matthew had gone north, and each of the boys described as best he could the territory he had covered. "I rode over just about all the area from here west to Beaver Creek," Mark offered. "I kept calling his name as loud as I could all afternoon, but I sure never got no answer. I even went to that old hollow tree where he shot them fifteen squirrels that time, but I didn't see no sign that he'd been there today."

"I did about the same thing up north," Matthew said. "I went everywhere I thought he might have gone, looking for him and calling his name. I was up on the river at Blue Hole when the sun went down, and it was dark by the time I got back here."

Seth turned the gray's head away from the hitching rail. "You boys put up your horses, then go to the house and stay with your ma," he said. He kneed the animal down the hill, adding over his shoulder, "Don't leave the house again till I get back."

A short time later, he framed himself in the doorway of the bunkhouse and motioned to his foreman, who stepped outside quickly. "I reckon we've got a problem, Rusty," he said, then explained that young Adam had failed to return from a turkey hunt that had begun long before daylight this morning.

Walker stood thoughtfully for a moment after hearing the story. "What do you think?" he asked finally. "Comanches?"

Seth shook his head. "Ain't no Comanches on this spread nowadays, Rusty. They ain't that dumb."

Walker stared off into the night for a few moments, then asked haltingly: "You . . . you think there's a possibility that it might have something to do with Adam's being a witness against Jim Bundy?"

"Hell, yes, I think it might," Seth answered. "That's the first thought that hit my mind after he didn't make it home by dark."

They stood in silence for a while. After it became clear that Seth had run out of words, Walker spoke again: "Ain't no question about what we've got to do, then." He left Seth standing alone and stepped inside the bunkhouse door. "Adam Copeland has come up missing, men!" he shouted. "We've got to organize a search party, and I expect every man here to be in the saddle in ten minutes! Light as many lanterns as you can find and meet me at the corral!" A few of the hands had been reading, while the others were involved in a card game. Every man dropped whatever he was doing and reached for his coat.

Walker stepped back into the yard. "You go on up and stay with your family, Seth, and leave this thing to us. If Adam is on this ranch, we'll find him."

"No, no," Seth said quickly. "I couldn't sit up there by that fireplace knowing that my boy might be lying out in the cold somewhere waiting for me to come looking for him. That could be it, Rusty; it could be that he just got hurt some way or another, that he can't do nothing but wait on us to find him."

"I'll get you a light," Walker said. He stepped inside the door quickly, not wanting his boss to see the expression of doubt on his face. A few moments later, he was back in the yard with a lighted lantern in his hand. "I checked the level of coal oil in this thing. It's full, so it'll burn all night."

Seth accepted the lantern, then climbed back into the saddle. "I'm gonna ride west first," he said, " 'cause I believe that's where Adam does most of his hunting. If you men'll ride north for about five miles, then spread out and start tightening the circle back toward the house, I'm thinking we're gonna find that boy pretty quick. He wouldn't have traveled no farther than five miles from home on a hunt. If he intended to do that, he'd have left here on horseback." He kneed the gray and headed west across the hillside.

A short while later, the eight men rode over the hill. Though five of them carried lighted lanterns, Simpson Bain did not. "You can't see nothing with a damn lantern," he had said, passing up a chance to carry one. "All one of them things does is light up whoever's holding it. Don't make no difference how high you carry it, either, you still can't see nothing but it." Since everybody knew that there was a certain amount of truth in what Bain was saying, nobody chose to argue with him.

They rode north for more than half an hour, then spread out, turned west, and began the circle. With at least fifty yards separating them, every man who did not have a lantern was situated between two riders who did; thus, each man was at all times aware of his own location in relation to the other members of the party.

Catching one cluster of sleeping cattle after another by surprise and sending them running, the men rode at a walking gait for hours, calling the boy's name over and over. It was past midnight when they finally dismounted at Gum Spring to water themselves and their mounts. Jud Welty, the oldest man in the group, heaved a sigh of relief as he stepped from the saddle. "Do you really think that boy is still alive, Rusty?" he asked.

Walker stood quietly for a moment, then spoke softly: "I'm not gonna answer that question, Jud. We've all got to act like we believe it whether we do or not, and keep right on looking till we've covered the entire ranch. Anything short of that is completely out of the question."

Welty shook his head. "I wasn't suggesting that we give up the hunt," he said. "I'll stick with it as long as the next man will."

Walker patted the man's shoulder. "I know that, Jud, but that cough of yours is getting louder and a whole lot more frequent. I think you oughtta go back to the bunkhouse and get under a stack of thick quilts, sweat some of that cold out of you before it turns into pneumonia."

"Well, I am feeling kinda poorly. If you think—"

"I know that's what you oughtta do," Walker interrupted. "We can cover the same amount of ground without you if we work a little harder, and we certainly don't want to take a chance on losing you." He pointed to Welty's horse. "Mount up and get on outta here."

Without another word, Welty climbed into his saddle and kneed his animal toward the bunkhouse. "Wake Pappy up when you get there!" Walker called after him. "I remember him telling me that he had a quart of medicine in his locker!"

Though none of the men had seen or heard anything to give them hope during the night, the remaining seven riders continued to move in a half circle hour after hour, their eyes glued to the ground and their voices calling Adam's name. When they finally halted at another spring a few miles southwest of the ranch buildings, the eastern horizon was already taking on a pink hue.

After men and horses had drunk from the spring, Walker put into words what every man in the crowd was already thinking: "It'll be daylight in a few minutes, fellows." He remounted, then pointed northeast. "The quicker we get on to the cookshack, the quicker Pappy'll fire up some breakfast." When the foreman did not lead off, none of the hands made an effort to head for home. After only a few moments, Walker was talking again: "Now, I ain't gonna order none of you to keep up the hunt after breakfast is over. Every man jack of you needs sleep and rest, 'cause you put in a hard day yesterday and you've been in the saddle all night.

"It's a decision each man is gonna have to make for himself. If he decides to go to bed, nobody's gonna feel hard at him. Of course, anybody who wants to keep on hunting can do that, too, and I'm sure the boss and his family will notice it." He blew out his lantern and kneed his animal toward the cookshack. The other riders followed close behind.

It was well past daybreak when they dismounted at the cookshack and tied their animals at its hitching rails. Even with the seriousness of the moment, Walker stood for a while taking in the remarkable view to the east. The morning sun had just come out of the ground on the far side of the hill, and had set the silvery waters of the fast-moving Leon to sparkling like fine wine. Even as he headed for the cookshack, he took another quick look over his shoulder.

Once inside the doorway, all of the men stopped suddenly, surprised to see that the entire Copeland family was there. Dan, Seth, their wives, and all of the children were seated about the room, some on the benches, others on chairs or empty boxes. All who wanted breakfast had evidently been fed, for an oversized dishpan on a small table was filled with plates and other eating utensils that had obviously been used. Emerald, whose plate still sat untouched and had long since grown cold, jumped to her feet at the sight of the seven men. She hurried over to meet them. "Did you see anything, Rusty?" Not waiting for an answer, she looked from one of the hands to the other. "Did any of you see anything? Did you hear anything?"

She looked down the line of solemn faces, then slowly dropped her eyes and began to stare at the floor, for every last man had shaken his head in the negative.

Mark suddenly got to his feet and walked across the room to his mother, placing his hand on her shoulder. "Ma, me and Matthew and Paul and Joseph all need to be in the saddle hunting Adam. We can't do no good just sitting up there at the house with you. I bet any one of us boys knows more about where to look for him than all these men put together."

Emerald said nothing, just placed her hand on top of her son's, then turned to face her husband.

Anticipating his wife's next question, Seth spoke quickly. "I reckon the boy's right," he said. "Let 'em go. They're all about as big as they're ever gonna be."

"I agree with that," Dan said, rising from the table. "Them boys are a whole lot younger'n the rest of us, and they know about every foot of this ranch. Let 'em go hunt their brother."

Mark had heard enough. He motioned to Matthew, Paul, and Joseph; then all four of the youngsters were quickly out of the building and headed for the corral.

Dan made a sweep with his arm, indicating all of the riders. "You men get some breakfast, then go to the bunkhouse and sleep till noon. You can go back to looking this afternoon if you feel up to it."

When the Copeland men and their wives had taken Rachel and Abel back up the hill, Walker and his riders seated themselves at the long dining table. "Looks like old Dan's done made the decision for all of us," he said. "I reckon we'll just eat a while and sleep a while, then go hunting again."

15

★

Every available man scoured the ranch for the next three days, but none saw any sign that young Adam Copeland had ever existed. Barnes and Drury, the line riders on the east boundary, said they had not seen the boy during the past several weeks, while Boone and Williams, the riders on the west side, said they had never seen him, that they did not even know him.

Sheriff Rountree and Deputy Winters arrived at the ranch just before noon on the fourth day, having been apprised of the situation by one of the 2C hands the night before. DanCopeland, who had been standing on the porch watching the approaching lawmen for several minutes, stepped into the yard and walked to the hitching rail to meet them, saying, "Howdy, Will, howdy, Jeff. You men get down and tie up."

The lawmen, neither of whom could remember Dan ever calling him by his first name, slid from the saddle with their right hands extended. "I'm awful sorry about your grandson,

Dan. We didn't find out about it till last night, or we'd have been here sooner."

Dan squeezed the sheriff's hand. "I appreciate your coming," he said. A gust of wind suddenly took the high-crowned hat from his head and deposited it against a small cedar a few yards away. He retrieved the hat, then added, "Don't reckon there's nothing you can do, though." He pointed to the house. "Let's move up on the porch and get outta this wind. Dinnertime ain't far off, and I reckon Pappy'll be dishing up some hot vittles over at the cookshack directly."

Once the men had seated themselves on the west end of the porch, Sheriff Rountree was the first to speak: "I suppose your riders have pretty well covered the ranch looking for that boy. Huh, Dan?"

Copeland nodded. "East, west, north, and south. I ain't said so to his ma, but I don't believe he's alive. Nor do I believe his body is on this ranch." He lowered his head and spoke against his chest, his words barely audible. "It's all so sad, and such a mystery. Adam wasn't old enough to have any enemies."

"He had one," Rountree said. "That's one of the reasons Jeff and I rode out here. You see, Jim Bundy knew that Adam was an eyewitness to the murder of Lefty Ingalls, and that the boy was gonna testify against him in court."

An expression of disbelief washed over Copeland's face. "You told Bundy about that?" he asked loudly.

"No," Rountree said. "I didn't discuss the case with him at all, but that young jailer I hired, a kid named Wally Newhouse, admits that he did. He says he got tired of listening to Bundy brag about how the jury was gonna turn him loose. When the prisoner kept talking about me not having any evidence, Wally says he couldn't resist the urge to shut him up. He not only told Bundy that I had an eyewitness, he even told him the boy's name.

"I hit the ceiling when I learned about it, raised hell with Wally and assured him that it was a stupid thing to do. He agreed with me after he thought about it a little bit, and promised never to discuss a case with a prisoner again. Don't reckon any of us oughtta hold it against him; he's just a kid and didn't know no better."

Copeland sat scratching his head as he digested the lawman's words. After a few moments, he turned halfway around so he could look directly into Rountree's eyes. "Do you think Jim Bundy had something to do with Adam's disappearance, Will?"

"Not directly," Rountree answered. "His ass is right there in jail, where it's been ever since I first locked him up. Now, what he might have done indirectly, I ain't got no way of knowing. Wally says he had two male visitors from Mills County a while back, and that they stood in front of his cell talking with him for quite a while. He says he couldn't make out none of what they were saying, 'cause they all talked too softly, sometimes even put their hands over their mouths when they spoke."

"Two men from Mills County," Dan repeated. "I wonder what they'd have in common with a man like Bundy. Did the jailer say what they looked like?"

"No, he didn't, Dan. I didn't ask him no more about 'em 'cause I didn't have no reason to. People visit prisoners in my jail just about every day of the year, and so far, there's never been any kind of problem with it. One thing I do remember Wally saying, though, is that the visitors were about the same age as the prisoner."

"Oh, well," Dan said, scratching his head again. "They're probably just two young fellows Bundy went to school with or worked with somewhere along the way. Whoever they are, they sure wouldn't have had no problem hearing about him being locked up, 'cause the fact that he's in your jail charged with murder ain't never been no secret. The newspaper published a story about it the very next day after you arrested him."

"I read the article," Rountree said, "and I have no doubt that Bundy's visitors did. Your guess about them just being acquaintances from bygone days is most likely right on the money, though, and nothing to be concerned about."

They sat in silence for a while. Then Dan pointed to the cookshack, where Pappy Wade had just stepped into the yard to ring the bell. The cook began to pull on the rope that set the conical chunk of iron to swinging back and forth, clanging the heavy clapper against one side, then the other, and producing a sound that could be heard for miles. "Dinner's ready,"Copeland said.

A short time later, the three men sat at the table eating roast beef, potatoes, and hot peppers, washed down with the strong coffee for which Pappy Wade was well known. "I don't have no way of knowing how many mouths I'm gonna have to feed," the cook said as he refilled the cups of all three. "Could be that none of the men was even in hearing distance of that bell."

"That might be true," Dan agreed, "but I doubt it. I think most of 'em have started looking closer to home the last day or two, and I expect 'em to be coming through that door before long. Close to home is the best place to look, too. Adam wasn't gonna walk no ten or fifteen miles to hunt no turkey. Round-trip, that'd be twenty or thirty miles." He opened two biscuits and laid them on his plate, then dipped gravy over them. "I say Adam didn't walk no more'n one mile before he sat down and started trying to call up a gobbler. He was smart enough to know he couldn't lug no turkey halfway across this ranch."

The sheriff and his deputy concentrated on their food quietly. Both men knew that DanCopeland's words made sense, but neither could think of anything to add.

When the meal was over, the lawmen thanked the cook and stepped through the doorway. Once outside, they began to amble toward the hitching rail and their horses. The elder Copeland was close beside them. "We've got to get on back to town, Dan," the sheriff said. "I'm sorry there ain't nothing we can do." He untied his mount, adding, "I reckon

I don't have to remind you that Bundy's trial is set for to-morrow. Judge Haynes is already in town, and I ain't got the slightest doubt about what he's gonna do at ten o'clock in the morning."

"Turn Bundy loose?" Dan asked.

"Exactly!" Rountree answered loudly. "Bundy is gonna swear that Ingalls went for his gun first, and without your grandson's testimony, there ain't a damn thing I can do to prove otherwise. When I have to stand up and admit that I don't have any evidence to refute Bundy's claim, the judge is gonna bang that gavel and send him on his way." He stepped into the saddle. "It's unfortunate, Dan, but that's the way it is. I've known Haynes for years, and I know what he's gonna do with this case. I've been through it all before."

As the lawmen rode down the hill, Jeff Winters turned halfway around in his saddle. "Tell Seth we're sorry we missed him," he said. "And tell him he has our deepest sympathy."

The sheriff and his deputy had no more than passed out of sight when Seth and the eight members of the bunkhouse crew rode out of the woods to the west. Dan stood on the porch watching as they rode across the hillside and dismounted at the cookshack. They held a short conversation on the ground, then the hands walked into the building. Seth remounted the gray and rode to the west end of his father's porch. He nodded a greeting to Dan, saying, "It's the same old story every day, Pa: nothing."

Dan shook his head. "There ain't gonna be nothing," he said. "Somebody's killed that boy, and there ain't no telling what they did with his body. I hate to say that, Seth, but I know you must be thinking the same thing by now."

Gaunt and exhausted, Seth sat his saddle tiredly, his bloodshot eyes staring between his horse's ears. "I've been thinking that from the very first day," he said finally. "I sure haven't said so to his ma, though. She's fit to be tied, Pa. Cries day and night."

"It's the same with your ma, son. I do all I can to keep her spirits up, but sometimes I think it's best if you just leave a woman alone and let her cry."

Seth nodded. He sat quietly for a few moments, then pointed up the hill. "The twins and Paul and Joseph are still prowling on the north side hoping to find something, but we've all been over that same ground before." He stared up the hill for a moment longer, then added, "I just now called off the search, Pa; told the hands to go on back to their regular duties tomorrow. There just ain't nowhere else to look."

Dan nodded. "Glad you did that, son. Them men need some rest, and you do, too. You look like you're about to fall outta that saddle right now."

"I could probably sleep for at least two days, Pa. As soon as I put this horse up, I intend to go to the house and find out."

"You do that," Dan said. "By the way, the sheriff and Deputy Winters just left here. Rountree says the judge is gonna turn Bundy loose in the morning when he finds out there ain't no evidence against him."

"That's what I was telling the hands a little while ago," Seth said, turning the gray around. "Ain't a damn thing any of us can do about it, either." He kneed the animal toward the corral.

Judge Haynes did indeed dismiss the murder charge against Jim Bundy next morning, and a rider named Andy Baker, saying he had been sent by Sheriff Rountree, arrived at the 2C Ranch just before sunset with the news. As was his custom, DanCopeland met the rider at the hitching rail just outside the yard. "The sheriff thought you folks oughtta be told right away how things went," Baker said, after being invited to dismount. He jumped to the ground and tied his mount. "Bundy stood up and told the judge his version of what happened, and when there weren't nobody there to dispute it, Haynes dismissed the case."

Dan nodded, and patted the young man's arm. "We expected as much, Andy. Thank you for coming."

Baker pointed to the left front foot of his bay. "He started favoring that foot about three miles back, and it turned out that he had a rock about the size of an acorn buried in the frog. I finally got it out, but it left a pretty bad bruise."

Dan pointed toward the barn. "Just turn him into the corral and put your saddle on one of mine, son. First time one of us comes to town, we'll bring your horse and switch back with you."

"I don't think that'll be necessary, sir." He smiled from one corner of his mouth. "I mean . . . not if you'll let me spend the night here at the ranch." He patted his horse's shoulder. "If I can borrow some liniment to put on that foot, I believe it'll be all right in the morning."

Dan motioned to the bunkhouse. "Plenty of room for you down there," he said. "The foreman's name is Rusty Walker. He'll be more'n happy to give you some liniment and put up your horse, then point you out a cot. Supper'll be in the cookshack about half an hour from now."

The young man thanked Dan profusely, then headed for the bunkhouse, his horse indeed showing a slight limp.

16

★

Adam had been missing for ten days now. And though the ranch hands had given up the hunt almost a week ago, the twins continued to saddle their horses every morning at sunup. Neither of the boys expected to find anything explaining their brother's disappearance, but they kept looking in order to please their grieving mother. Today they had searched the area north of the ranch houses all morning, then circled to the west. At noon, they dismounted at a spring three miles from home to water their horses and eat their lunches. When their ham and biscuits were gone, they seated themselves on the ground with their backs against a log.

"Let's just sit here and rest the horses for a while," Mark said. "Ain't nowhere on this ranch that we ain't already looked, nohow." Standing six foot two, he was an inch taller than his twin, and twenty pounds heavier. He was by far the more confident, talkative, and outgoing of the two, and Matthew had always looked upon him as the leader, passively allowing him to speak and make most of the decisions for both boys.

Mark was also considered by many to be the more handsome, having the same dimples, dark hair, dark complexion, and steel gray eyes as his father. His broad shoulders, thick chest, and muscular arms suggested abnormal strength, and more than once his twin had seen him throw a four-hundred-pound calf to the ground with his bare hands.

Other than the fact that he was much taller than the average boy of sixteen and one-half years, Matthew's body was quite normal. Nor was he anywhere near as athletic as his twin, seeming to prefer easing through life as quietly and as effortlessly as possible. He bore a strong resemblance to his grandfather, with the same big brown eyes and leathery complexion. And like Dan, he usually spoke only when he had something to say, always getting right to the point. Now, he stretched out his long legs and laid his head on the log, pulling the brim of his hat over one eye. "Let me know when you get ready to move on, Mark," he said.

Several minutes passed and Matthew was almost asleep when his twin tapped him on the shoulder. "Why do you reckon them buzzards are circling up yonder?" Mark asked.

"Probably a dead cow," Matthew answered drowsily, without looking up. "We'll check on it after a while." A moment later, he suddenly jerked the hat off his eyes and jumped to his feet. "Buzzards?" he asked loudly. "Where?"

Mark pointed north. "At least three of 'em off there about a quarter mile. They're behind the trees right now, but they'll be coming around again pretty quick."

They stood watching the broad-winged vultures circle for a while, each pass bringing them a little closer to the ground. "Are you thinking what I'm thinking?" Mark asked, already moving toward his horse.

"Probably," Matthew said. "I believe they're circling above Dry Creek, and it's plenty dry right now. Ain't been no water in it since all them heavy rains last winter." He untied his own mount and stepped into the saddle. When they had ridden a few hundred yards, he pulled up. "Don't you think we oughtta go the rest of the way on foot so them buzzards won't see us?" he asked.

Mark shook his head. "You can't sneak up on a damn buzzard, Matt. They're up there looking down on the whole world, and they know exactly where we are right now. Ain't no doubt in my mind that they saw us a long time before we saw them." He pointed north. "Like you said, they're circling over Dry Creek, so let's just go on up there and see what they've found." They kneed their animals and rode deeper into the woods.

Finding the location of the vultures' objective proved to be no problem. As the twins rode into the clearing above the dry creek bed, three of the big birds rose toward the treetops, flapping their wings noisily.

The boys trotted their animals across the clearing and brought them to a halt at the creek bed. They sat their saddles without speaking for a long time, for the sorry spectacle before them had momentarily left them speechless: someone had caved in a small cutbank over a corpse, and the body had recently been unearthed by animals. The arm, leg, and part of one shoulder that had been uncovered had been partially eaten, then abandoned to the winged carrion eaters. Matthew had finally found his voice. "That's Adam's boot," he said, pointing.

"Sure it is," Mark said quickly. "I'd bet a million dollars that his foot's in it, too." He jerked his thumb toward home. "Go to the house and get Pa, Matt. Tell him to bring a shovel and a wagon and some blankets. I'll keep them damn buzzards away till you get back."

Matthew nodded, and whirled his horse. As he rode away, Mark called after him. "Don't let Ma hear you when you tell Pa that! Grandma, neither!"

Mark continued to sit his saddle. He stared at Adam's booted foot for a while. Then, feeling that he was about to lose his dinner, he kneed his horse farther up the creek. A short time later, he slid from the saddle, dropped the reins to the ground, and began to vomit. He continued to heave long after emptying his stomach, then sat down on a large rock to recuperate. Even though he began to feel better right away, he kept his seat for a long time.

After an hour, with no sign of Matthew or his father, Mark mounted and began to ride around the immediate area, his eyes glued to the ground. Reading the hoofprints of a dozen horses going in as many different directions was an impossibility, especially since they intermingled with those of twice as many cattle. Finally, he halted on the opposite side and sat staring across the creek bed at the cave-in, wondering how many of the hands had rested their horses almost on top of the makeshift grave during the search. He began to shake his head. He himself had ridden right by it several times, and he had no doubt that his brother Matthew had done likewise.

Matthew had been gone for almost three hours when Mark saw the wagon come out of the trees and into the clearing. The boy had obviously left his horse in the corral, for now he was sitting on the seat beside his father. Seth guided the team alongside the cave-in, then stepped down from the wagon.

Matthew jumped to the ground, then walked to the rear of the wagon and dropped the tailgate. "The reason we took so long getting here was 'cause Pa wanted to build this coffin," he said, pointing to the long pine box in the wagon bed. "We didn't tell Ma nor Grandma nothing about it, neither."

Mark nodded, and said nothing.

With an expressionless face that could have been carved from granite, Seth stood staring over the bank through steel gray eyes that appeared to see nothing. Finally, he wiped a tear from his cheek and pointed to the wagon. "You boys get that coffin and them two shovels. We'll finish digging him up, then bury him up there on the hill with Lefty." He was quiet for a moment, then added, "We'll do it without saying a word to anybody, too. I'll tell your ma and the rest of the family about it after it's been done."

The twins moved the box into the creek bed, then picked up a shovel apiece and started to dig. In less than five minutes, they had uncovered the body of their brother and placed it on a quilt inside the coffin, covering it with a thick blanket.

Seth laid the lid on the long pine box, then got on his knees with a hammer and a handful of tenpenny nails. He hammered for a while, then pointed to the cave-in. "You boys poke around in that hole a little more with your shovels," he said. "Whoever put Adam in there might have thrown his rifle in, too."

The twins picked up the shovels and resumed their digging. Two minutes later, Mark held up his brother's rifle. "It looks to be in good shape, Pa. Action's probably fouled with dirt, but I can fix that easy."

Seth nodded. "Wash it out with water and oil it good. Then it'll be just like new."

Darkness was on them before they reached the burial ground. Shortly after sunset, Seth lit the lantern and spoke to Matthew, who was driving the team: "When you get a little closer, circle around the hill so you come up on the burial ground from the north, son. I don't want none of the folks at home to see this light."

Matthew complied and, half an hour later, brought the wagon to a halt beside the two existing graves. Knowing that the flat contour of the land at the top of the hill prevented anyone down below from seeing the burial ground, Seth was no longer concerned about the lantern. He immediately chose a space on the south side of Lefty Ingalls's mound, then began to break up the earth with the broad end of his mattock. The twins stood by waiting, knowing that when their father finally stopped to rest it would be their job to shovel the loose dirt out of the hole.

After a considerable length of time had passed and the hole was still less than two feet deep, Mark talked his father into trading tools with him. With Mark now wielding the mattock and the hard earth yielding at a much faster rate, the grave was at its proper depth within the hour.

The coffin was lowered into the grave with ropes, and a short time later, Seth threw the last shovelful of dirt on the mound and patted it down. Then he threw his shovel in the direction of the wagon and doffed his hat. His sons, knowing that their father was about to say a few words over their departed sibling, stepped up beside the grave and removed their own headgear.

"Lord," Seth began, "I don't know much about this kinda stuff, but I don't reckon my pa could do no better. Anyway, I'm giving you back what's left of my fifth-born son, and I'm asking you to treat him good. One more thing, Lord: Please stand watch over the rest of the family and don't let nothing like this ever happen to us again." He wiped his cheek with the heel of his hand, then put his hat back on his head. "Amen," he added.

With the exception of Seth and the twins, the Copelands spent most of the morning at the graveside next day. Paul, Joseph, and Abel had walked up the hill, while Dan, Rachel, and the women rode in a two-seated spring wagon. Paul had hitched up the team early, for he knew that walking up and down that hill on his artificial leg would be extremely difficult for his grandfather. The women had ridden with Dan because he had asked them to, and Rachel had climbed aboard because it made her feel more like a grown-up.

The elder Copeland said a few words over the grave early on. Then the family members either knelt beside the mound in silence or sat on the ground beside the wagon with long faces. Though Emerald held up well for the first hour or so, she finally broke down and threw herself on the yellow mound of clay, screaming, sobbing, and beating her tiny fist against the ground. Even after she calmed down, she continued to sit on the grave. She finally got back on her feet an hour before noon, by which time Dan had convinced her that it was time to go home. As he helped her to the wagon, she pointed to the mound with a shaky finger. "Do you think we could put up a headstone pretty soon?"

Dan hugged her tightly. "It'll be done, little girl," he said. "A big headstone."

Seth ate a late breakfast at the cookshack next morning. Though he had not said so to anyone, he intended to head for Gatesville within the next few minutes. He finished his meal and dropped his utensils in the dishpan, then walked to the doorway, where he turned and spoke to the cook: "Do you need anything that I can bring back from town on horseback, Pappy?"

The old-timer fished around in his pocket and produced a dime. "You can bring me back two bags of smoking tobacco," he said, laying the coin in his boss's hand. "Reckon I got about everything else I need."

Seth nodded, then headed for the corral. Twenty minutes later, he rode down the hill and took the road to Gatesville, where he intended to visit the county jail. He wanted to talk with a part-time deputy sheriff named Wally Newhouse, the young man who had been the appointed jailer the day two men from Mills County had visited Jim Bundy.

Although Bundy had been in the county jail when Adam disappeared, there was nonetheless no doubt in Seth's mind that the man was responsible for his son's murder. According to what the sheriff had told Dan, the jailer himself had supplied Bundy with the information that Adam was going to testify against him, and that had been before the men from Mills County had visited the prisoner. It would have been a simple matter for Bundy to instruct his visitors to silence the witness, and not only could he have told them who Adam was and where to find him, but also that the boy often hunted turkeys and other game several miles from home.

It was close to noon when Seth arrived in town, for he had allowed the gray to set the pace. As he rode down the street toward the jail, he could see even at a distance that Sheriff Rountree was at the hitching rail about to mount his horse. Seth kicked the gray to a canter, and arrived just after the lawman stepped into the stirrup and threw his leg over the saddle. "Howdy, Seth," Rountree said. "You seem to be in a hurry. Is there something I can do for you?"

"I just wanted to tell you that the twins found Adam's body yesterday. Some no-good son of a bitch killed him and caved a cutbank in over him."

The sheriff's face took on what appeared to be a genuine look of sympathy. "Lord, I'm sorry to hear that, Seth. What did they kill him with? Did they shoot him?"

Seth shook his head. "Wasn't enough left of him to tell."

"Damn!" Rountree said. "I reckon we all know that Bundy couldn't have done it, but there ain't no doubt in my mind that he knows who did. Ain't no way to ask him, though. He left this town at a gallop about two minutes after the judge told him to."

Seth nodded. He sat quietly for a few seconds, then steered the conversation in another direction. "That young jailer of yours named Wally Newhouse, Sheriff. If I wanted to talk with him, where would I find him?"

Rountree chuckled, then pointed to his office. "You'd find him right in there behind my desk, and I'm sure he'll be glad to talk with you." He reined his horse away from the hitching rail. "I'd like to stay around and talk with you a little bit longer, but I've got to take a quick ride out in the country. Two old men arguing over a land line, and I'd like to get there before they stop arguing and start shooting." Then he was gone down the street at a canter.

Seth dismounted and tied his animal, then stepped into the office. The young deputy, who had been sitting behind the desk reading, was on his feet quickly. He stepped halfway across the room with his right hand extended. "How do you do, sir?" he asked in a high-pitched voice. "I'm Deputy Sheriff Wally Newhouse. Can I help you?"

Seth grasped the hand with a firm grip. "I'm Seth Copeland," he said, "and I'm hoping you can answer a few questions for me."

"Seth Copeland," the deputy repeated, pointing to a chair. "You're the man with the missing son."

"Not anymore," Seth said, taking the seat he had been offered. "We found him two days ago . . . found his body."

"Oh, I'm so sorry," Newhouse said. He was a tall man, almost as tall as Seth, and looked and sounded even younger than his twenty-one years. Appearing to weigh about a hundred forty pounds, with a chalky complexion, crooked teeth, large ears, and cowlicks sticking out from under his hat in all directions, he was not a handsome man. He continued to stand for a few moments, then reseated himself behind the desk. "I'll be happy to help you any way I can, sir. Go ahead, ask your questions."

Seth moved his chair a little closer to the desk. "Well, Sheriff Rountree told my pa that Jim Bundy had two visitors from Mills County while he was locked up here, and that you were the jailer on duty that day. I was wondering if you could tell me what they looked like, and maybe where they live."

Newhouse nodded. "I remember 'em well, sir. They didn't say nothing about what part of Mills County they lived in, but I can sure describe 'em for you. I paid mighty close attention to both of 'em. The tall one, about as tall as me, I reckon, had a mop of stringy chestnut-colored hair that hung all the way to his shoulders. He had freckles sprinkled all over his face, ears and all, and probably the widest mouth I've ever seen. He spoke unusually soft, like what he really wanted to do was whisper. He said his name was Buddy Banks.

"Now, the fellow with him, who claimed to be Tom Ripley, was several inches shorter, and a whole lot thicker. A fellow could see with one eye that he was as strong as an ox, and it looked like the buttons might pop off his shirt at any minute. I tell you, that fellow looked like he might even have muscles in his shit."

When the deputy grew quiet, Seth prompted him. "Did you notice anything else about him?"

"Yes, sir. He had black, curly hair that was cut short, and one of the deepest voices I ever heard. It wasn't easy to understand every word he said, though. He had a real bad harelip that made him lisp when he talked. His buddy did most of the talking."

Seth nodded. "Did you overhear any of their talk with Bundy?"

"Oh, I could hear 'em all right, but I couldn't understand what they were saying. They all spoke real soft, and I think Bundy was doing most of the talking. At least, every time I looked back there, it was his lips that were moving."

"I see," Seth said. "Did you happen to notice the brand on the visitors' horses?"

"They didn't have no horses. I'd have thought they had just walked down here from one of the saloons if it hadn't been so early in the morning. Anyway, I stood in the doorway and watched 'em when they left. They walked up the street toward the west, then turned north at the corner, and I ain't seen 'em since."

Seth sat staring at the wall behind the deputy. He had listened to the young man's descriptions closely, and in his mind's eye, he could see Bundy's visitors clearly. He also believed he knew who the men were. He spoke to the deputy: "Could you positively identify the men if you saw them again, Wally?"

"Absolutely," Newhouse answered quickly. "I can close my eyes and see 'em as pretty as you please right now."

Seth got to his feet and walked to the door. He stood watching the street traffic for a few moments, then turned halfway around. "Thank you, Deputy," he said, then walked to the hitching rail. He did not mount, however, nor did he even untie his horse. Instead, he stood leaning against the rail thoughtfully for a good five minutes, then suddenly snapped his fingers and stepped back into the office. "Wally, could I ask you for one more favor?" he asked from the doorway, then walked on to the desk.

The deputy nodded. "Of course."

"All right," Seth began. "Tomorrow's Saturday, so I know you'll be on duty. What I want you to do is walk into the saloon at the Durant Hotel tomorrow afternoon at two o'clock. I'll be sitting at a table with two men, and I want you to walk by and look them over. Don't speak to any of us, just keep on walking. I'll follow you on to this office a few minutes later. What I'll be wanting to know is whether or not the two men you saw sitting at my table are the same ones who visited Jim Bundy in jail."

Newhouse was on his feet offering a parting handshake. "I'll be happy to do that, sir. Two o'clock sharp."

Seth shook the young deputy's hand. "Not a word of this to anybody, Wally. Don't even tell the sheriff." Then he was out the door. This time he did mount, and rode back the way he had come. All he had to do now was pick up two bags of tobacco for Pappy Wade, then strike out for home.

17

★

Seth did not ride straight home after leaving the sheriff's office. A few miles out of town, he left the road and headed cross-country to the line shack on the 2C's southwestern boundary. He wanted to have a short talk with Eldridge Boone.

The sun was still an hour high when he reached the property line, and the sound of someone chopping wood reached his ears long before the shack came into view. When he rode around the corner of the building a few minutes later, the line rider was on his knees beside the woodpile. "Howdy, Seth," he said, getting to his feet with an armload of firewood for his cookstove. "You're just in time for supper. Won't take me but a few minutes to heat up some beans and bacon."

Seth shook his head. "I appreciate the offer, but I've got to keep moving. Even now it's gonna be dark long before I get home. I just rode by to tell you that I'm giving you and Clint Williams the day off tomorrow. You've both been working seven days a week since the first of the year, and it's time you had a Saturday off. In fact, the food and drinks are gonna be on me at the Durant Hotel tomorrow. You and Clint just ride into town about dinnertime, and I'll meet you in the saloon. We'll all have a big beefsteak, then try to drink the place dry." He reined his horse around. "Can you get the word to Clint tonight?"

"Sure can," Boone said. "I was intending to ride up to his shack after a while, anyway. I do that two or three nights a week, and he comes down here about that often. It gets mighty lonesome being by yourself all the time, and that relieves the monotony for both of us."

Seth nodded. "I can understand that," he said. He glanced at the sun, now barely above the treetops. "I'll be on my way now. See you fellows tomorrow." He kicked the gray in the ribs and headed east at a canter.

He held the same pace till the gathering darkness began to hamper his vision, then slowed his animal to a fast walk. He reached the ranch buildings two hours after dark. He fed and cared for the gray by lanternlight, then walked to the bunkhouse, where the lamp was still burning. He poked his head through the doorway and spoke to his foreman, who sat on his cot working on a bridle. "Everything going all right, Rusty?"

Walker smiled. "About like they oughtta go, I reckon. Best I can tell, them Hereford bulls are working around the clock. Just about every cow and heifer on the ranch is beginning to swell."

"Good," Seth said, and closed the door. Then, seeing that the cook's lamp was still burning, he walked up the hill to the cookshack. He stepped inside the building, then spoke to the aging man, who was busy chopping up vegetables for tomorrow's soup. "I'd have thought a hardworking man like you would have been asleep hours ago, Pappy," he said.

The old-timer laid his broad-bladed knife aside and met his boss at the end of the long table. "Done been to bed once tonight," he said. "Didn't do me no damn good, though.

The minute I laid down, my eyes popped open and felt like they never would close again."

Seth smiled. "That happens to me once in a while, too," he said. "Sometimes it seems like the harder I work, the harder it is for me to go to sleep at night."

"Well, I reckon my problem's a little simpler'n yours," Pappy said. "Here lately I've been taking a nap just about every afternoon, and that plays hell with my nights. I said I was gonna quit doing it, but it ain't all that easy. Soon as I get dinner over with every day and get everything cleaned up, I get so damn sleepy I start running into things." He seated himself on the end of the bench. "Anyway, when I couldn't go to sleep tonight I decided to get back up and fix a pot of soup for tomorrow."

Seth doffed his coat and hung it on a rack just inside the door. He took two bags of tobacco out of one of the pockets and handed them across the table. "I almost forgot to give you this."

The old-timer shook his head. "I wasn't gonna let you forget it," he said. "I'm completely out, and I ain't had a cigarette since right after dinner." He tore the seal off one of the bags, then selected a paper and began to roll a smoke. A few moments later, he licked the paper and gave it a final twist, then touched the end of the finished product with a burning match. "Could you eat something?" he asked, sending a billow of smoke toward the ceiling. "Let me fix you someting to eat."

Seth did not argue. "Now that you mention it, I reckon it has been a while since breakfast this morning. You still got some of that sugar-cured ham?"

Pappy was on his feet quickly, his cigarette dangling from his lips. "You mean you've been running around all day without eating anything?" Not waiting for an answer, he lifted an eye off the cookstove's firebox, then reached into the woodbin. When he had kindled a fire, he cut several slices of ham into a skillet, then broke half a dozen eggs into a bowl, beating them vigorously with a fork. A short while later, he placed a platter of ham, eggs, and warmed-over biscuits on the table before his boss, then delivered the glass of water that Seth had requested.

Seth looked at the platter for only a moment, then dug in. "I reckon us folks here at the 2C eat about as good as anybody does, Pappy," he said between bites. "Don't seem to matter whether I eat down here or up at my wife's table, either. You and her both put out better grub than any restaurant in Gatesville."

Pappy smiled. "Learning to put a good meal together is mostly just trial and error," he said. "Your wife and I both have had plenty of experience." He lit another cigarette and dropped the spent match into a tin can. "Cooking for a big family like she's done all these years, and being her own boss, the lady was just naturally gonna get good at it." He took a deep drag from his cigarette and blew a cloud of smoke over his shoulder. "You mentioned restaurants, Seth. Let me tell you something about restaurants:

"It's altogether possible for a restaurant to have the best cook in the country without the people who eat there ever even knowing it. You see, the owner almost always insists that everything be done his way, and that's usually the difference between outstanding food and something ordinary.

"I've certainly seen more than my share of that. I've worked in so many restaurants that I've lost count, but I've never had a free hand in one yet. I mean, you can't put a good meal together with somebody looking over your shoulder telling you how to do it. It's usually the same man who pays your wages, too, and most of them just barely know how to boil water!" The longer the cook talked, the louder his voice became. He emphasized the last sentence by banging his fist against the table.

Seth smiled. "You've got me convinced, Pappy," he said, breaking into laughter. "And I sure didn't have no trouble hearing what you were saying." He got to his feet and put his empty plate in the dishpan, then walked to the rack and stood buttoning up his coat. "I'll have breakfast with you again in the morning. Got some more business in town tomorrow." He stepped through the doorway and headed up the hill. Having been in the saddle all day, he was very tired, and knew that his feather bed and the arms of his loving wife would put him to sleep.

After eating a large breakfast at the cookshack, Seth was back at the corral shortly after sunup next morning. He had decided to let the gray have the day off, and dropped his loop around the neck of a big chestnut that he had never ridden before. As far as he knew, none of the 2C hands had ever ridden the animal either, for cowboys preferred smaller horses for working cattle. Last month Walker had bought eight horses from Lester Burbank, their neighboring rancher to the west, and the chestnut had been among them. The big saddler had been loafing in the corral since then.

Seth first inspected the horse's teeth, then slipped on the bridle. The bill of sale stated that this particular animal was five years old, and after looking in its mouth, Seth believed that to be the case. He wrapped the reins around a fence post and smoothed the saddle blanket out on the horse's back, then laid the saddle on and cinched it down. He shoved his Henry in the boot, then mounted and headed down the hill. The big chestnut took to the road at a trot, then gradually eased into a slow canter, a pace that suited its rider perfectly.

He arrived in town at midmorning and tied his mount to the hitching rail in front of the billiard parlor. Not only did he know that there was always a pot of coffee on the stove, but this morning Dan Copeland had given him some money to deliver to the proprietor. He stepped inside the large hall and knocked on the office door, which opened quickly. "Seth Copeland!" Runt Bailey said loudly, a broad smile appearing to stretch his mouth. "Seems like years since I've seen you. Come on in here."

It was the local custom for anyone visiting Bailey to help himself to the coffeepot, and Seth did so now. "I don't spend much time in town, Runt; usually just come in and get what I need, then head on back to the ranch." He stirred a spoonful of sugar into his coffee, then seated himself in the chair he was offered. He chuckled. "I've got a little time to kill this morning, and you've got the only free coffee in town."

With shoulder-length blond hair and small copper-colored eyes, Runt Bailey was a giant of a man who stood six feet seven inches tall and weighed well over three hundred pounds. And like most men of such physical dimensions, he had a disposition that was easy to digest, and the majority of the local men came by his place to visit fairly often. Now seated in his oversized chair, he pointed to the coffeepot. "I brew up a fresh pot at least three times a day whether anybody comes by to drink it or not. Can't think of many things that taste worse than stale coffee."

Seth was quiet for a while, then set his cup on the desk and began to fish around in his pocket. "I've got something here for you, Runt," he said. He laid five double eagles in the big man's hand. "Pa sent this hundred dollars to you, said you put it on him pretty bad the last time the two of you played dominoes together."

Bailey accepted the money and dropped it into a desk drawer. "Naw, naw," he said. "I ain't never beat Dan Copeland bad. Fact is, the last time we played is the only time I ever finished a game ahead of him. Only reason I was even in that game at all was because nobody else was in here to play him. It was no doubt his unlucky day and I just happened to catch some good rocks." He shook his head several times. "No, sir. If I had to play dominoes with Dan Copeland for a living, I'd have been in the poorhouse a long time ago."

Seth spent the large part of an hour in the billiard parlor, then rode to the livery stable, where he seated himself on an upended nail keg and watched his friend Jesse Hunter shoe a team of draft horses that appeared to weigh at least two thousand pounds each.

"Percherons," Hunter said, in answer to Seth's question

about the oversized animals' breeding. "Some folks call 'em Percheron Normans. The breed comes from France, and they're just as damn stout as they look. Ain't many of 'em been shipped into this country yet, but I bet they'll be everywhere you look a few years from now. This team here belongs to the county, and they've been assigned to the road-building crew."

Amazed by the size of the grayish black beasts, Seth continued to look them over. "Their feet are as big as dishpans, Jesse," he said. "What size shoes are you putting on 'em?"

Hunter went around the edges of the hoof he had been working on with a coarse file, then dropped it to the ground. "There ain't no size to 'em," he said. "I didn't have no shoes nowhere near big enough for these boogers, so I just had to make some. Took me about all day yesterday to do it, too."

Seth sat watching till the blacksmith had finished shoeing one of the animals. Then he got to his feet, put the keg back against the wall where he had found it, and made a few steps toward the front door. "I'd sure like to know how much a team like that could pull," he said.

"Just about any damn thing you hitch 'em to," Hunter said, picking up a front hoof of the second animal.

Without another word, Seth continued on through the doorway. He walked to the hitching rail and untied the chestnut, then looked at his watch. The time was half past eleven, about time for the line riders to be arriving at the saloon. He stepped into the stirrup and threw his leg over the saddle, then headed up the street toward the hotel. As he neared the Durant he could read the 2C brand on the hips of two black horses in front of the establishment. A few moments later, he dismounted and tied the chestnut beside them.

He avoided the hotel lobby, and entered the saloon through a side door that opened off the street. Even as he stood in the doorway he could see his line riders at the end of the bar waving their arms. As he moved in their direction both Boone and Williams slid off their stools and stood waiting in the aisle. "Where do you want to sit at, boss?" Boone asked.

Seth pointed to his right. "Take that table and order up three T-bone steaks," he said. "I'll get a bottle and some glasses, and be right with you." He headed for the bar while the line riders, both wearing Colt revolvers low on their hips, seated themselves at the table their boss had indicated. A waiter took their order quickly, then returned to the kitchen.

Boone and Williams had both originally come from the San Antonio area, but had become acquainted only after going to work on the 2C spread. Boone had been on the ranch a little more than a year, and Williams about half that long. A few months ago, the men had requested line-riding duty on the west boundary, a job that normally rotated among several different hands.

Most cowboys detested living in line shacks, and since none of the 2C hands had objected to giving up his turn in the rotation, Boone and Williams had been assigned to the west boundary on a somewhat permanent basis. There, they were free to practice the fast draw as many hours a day as they wished, with nobody to see them. And unbeknownst to the rest of the hands, the two men were visited at least twice a week by Jim Bundy, who very happily spent several hours at a time exhibiting his own prowess with a six-gun and filling their heads with tall tales.

The gullible line riders had bought Bundy's wild stories, and had quickly begun to idolize him. Both men now spent a large portion of their waking hours practicing the quick draw and the gunfighter's stance that they had learned by watching him. Williams had even begun to practice standing like Bundy, and to emulate his walk. Even now, sitting at the table waiting for his boss to bring him a drink, he was thinking about his idol, and wondering if Bundy could really be counted on to do all the things he had promised.

"Did you fellows order our steaks yet?" Seth asked as he set a bottle of Kentucky whiskey and three glasses on the table.

Boone nodded. "With mashed potatoes and gravy," he said.

Seth seated himself and poured drinks for all three. "The bartender says this is the best whiskey he's got, so I suppose it's drinkable."

Williams raised his glass to his lips, then set it back on the table. "Tastes mighty good to me," he said. "First drink I've had in more'n three months." He looked across the table at Boone. "Ain't it been about that long since the last time we were in town, Eldridge? About the middle of January?"

Boone nodded. "Middle of January. Along about the fifteenth, I believe."

Seth had been listening; now he sat thinking. Had he been barking up the wrong tree right from the start? Were Boone and Williams simply two men who enjoyed the isolation of the boundary work? Men who, despite having a pocketful of money, could spurn the nightlife and concentrate on their jobs seven days a week? Maybe. If they had spoken the truth just now, they could not possibly be the men who had visited Jim Bundy in jail. Seth sat scratching at the label on the whiskey bottle with a thumbnail. "I don't know how you fellows do it," he said. "I don't think there's any way in the world that I could stay in a line shack for three or four months without coming to town."

Boone opened his mouth, but it was Williams who spoke. "Any time you start wondering what's going on in town, you've gotta push the whole thing right outta your mind. If you're gonna take a rancher's money, you're supposed to give him all you've got, and that means staying on the job even if you'd rather be someplace else."

Boone nodded. "That's right," he said.

Though Boone and Williams gobbled their food down quickly and resumed their drinking, Seth took close to an hour with his meal. He paused after each bite to talk or listen, for he had no intention of getting drunk. Even after the waiter had taken his empty plate back to the kitchen, Seth continued to sip very slowly.

Though the whiskey eventually loosened the tongues of the line riders, most of their conversation was aimed directly at each other, and Seth sat through two hours of boredom. When he finally looked at his watch for the third time, he saw that two o'clock was only one minute away. Even as he slid the timepiece back into his pocket and looked toward the front of the building, he saw Deputy Wally Newhouse step through the batwing doors. He picked up the whiskey bottle, which was now almost empty. "Let's polish the rest of this stuff off," he said, pouring the remainder of the brown liquid into the men's glasses. "Drink up so I can get us another bottle."

Seth continued to chat idly in an effort to hold their attention, for he knew that the deputy was at this very moment walking down the aisle toward their table. The seconds passed slowly, and though Seth neither raised his head nor his eyes, he was nonetheless aware of Newhouse's whereabouts. And though he had heard no footfalls, he knew that the deputy had already passed the table once, and would turn around when he reached the end of the bar and walk past again. On the young lawman's second pass, Boone and Williams suddenly found something interesting on the barroom floor. Both men sat with their hands over their faces and their eyes staring between their legs.

Seth sat quietly till he heard Newhouse leave the building. Then he drained his glass and reached for the empty bottle. "Time for a new one," he said, getting to his feet. He bought a quart of the same brand at the bar, then returned to the table. "It's exactly like that bartender claimed," he said. "This is mighty good stuff." He pulled the cork out of the bottle with his teeth, then poured whiskey in all three glasses. Continuing to stand, he set the bottle on the table, then inhaled his drink in one gulp. "I'm gonna be leaving you for a while, men," he said. "I've still got a little business to take care of, but it won't take me long. You fellows just sit tight. I'll be back." Then he was gone through the front door.

When Seth reached the sheriff's office, Deputy Newhouse was standing on the boardwalk out front, leaning against one of the posts that held up the awning. "It didn't really take but one glance," Newhouse said, "but I looked 'em over good anyway. That's the same two men who came to see Bundy in jail."

Seth nodded, then stood looking down the street toward the saloon. After a few moments, he turned back to the deputy. "Are you positive, Wally?"

"Absolutely," Newhouse answered quickly. "They've even got on the same clothes they wore that day."

Seth stood thoughtfully for a while. "I can't figure it, Wally," he said finally. "Both of 'em just told me that today was the first time they'd been in town since the middle of January."

"They're lying through their teeth, then. Banks and Ripley are the names they used, and they stood in front of Bundy's cell whispering back and forth for at least twenty minutes. I'll walk in that saloon with you and give 'em the lie right to their faces if you want me to."

Seth shook his head. "That won't be necessary, Wally. I believe what you've told me, and that's all I'm concerned about." Then he took the deputy into his confidence, telling him that he believed one or both of the line riders had killed his son, that the plan had been hatched during the jailhouse visit, and that Bundy himself had supplied the information that Adam went hunting alone several times a week. "It's an idea I'll have to stay after," Seth added, "but I don't intend to quit till I know the truth." He placed his hand on the young man's shoulder. "Once again, I'm asking you to keep all this under your hat, Wally. Don't mention it to a soul, not even the sheriff." He squeezed the shoulder and shook the man slightly. "All right?"

The deputy nodded. "All right," he said. "Not a soul."

Seth spun on his heel and walked back to the saloon. Boone and Williams were still sitting at the table concentrating on the bottle, which was half empty now. "There's been a change in my plans, fellows," Seth said. "I'm gonna ride a few miles north of town and talk to a man about some cows. When I'm done, I'll just cut across the country and go home from there." He laid two dollars on the table. "Here's some money for another bottle when that one runs dry. You two stay as long as you want and enjoy yourselves. Just make sure you're back on the job at sunup." He turned and headed for the door.

"We'll take care of our jobs!" Boone called after him. "You can count on us!"

Moments later, Seth mounted the chestnut and rode north at a canter. After about a mile, he circled around to the northwest and headed home.

18

★

Seth slept almost around the clock. When he finally did get out of bed next morning, he spent the first half of the day hanging around the barn waiting for the right time to put the next part of his plan into action. Aside from his wife and the deputy, he had mentioned his suspicions to no one. Nor had he told anyone about his own activities during the past two days. He watched the hands go in and out of the cook-shack at dinnertime, then stepped into the building himself after he knew the cook was alone.

"I expected you to come straggling in," Pappy said jokingly. "That's why I kept everything hot." He pointed to the bench. "Have a seat right there, and I'll fix you up."

Though the cook placed a platter of ham, venison, and potatoes on the table, Seth made a meal of beans and corn bread. "I'm gonna be needing a big lunch, too," he said as he cleaned his bowl for the second time. "I've got some prowling to do, and I ain't got no idea when I might be back." When the cook nodded and started to rise, Seth laid a hand on his arm. "Now, I want to keep this between you and me, Pappy. It ain't none of nobody else's business."

The old-timer chuckled, and pushed himself to his feet with his elbows. "Damn sure ain't nobody gonna hear it from me," he said. He pointed to the platter. "Looks like you ain't gonna eat none of that ham or venison right now, so I'll just wrap it up with some biscuits. Got some of that apple pie left, too." He wrapped the food in an old newspaper he had been saving for that purpose, then tied it with a string.

Seth accepted the bundle, then filled both of his canteens from the cook's water bucket. "Thank you, Pappy," he said. "I'll see you again whenever I do." He was out the door quickly.

At the corral, he caught up the big gray and led the animal inside the barn, where he cinched down his saddle and tied a bedroll and an extra blanket behind the cantle. Then, instead of the Henry rifle that he usually carried on the saddle, he shoved a double-barreled ten-gauge shotgun into the boot. A short time later, he led the gray through the corral gate, then mounted and headed southwest. He was out of sight in less than two minutes.

Three hours of riding at a walking gait brought him within a mile of Eldridge Boone's line shack. Deciding to lead his animal the rest of the way, he dismounted and began to move forward at a slower pace. The sun was still more than an hour high, so he was in no hurry. His aim was to eavesdrop on a conversation between Boone and Williams when they thought no one else was around, and he believed that he would soon be getting his chance.

Boone had said that he rode up to Clint Williams's shack two or three nights a week, and that Williams visited him about as often. Which meant that the two men were together at one place or the other almost every night. All Seth had to do was select a good listening post for himself, then keep an eye on Boone's shack till Clint Williams came calling.

Seth knew the terrain very well, and had already decided that he would leave the gray tied in a thick cluster of cedars about three hundred yards east of the shack. And although he had no grain to put in it, he would tie on the nose bag to discourage the animal from neighing when it sensed other horses in the area.

That done, he could easily make his way to the rear of the small building undetected after dark, for although the shack was located at the edge of a clearing, the bushes and saplings growing behind it had all been left standing. The fact that the vegetation was now in the process of putting on new leaves would also work in his favor.

Before he put his ear to the wall, however, he must first determine that the two men were actually inside the building, and he could do that only if he counted the horses in the corral or saw Williams ride down from the north.

He continued to walk west at the same slow pace, using as much cover as possible and keeping an eye out for anything that looked human. Though he owned the land he was walking on, and knew that he would owe neither of the line riders an explanation if they happened to become aware of his presence, he also knew that this was likely to be the only chance he would ever get to determine their guilt or innocence: if either man ever caught a glimpse of him sneaking through the woods, their lips would be sealed forever.

He saw the smoke coming from the flue when he was still several hundred yards from the shack, and supposed that Boone was not only using the stove to warm up his supper, but to ward off the growing chill of the evening as well.

When Seth led his animal into the cedars a short while later, he came to a halt immediately, for at least a dozen cows lay on the ground chewing their cuds and blocking his way. He tied his mount, then stood still, for he knew that after sighting a human being in close proximity, longhorns would sometimes bolt and run as if the devil himself were after them. The last thing he wanted to do was excite the beasts, for any time a line rider saw a bunch of cattle looking like they were running for their lives, he would immediately set out to determine the reason behind their fear.

Seth stood for a while longer; then, when it began to look as if the cows had decided to make a night of it, he bent to the ground and picked up a few pebbles. He tossed one of them at an old white cow that he had decided was most likely the boss. After missing his target with both the first and the second pebbles, he hit the old cow on the rump with the third. She first switched her tail as if she thought an insect was on her back, then shook her head and slowly pushed herself to her feet.

Seth knew right away that he had been correct in assuming that the old cow was the boss, for the others immediately followed her lead. She stood staring at him for a few moments, then wandered off in search of a new bedding ground, the rest of the bunch close on her heels.

He put the bag on the gray's nose, then slid the shotgun out of its scabbard. A few moments later, he was circling around to the north side of the shack, where he could count the horses. He was still unable to see the corral when he came to a halt behind a large oak, but he did have an unhampered view of the clearing to the west and the northwest. Knowing that few men would choose to travel through the woods on horseback when they had the choice of riding across a treeless plain, he believed that he would be able to spot Clint Williams long before he reached the shack, providing the man came along before dark. No doubt about it, he was thinking as he stood peeking around the tree, squinting at the setting sun. When and if Williams came calling, he would ride out of those trees about a mile to the northwest, then across yonder clearing.

It happened even as Seth was thinking about it: out of the woods on the north side of the clearing stepped two horses, one of which appeared to be riderless. Seth held his position for the next several minutes, for he had plenty of cover around him. He continued to watch, and a few minutes later he could very easily make out the form of Clint Williams slouching in the saddle. He was riding one bay and leading another, with the second animal carrying a pack on its back.

A packhorse? Seth asked himself. Why in the hell would Williams need a packhorse? He suddenly began to retrace his footsteps as the answer hit him: the two men were about to skip the country, and intended to take Seth's horses and anything else they could steal along with them.

Darkness was coming on fast by the time he got back to the clump of cedars. He paused for a while and patted the gray's neck reassuringly. Then, with his Colt revolver strapped on his hip and the double-barreled ten-gauge in his hands, he eased off into the brush and began to make his way toward the shack. He was almost there when he heard a rattling, metallic noise from the corral that sounded like Williams dropping his pack of pots and pans to the ground. "I'm just gonna leave this pack out here under the shed!" Williams called out loudly. "You ain't gotta worry about nothing but your bedroll; I've got everything else we're gonna need!"

"Good!" Boone's deep voice answered from the doorway. "We'll carry that sack of grain with us, though! It ain't late enough in the year to count on grass!"

Positioned behind a clump of leafy bushes, Seth suddenly saw light shining through the cracks in the cabin. Boone had lit his coal-oil lamp for the night, and Williams would be joining him at any moment.

Seth moved out stealthily. Since the cabin door, the corral, and the shed were all on the south side of the building, he approached the shack at its northeast corner. Crouching close to the wall, he had no choice but to remain still until he knew that Williams was inside.

After several minutes had passed, he began to hear the men's voices inside the building. He quickly moved to the southeast corner, then up the south side of the building, halfway to the door. The walls were thin and uninsulated, and now that he was closer he had no problem understanding every word he was hearing:

"We can turn them two extra horses into money mighty easy if we ever need to," Clint Williams was saying. "I can forge a damn bill of sale good enough to fool anybody."

"Well, I'll leave all that to you," Boone said. "I don't write very good."

Both men were quiet for a while. Seth had no problem identifying the other sounds he was hearing, however: the lid from the iron pot had first been laid on the stove noisily, followed by the rattling of spoons, tin plates, and tin cups as they were placed on the table. When he heard the sound of chairs scraping along the floor a few moments later, he knew that the men had dished up their food and poured their coffee, and were now seating themselves at the small table to eat their supper.

Seth kept his ear to the wall. "Do you really believe Jim'll meet us in San Marcos?" Williams asked around a mouthful of food.

"Ain't got no reason not to," Boone answered. "Anyway, he needs us to help him pull off that job in Arizona Territory. If it's anything like he said it was, he damn sure can't handle it by himself."

Several seconds of silence followed. Then Williams spoke again: "No matter whether Bundy meets us or not, I'm gonna be glad to get away from this place. I don't like the way Seth's been acting lately, and for all I know, that damn deputy told him about us talking with Jim while he was in jail."

"That wouldn't prove nothing even if he did," Boone said. "Ain't no law against visiting somebody in jail." Seth could hear a spoon scraping the bottom of a tin plate, then someone slurping coffee. "I'm just like you are about wanting to get away from here, though," Boone continued. "Seth's a nice enough fellow, but he looks to me like he might have a mean streak in him. If he ever found out that we put his boy under that Dry Creek cutbank, we'd have to kill him, too."

Seth had heard it with his own ears! His hands tightened on the shotgun as a streak of rage ran through his entire body. He suddenly had the same feeling he had experienced many times during the Civil War after watching a beloved comrade fall to enemy fire. He had reacted with violence then, and so would he now.

He cupped his left hand over his right thumb to muffle the sound, then pulled both hammers of the shotgun to full cock. Then he eased forward till he was standing directly even with the door. He had built this shack himself, and well remembered the layout inside. He knew that the small table set against the north wall and catercorner to the stove, which was situated in the northwest corner. He also knew that the door had no lock, but a flimsy latching device consisting of a string wrapped around a nail that had been driven into the doorjamb.

He kicked the door open and stepped into the doorway in one fluid motion, the shotgun pressed against his shoulder tightly. "No!" Williams shouted loudly, his eyes wide with fright at the sight of the big ten-gauge. "No, Seth, we never—" He did not live to finish the sentence. A full load of double-aught buckshot took him in the face, slamming both him and his chair against the north wall. Then, even as the deafening sound reverberated throughout the building, a second shot sent Eldridge Boone bouncing off the wall on the opposite side of the table. He never moved after he hit the floor, and was still holding his soupspoon in his hand when he died.

When Seth stepped to the table, one glance told him all he needed to know. The faces of the men appeared to have been turned inside out by the big weapon, and it was obvious that both had departed for another world. Neither man had been wearing a six-gun when he died, and Seth could see their gunbelts hanging on pegs near the heads of their bunks.

Two rifles and a shotgun also leaned against the wall in the
southeast corner. Seth blew out the lamp and left the building.

He rented a room at the Durant Hotel at midnight and
slept soundly. The first thing he saw when he opened his
eyes next morning was the sun shining around the edges of
the window shade. He was on his feet quickly. He dressed
himself and washed his face and hands, then headed for the
stairway. He ate a ham-and-egg breakfast at the hotel restaurant, then went looking for Sheriff Rountree.

He met the lawman halfway down the block, headed for
the restaurant to eat his own breakfast. After the usual greeting and handshake, Seth volunteered to walk back to the
establishment with Rountree, saying he would have another
cup of coffee while the sheriff ate. They seated themselves at
a table along the rear wall, and as soon as the waiter had
poured their coffee, taken the sheriff's order, and departed,
Seth said bluntly: "I killed two men last night, Will."

Rountree sat slurping his coffee noisily for a moment,
then set the cup on the table. "The hell you say!"

Seth nodded, then began to describe the situation slowly
and deliberately. He told of how he had immediately become
suspicious of his line riders after learning that they had visited Jim Bundy using names other than their own. Finally,
he repeated what he had overheard at the line shack the night
before, then gave an account of his own actions with the
shotgun.

Rountree listened attentively, and did not interrupt once.
He looked over his shoulder to see that his breakfast was
coming, then said, "I'll get one of my deputies as soon as I
get through eating, then we'll take a ride out there."

It was well past noon when Seth, Sheriff Rountree, and
Deputy Jeff Winters arrived at the line shack. They dismounted and tied their animals to a corral pole, then walked
the few steps to the cabin. When the sheriff opened the door,
all three men stepped back quickly, shaking their heads from

side to side. The smell of death was so overwhelming that even the horses began to snort and stomp their feet.

Finally, Rountree spoke to his deputy: "It's part of the job, Jeff; we've got to go in." Winters nodded, and followed his boss through the doorway. Since Seth had already seen the picture inside the building, he retraced his footsteps and waited beside the horses.

The lawmen stayed inside the shack longer than Seth had expected, and both emerged inhaling the fresh air in short, deep gasps, coughing and blowing their noses as they hurried away from the shack. When they reached the corral, the sheriff said, "I want you to repeat word for word what you heard Boone and Williams say before you shot 'em, Seth. Jeff ain't heard it yet."

Seth complied. The deputy listened closely, but made no comment when the narrative was over.

The sheriff turned to Seth again. "Them your guns in that shack?" he asked.

"Nope. Reckon they belong to the men who had 'em. The horses are mine, and all this equipment is mine, but I don't furnish firearms for nobody."

The sheriff nodded, then patted his vest pocket. "Well, they both had more'n enough money on 'em to pay for their own burial. I'll send the undertaker after 'em with a wagon tomorrow." He pointed to the shack and winked at his deputy. "Looks like a clear-cut case of self-defense to me, Jeff. What do you think?"

Winters nodded, a smile playing around one corner of his mouth. "Self-defense," he answered. "Pure and simple."

PART THREE

★

19

★

Rachel Copeland enrolled at the women's college in Dallas in 1875, and the following year, both Paul and Joseph took up residence at a school of higher learning in Waco. The twins, neither of whom had shown any interest in acquiring a college education, continued to live on the ranch, though they obviously had little concern for its day-to-day operation. First Mark, then Matthew had taken up the fast draw after their brother Adam was killed, and a year ago both had begun to drink hard liquor, keeping their bottles stashed in secret hiding places around the ranch.

Keeping such activities a secret from one's family members is difficult if not impossible, however, and even nine-year-old Abel knew that his older brothers were sometimes drunk. Seth had been aware of their drinking for more than a year, and back in the fall he had learned that they not only sat around in the saloons of both Gatesville and Waco with drinks in their hands, but had begun to spend a considerable amount of time at the gambling tables as well.

When Mark once boasted to his mother that he had won

more than a hundred dollars playing poker over the weekend and that he had figured out a lucky system that was going to make him rich, Emerald went straight to her husband with the problem. And though Seth had immediately eliminated himself as a source of gambling capital for the twins, their activities appeared to continue unabated, for both had been earning money working for neighboring ranchers ever since they had been old enough.

Seth had smelled liquor on Mark's breath on several occasions, and had once seen him get his feet tangled up in one of the stirrups and fall to the ground while trying to saddle his horse. Seth had stood behind the chicken house watching while his son got to his feet, looked around quickly to see if anyone had seen him, then saddled his horse and rode off toward Gatesville much like a sober man.

Hoping that Mark would of his own accord come to realize that drinking to excess was not a good thing, his father had never mentioned the incident. It had long been Seth's policy not to forbid his children to do anything that he did himself, and he had certainly been known to hoist a glass of good whiskey on occasion. He had been drunk only twice in his life, however, and seriously doubted that it would ever happen again.

He had passed out from drinking home brew on his eighteenth birthday, and the second and last time he had drunk too much was two days after coming home from the war. So blind that he could scarcely see the road on his way home from town, he had vomited into the ditch time after time, then crawled off into the woods to recuperate. While lying under a leafy bush with his head swimming round and round, he asked himself a question that men had probably been asking for hundreds of years: Why in the hell would a man pay so much money to feel so bad? He was sick all night and had a big head for several days, and he had never taken more than a few drinks at a time since.

Emerald had been less tolerant of the twins' behavior. "I've always been told that most gamblers end up in the gutter," she said to Mark on a day when he was sitting at the kitchen table bragging about all the money he had won. "And you there, Matthew!" she added in a cold voice. "I can smell that whiskey on you way over here!"

She stepped to the stove and stirred the contents of a pot, then reseated herself at the table. "Let me ask you both something," she continued. "Do you really think them gamblers are gonna just keep on letting you take their money? And do you really think you can keep on swigging all that liquor without it finally taking aholt of you?" She bounced her fist on the table. "If either one of you can name me one good thing that ever comes outta drinking whiskey, I'll have a glass of it myself. And if you can teach me to play cards so good that I can't lose, why, I'll be at them tables every day and every night." Getting no answer, she put a lid on her pot and pulled it to the side of the stove, then left the building.

Spring came to central Texas early in this year of 1876, and by the middle of March the 2C hands were walking or riding around in shirtsleeves. Rusty Walker wore an old shirt that he had cut the sleeves out of with a pocketknife, revealing muscular, hairy arms that were as freckled as his face. A powerfully built six-footer who knew the cattle business inside and out, Rusty looked older than his thirty-three years when he was not wearing a hat, for he had lost almost all of his hair since becoming ranch foreman.

This morning Walker was sitting under the shed talking with his boss about an upcoming cattle drive to the rails. "I think we oughtta count on sending about twenty-five hundred head, Seth. We've got more'n a thousand head of three-quarter-blood steers, and at least fifteen hundred half-blood cows. Every one of them cows has dropped at least one calf from the Hereford bulls, so we need to get 'em on outta here. The sooner them bulls ain't got nothing to breed but their granddaughters and great-granddaughters, the sooner we'll be completely rid of the longhorn strain."

"Makes sense," Seth agreed. "I don't reckon we've got

none of the pure longhorns left. About a dozen head of 'em have turned up since we thought we sent 'em all to Kansas on that community drive two years ago, but there ain't nobody seen one in a long time now."

Walker shook his head. "Ain't no more of 'em around. That tough old cow we butchered and ground up last summer was the last of 'em."

Seth rose from his seat on a wagon tongue, then leaned against a post. "The reason I hired Bill Penny to boss the drive is 'cause we've had some awful good luck with him before."

Walker chuckled. "I hate to say this, boss, but I don't think it had anything to do with luck. Penny's a man who knows exactly what he's doing, and everybody who hires him to move a herd seems to get about as lucky as you did. I hear he charges more than some, but the old saying that a man who can deliver the goods is worth a little more salt sounds about right to me."

Seth nodded, then stood thoughtfully for a while. "Penny'll be here with his crew next week," he said finally. "With his ten men and our twelve, it shouldn't take us more'n about two weeks to round up and cut out the ones we want to send up the trail."

"Sounds about right," Walker said. "If it takes longer, it just does."

Seth stared up the hill for a few moments. "Mark keeps on asking me about letting him and Matthew go up the trail with the herd," he said. "I want you to give it to me straight, Rusty. Do you think they can hold down jobs as drovers?"

"Either one of 'em can handle the work," Rusty said, "but their dispositions might be another matter. Both of 'em are a little mouthy, and Bill Penny ain't too likely to appreciate it. He don't put up with no shit out of nobody, and I figure he'd set both of them straight the very first day. I know for sure that he won't tolerate their drinking."

"No," Seth said, "I wouldn't expect him to. Anyway, I told Mark and Matthew both that I wasn't gonna mention it to Penny myself, that if they wanted to go on the drive they'd simply have to ride into Gatesville and ask him for a job themselves. They left for town before sunup this morning, so I reckon we'll find out when they get back."

Their conversation over, Seth walked up the hill to his house while Walker saddled a big buckskin and headed for the west boundary.

A mile east of Gatesville, the twins found Bill Penny busy replacing some pickets in the fence that surrounded his front yard while his wife piddled around in a nearby flower bed. Recognizing his visitors instantly, Penny laid his hammer aside. "Howdy, boys," he said, stepping over the fence and pointing toward the hitching rail. "Get down and tie up."

Bill Penny was an impressive man. Though not as tall as the twins, he was at least as broad and as thick, with a leathery, well-seasoned look that suggested he might be able to back up a verbal order with physical force if the need ever arose. He appeared to be about thirty-five years old, with brown eyes and a full head of dark brown hair. "How are things going out at the ranch?" he asked as the boys dismounted.

"Everything's hunky-dory," Mark said, offering a handshake. "Pa said he thought you might need some help for the trail drive, so he sent us over here to tell you that we'd be more'n happy to make the trip to Kansas with you."

Penny shook hands with both boys, then spoke to Mark. "Kinda funny," he said, "because Seth already knows I've got a full crew. I told him when I agreed to take the herd up that I'd use the same ten men I used last time. Now, I ain't got no written contract with none of them fellows, but I reckon they're all counting on me for work." He shook his head. "Naw, boys, I reckon I'm full up on drovers. Besides, the price me and your pa agreed on wouldn't cover the wages of two extra men. Maybe he didn't think about that."

The twins remounted quickly, and Mark continued to speak for both. "I'll tell Pa what you said, but I don't reckon there's nothing I can say to help his feelings. He sure had his heart set on us going to Kansas, learning about a trail drive and seeing some new country." He reined his horse around and spoke to his brother. "Let's go home, Matthew."

As they rode away, Penny called after them: "Tell your pa it's all right with me, if he wants to kick in the extra money to pay your salaries!"

Twenty minutes later, Mark tied up at a run-down saloon and bought a bottle of whiskey. "I've been wanting a drink all day," he said as he shoved the bottle into his saddlebag and remounted. "And now that the meeting with Bill Penny is over, I can't think of no reason not to have one."

"Me either," Matthew said.

A quarter mile from town they began to pass the bottle back and forth. For every sip taken by his brother, Mark took a full swallow, and he became even more talkative than usual. After a few miles he dismounted at the side of the road, where he picked up a chunk of charred wood a little smaller than a man's head. "Probably floated outta the campground when we had all that high water a month ago," he said, remounting. "I'm gonna ride into that arroyo up ahead and get in some shooting practice. Bet I can put more shots into this chunk at twenty yards than you can."

"I ain't gonna do no betting," Matthew said. "You're not only quicker on the draw than I am, but you've got a better eye."

A short time later, with their horses tied to a short cedar on the otherwise treeless plain, the twins were down in the deep gully with Mark blasting away at the chunk of wood. "I hit it all three times!" he exclaimed, no doubt speaking louder than he realized. "Dead center!"

Matthew shook his head. "I believe you missed it twice," he said. "I was watching that thing mighty close, and I didn't even see it quiver the first two times you fired."

"By God, I'll show you," Mark said. He covered the fifty feet or so to the target in long strides, then retrieved it from its leaning position on the outer bank of an abrupt curve in the gully. He stood looking it over for a few moments. "I can see what happened here mighty easy, Matt," he said. "I hit it dead center the first time, then my other two shots went through the same hole." He brought the block to his brother. "See?" he said, pointing. "See? That hole's too big to have been made by one bullet. The other two widened it out a little on both sides."

Though Matthew seriously doubted the accuracy of the assessment, he could not remember ever winning an argument against Mark. "Maybe so," he said. "I'll tell you one thing, if that's what really happened, it's the best shooting I ever saw."

"Well, that's exactly what happened," Mark said. "You can bet your bottom dollar on it." He tossed the chunk back to its former position, then replaced the spent shells in his six-gun. "Anyway, Matt, what did you expect? Ain't I been practicing with this thing for more'n two years now?" When he got no answer to either question, he holstered the weapon and seated himself cross-legged on the ground. He jerked the stopper out of the whiskey bottle with his teeth, then took a long pull. He wiped his mouth on the heel of his hand, then held up the bottle of brown liquid, two-thirds of which was by now long gone. "I can draw a lot faster after I've had a little of this," he said. "Loosens me up and relaxes me; makes my reflexes a lot quicker, too."

Matthew took a small sip from the bottle, then shoved the cork back in the neck. "I ain't gonna argue about that one way or the other, Mark, but it seems to me that a fellow oughtta be able to do everything better when he ain't drinking."

"You didn't hear me right, Matt," Mark said with a thick tongue. "I wasn't talking about getting drunk, I was just saying that I can draw and shoot better after I've had a few drinks to relax me, like right now." He got to his feet unsteadily, spread his legs and bent forward slightly, then pointed to the block of wood against the bank. "Keep your eye on that target and count to three."

Matthew complied. Mark drew his weapon considerably slower than his twin had seen him do on many other occasions, and when he fired, Matthew saw dirt kick up about two feet to the right of the target. "Dead center again!" Mark said loudly. He holstered the Colt, then reached for the bottle. "Another bullet right through that same hole, Matt. That's exactly what I've been talking about, and you just saw it with your own eyes." He took another long pull, then licked his lips. "Ain't many men around who could match that draw I just made, either."

Leaving the empty bottle in the arroyo, they mounted and rode toward the ranch at a slow walk. Though he had clearly been drunk when he left the gully, Mark, thanks to the remarkable recuperative powers of the young, was already sober enough to fool Seth when he got home three hours later. "Mr. Penny said he'd been thinking about us all along," he said, in answer to his father's question about how the meeting had gone. "He said he never did mention it to you 'cause the deal didn't pay enough for him to afford two more riders. He said he needed me and Matt real bad, though, and that if you'd add enough money to the contract to pay our salaries, he'd put us to work and take us right on to Kansas."

Seth nodded. "Don't reckon that'll be no problem." He stood thinking and scratching his chin for a moment, then added, "That's the way we'll do it, then. I'll just up his money a little." He headed up the hill to tell his wife that her firstborn sons were about to become respectable cattle drovers.

"Pa ain't gonna find out that Penny didn't say all that stuff," Mark said as he loosened the girth on his horse's belly. "They ain't gonna have no big discussion about it nohow. Pa'll just tell him that he's gonna give him some extra money to pay our salaries, and that'll be the end of it."

Matthew nodded. "Seems like you always know exactly what to say, Mark. You always could handle Pa."

The twins unsaddled and cared for their animals, then climbed the hill above the house. They had a bottle hidden about a hundred yards from the spring.

20

★

Bill Penny was one of a growing number of trail bosses who used his own men, horses, and other necessary equipment, and contracted to deliver herds of cattle to the rails in Kansas, with the rancher having to furnish nothing but the cattle. And though their compensation was usually a set fee that had been agreed upon by all parties beforehand, some of the bosses with a great deal of confidence in their ability to haggle with the Kansas buyers might make a deal with a rancher for a percentage of the selling price.

Bill Penny was not among the latter, however. He commanded a flat rate of a dollar fifty per cow, with a minimum of two thousand head, and had made a very comfortable living with the arrangement over the past several years. The fact that he might leave a ranch with two thousand steers did not necessarily mean that he was going to receive three thousand dollars for the trip, however. The dollar-fifty-per-head contract stipulated live delivery, and trailing a herd from Texas to Kansas without losing a few head was unheard-of. "Every time you lose a cow, it's a buck fifty right outta my ass pocket," he had told his drovers on more than one occasion. "I expect every one of them critters to be looked after like helpless orphans."

Bill Penny arived at the 2C Ranch on the first Monday in April. Leaving two young wranglers at the river with the horse herd, he was followed up the hill by the cook, who drove the chuck wagon, and a crew of eight drovers. They came to a halt between the corral and the cookshack, where Rusty Walker and Dan and Seth Copeland stood waiting. In strict adherence to the unwritten etiquette of the West, all remained in their saddles till Dan invited them to dismount.

Once the handshaking was done, Penny turned to Seth. "The quicker we get 'em on the trail, the better trip we're gonna have," he said. "All that rain I was cussing about a few weeks ago is gonna work in our favor." He pointed north. "With all that moisture in the ground, and all these sunny days we've been having, that grass is gonna be right. Sure would be nice if we could get to it before the other trail herds eat it up; cows are a whole lot less trouble when they've got green grass right under their noses."

"We're gonna have about twenty men in the saddle," Rusty Walker said, "so it shouldn't take forever to get a herd ready for the road. The twins and two line riders have been holding about five hundred head of steers up on the north plateau for nearly a week now, and two days ago we drove a couple hundred of them half-blood cows up there with 'em.

"We'll get after 'em early in the morning, and every morning after that. Every afternoon we'll drive the ones we've cut out on up to the mesa, 'cause it's the best place on the ranch to put a herd together. Plenty of grass and water, and you can sit in your saddle and see for at least three miles in any direction. Them four men up there ain't gonna have no trouble at all holding as many as we can bring 'em.

"Now, we'd like to find all of them young steers, but every one of us knows that them bastards can hide out better'n bank robbers. We're bound to miss some, but they'll just be worth a little more money when we find 'em next year." He paused for a moment, then spoke directly to the trail boss. "We ain't nowhere near as concerned about the steers as we are them half-blood cows, Bill. As you know, we're trying to get rid of every drop of longhorn blood on this ranch, and getting them bitches outta here'll be a big step in that direction."

Penny nodded. "We'll get all of 'em we can find," he said. "Then we'll check, double-check, and triple-check."

Being nowhere near as familiar with the ranch as was Rusty Walker, Penny informed his men that the 2C foreman would be in charge of the roundup, and that they were expected to follow his orders without question. He himself would be working right beside them, he added, and taking orders from the same man. Penny knew that there was only room for one boss at a time, and that until the herd was finally bunched and ready for the road, the only things he could add to the effort were his stamina, his extensive cattle savvy, and the services of a cow pony that could turn on a dime. He said as much to Walker.

Half an hour later, the foreman assembled the combined crews in the yard in front of the bunkhouse. With four of the 2C men tied up holding the cattle on the north plateau, and Penny volunteering to work as an ordinary cowboy, Walker now had eighteen men and himself for the roundup. He began by splitting the men into two groups, four of Penny's riders and five 2C men in each bunch. "We'll head southwest this afternoon and make camp a few miles north of the southwest boundary," he said to his attentive audience. "Early in the morning we'll start making a sweep due north.

"I expect to have a sizable herd cut out by noon, then half of us can drive 'em on up to the plateau. Next day, we'll do the same thing, only the other team'll drive the steers and the half bloods to the plateau, while the ones that done it the day before lie around telling jokes and resting their bones." He swept the crowd with his eyes. "Anybody got a better idea?"

When he got no answer, he pointed to the cookshack and chuckled. "That fellow in there might be lying to me, but he claims to have about five gallons of stew and several pones of corn bread waiting for us. Let's go see for ourselves."

The roundup took thirteen days, and on the third Monday of April, all of the 2C hands gathered on the north plateau to help Penny's crew get the herd moving. "Ain't none of these cattle ever trailed before," Penny was saying to the assembled riders, "so they ain't gonna have the slightest damned idea what we're trying to get 'em to do." Then he addressed the 2C men in particular. "I sure appreciate you fellows coming up, 'cause I know we're gonna need your help to get 'em started. Even then, it's gonna be mighty slow going for the first day or two."

An old spotted longhorn steer that had somehow managed to escape several earlier roundups had been found and deliberately thrown into the herd. "I'm gonna put that old fellow up front and hope the others will follow him," Penny said to Seth. "No matter whether he makes a good leader or not, I can probably get you twelve or fifteen dollars for him in Dodge City."

Seth chuckled. "Get him outta here," he said.

Dan Copeland sat his saddle a hundred yards from the herd, accompanied by his grandson Abel. Now three months past the age of nine, Abel had been born on the 2C Ranch in January of 1867. And although no one had mentioned it or even thought about it, the boy was the only native Texan in the entire crowd. Aboard his own small bay, he had been sitting beside his grandfather for more than an hour, watching the men riding back and forth, talking out their strategy for getting the herd on the move. "I sure hope I can do something like that when I get bigger, Grandpa," he said, motioning toward the drovers.

"Why, you look big enough to me right now," Dan said. He reached for his grandson's arm and squeezed the biceps. "Anybody with a muscle that hard oughtta be able to handle a dumb old cow." He pointed to Bill Penny. "Ride over there and tell that man you'd like to help. Ask him if there's anything you can do." Abel smiled broadly, then kneed his bay across the clearing.

Dan sat watching as the boy had a discussion with the trail boss, who nodded, then pointed to the rear of the herd. Penny was obviously going to allow Abel to tag along with the men riding drag for a while. The young man kicked his bay and headed down the quarter-mile-long line of cattle, where several men were already sitting on the ground holding the reins of their cow ponies.

Though Penny's men were all experienced drovers who knew the way to Dodge City, this morning the trail boss had taken the time to describe the route to Dan and Seth. "We'll cross the Leon River a few miles east of Hamilton," he began, "then continue on north till we hit the old Chip Hankins feeder trail, which runs in a northwesterly direction all the way to Fort Griffin. We'll take up the Western Trail at Griffin, and it's almost a straight shot from there to Dodge City."

With Bill Penny leading the way, the riders began to move the cattle north at midmorning. Even with twenty men in the saddle, it took more than three hours to get the herd off the plateau. Penny's idea of using the spotted steer as a leader had paid off early on, for as soon as the riders got the old longhorn pointed in the right direction, first the cows, then the younger steers fell in with little prodding behind the rawboned animal.

When the herd had finally moved across the clearing, both Dan and Seth fell in behind the animals and followed them till they were off the plateau. Once there, Seth informed Abel that his role in the drive had come to an end, then brought his horse to a halt. His father and his son did likewise. Dan sat quietly for a while watching the receding cattle, which were now moving briskly ahead in a column of four. "If I was a young man, I'd be right in the middle of that," he said.

"I wish I was old enough," Abel said wistfully. "I might even be leading it."

Seth turned his horse's head toward home. "I never did like breathing dust," he said, "and they'll stir up many a ton of it before they reach Kansas. Let the men who like that kind of work do it, then bring the money back to us."

When they reached Seth's house, Dan dismounted and handed the reins to his son. "Em says we're all gonna eat dinner with her, so I'll just get off right here and let you two go on to the barn without me. Getting back up this hill afoot ain't near as easy as it was when I had two good legs. Just unsaddle my horse and turn him into the corral. I'll feed him later on."

Abel moved off at a trot while Seth led his father's horse down the hill at a walk. And although Seth curried and fed his own mount, he merely turned Dan's animal into the corral, as he had been instructed. Abel cared for his own horse without being told, for he had been taught early on that a bucketful of oats should always follow a good workout.

Father and son walked back up the hill a short time later, and while Seth took a seat on the front porch beside Dan, Abel was quick to disappear inside the house, no doubt anxious to tell his mother and his grandmother about his busy morning in the saddle. As soon as the boy was out of earshot, Dan turned to Seth. "Do you think the twins're gonna make it on that drive?" he asked.

Seth had been daydreaming, biting his fingernails and staring at the western horizon. "I don't have no way of knowing," he said, spitting a small fragment of thumbnail over the railing. "Rusty talked like it would surprise him if they even get to stay with the herd. He says if they start drinking, playing with their guns, or mouthing off, Penny'll put 'em both on the road in a hurry."

"Couldn't expect him to do nothing else," Dan said. He

was quiet for a few moments, then added, "That's exactly what's gonna happen, too, Seth. You mark my words."

The front door opened just then, and Emerald poked her head through to announce that dinner was ready. "You men can wash up on the back porch," she added. "There's a clean towel hanging on that post above the washpan."

The five Copelands were soon seated at one end of the long dining table. As she had been doing since she was sixteen years old, Emerald fixed her husband's plate and set it before him. "This is some of them mustard greens I canned back in the fall," she said, "and there ain't but two more jars of 'em in the cellar. Now, you know how much you and all the rest of us like 'em, so it's time we put some more seed in the ground."

"What Em is trying to say is that we want you to hitch a team to the turning plow and break up our garden spot, son," Elsie said. "Just turn it over and harrow it, then lay off about twenty rows on the west end for corn and beans. Once you get that done, we'll do the rest ourselves. We'll be planting tomatoes and melons in the middle, so we'll build up the hills for them with our hoes. Then we're gonna broadcast a mixture of mustard and turnip seed over the whole east end of the plot. Maybe that way we won't run out of greens so early next year."

Seth nodded. "Yes, ladies," he said. "Far be it from me to stand in the way of somebody wanting to plant something good to eat. I'll get on it right after dinner. I'm gonna have to haul in some new poles to patch up the northwest corner of that garden fence, though. One of them old bulls just about tore it up last summer trying to get to that green corn. I'll cut some poles stout enough to make a believer out of him this time."

A short time later, after eating his fill of smoked pork, mashed potatoes, corn bread, beans, and mustard greens, followed by two slices of sweet potato pie, Seth harnessed a team and dragged a turning plow to the garden, which consisted of about one acre of land. The fence encircling the plot was composed of several different species of slender poles that, with the exception of a ten-foot section at the southeast corner, were anchored to large cedar posts with twenty-penny nails.

The section where the poles had not been nailed was the gateway, and would even allow a team and wagon to pass through once the poles were lifted out of their notches, which had been created by nailing short sections of forked limbs to the posts.

Seth spent three hours breaking the ground, then exchanged the plow for the harrow, a homemade device consisting of three cedar posts bolted together in a triangle, then equipped with rows of protruding railroad spikes that helped to level the ground, break up clods, and uproot weeds. He placed a board across the harrow and stood on it as the team pulled it first one way, then another across the plowed field, for the extra weight added to the effectiveness of the apparatus.

When the harrowing was done, he bolted two Johnson Wings on a curved wooden plow stock, then laid off the twenty rows his mother had requested. When he left the garden for the last time a few minutes before sunset, the plot was ready for planting.

Next morning at sunup, with Abel sitting on the seat beside him, Seth forded the river in a wagon and pointed the team due east. He was headed for a stand of hardwood saplings about three miles away, for all of the poles closer to home that were long enough and straight enough to be used for fencing had long since fallen to the ax and the saw.

Holding the horses to a walking gait, Seth was riding along counting cows when Abel let out an audible sigh and spoke in a high-pitched voice. "Mark and Matthew are sure gonna know a lot when they get back here," he said softly, as if talking to himself. "I'm gonna get 'em both to tell me about it, too."

Seth chuckled. "Shouldn't be no problem there," he said.

"They'd probably be happy to spend several hours a day telling you about it."

"I hope so," Abel said. "I sure wish Adam was still alive to hear 'em tell it."

Seth suddenly stiffened. Though the mention of his dead son's name was like a dagger in his heart, he also knew that Abel was at this moment feeling very sad and that it was he, not Adam, who needed comforting. He put his arm around Abel's shoulder and drew him close. "Adam don't have to be alive to hear it, son. I figure he's in a place where he sees and hears everything." He pointed skyward. "I bet he's up there looking down on us right now."

"Hope he is," Abel said. "I sure do miss him, though."

Less than two hours after reaching the stand of hardwoods, they had twenty ten-foot poles in the wagon, for young Abel had handled his end of the crosscut saw very well. "This is all we need, son," Seth said. "We'll leave the rest of 'em for another day." They headed home, and before the day was out, the garden fence was sturdy enough to turn back the strongest bull on the premises.

21

★

Two weeks after the herd left for Kansas, Seth decided that he and Abel would cut and haul in enough wood to fire the stoves and heaters for the rest of the year. An hour before sunset, he was underneath the shed greasing the wheels of the wood wagon when he heard his father's buggy leave the main road and head up the hill. Dan had been in Gatesville for the past three days, visiting and playing dominoes with his friends. Seth got to his feet and wiped the grease from his hands with a gunnysack, then stepped out to meet the approaching vehicle. "I told you two weeks ago to mark my words," Dan said as he pulled the mare to a halt, "and I hope you did."

Seth stood quietly for a moment, then said, "I'm having a little trouble figuring out what you're talking about, Pa."

Dan climbed to the ground with no assistance. "The twins didn't stay with that herd till the water got hot," he said. "When a fellow told me this morning that they were in the Branding Iron Saloon playing poker, I walked straight over there 'cause I wanted to see it with my own eyes. There they sat just as pretty as you please: Mark playing five-card stud, and Matthew taking a hand in a draw poker game at another table."

Seth stood staring at his callused hands. "I wonder what happened on the drive," he said finally.

"Exactly what I told you would happen," Dan said quickly. "Them boys ain't got no respect for nothing nor nobody, and just as soon as Bill Penny found that out he sent their asses packing."

Crestfallen, and growing more dispirited by the moment, Seth led the mare to the opposite end of the building and backed the buggy under the shed. Dan followed, and stood watching his son unhitch the mare. Seth unhooked a trace chain from the singletree, then hung the chain on one of the hames. "Did you speak to either one of the boys?" he asked.

Dan nodded. "Tried to talk to Mark, but he didn't want to listen. He kept waving me away like he wasn't gonna talk to me at all to start with. Then he finally threw his cards down and walked over to the bar where I was standing. When I asked him why him and Matthew left the herd, he said Bill Penny was too hard to work for, that he singled them out from the very first day and barked at 'em from daylight till dark."

Seth finished unhitching and unharnessing the mare, then led her out from between the shafts. "You go on to the house and get some supper, Pa. I'll feed and curry ol' Bess, then turn her into the corral." He took a few steps toward the barn, then stopped and turned halfway around. "I'll go into town tomorrow and hunt them boys up," he said. "See if I can get any sense out of 'em."

"There's something else I didn't mention, Seth," Dan said, then walked back down the slope. "I wasn't gonna say nothing about this, son, but now I've decided to go ahead and tell you about it. Mark told me right to my face that I was too old-fashioned to understand him and Matthew.

Now, there might be a certain amount of truth in that, but what he said next hurt me so bad that I walked outta there with tears in my eyes."

Seth stood waiting for his father to continue. When it did not happen, he said, "I'm sorry to hear that, Pa. What was it? What did Mark say?"

"He said life had already passed me by, and that the only thing left between me and a hole in the ground was a few more games of dominoes. Then he . . . called me an old codger."

Seth dropped the mare's reins to the ground and put an arm around his father's shoulder. "I reckon that hurts me about as much as it hurts you, Pa," he said. "I never would've dreamed that one of my children would say something like that to you, especially one of the twins. Ever since they were born, you've been giving 'em everything they needed and a whole lot of stuff they didn't need, and I've certainly never heard you speak unkindly to one of 'em." He stood shaking his head. "I can't figure out what's got into Mark."

"It's in their blood, Seth, and I expect 'em to just get worse and worse till somebody kills 'em. I ain't never told you this before 'cause there ain't been no reason to, but now I reckon the time has come.

"You see, your great-grandpa's three brothers weren't worth killing, and a few people even had their doubts about Grandpa." He shook his head and waved his hand as if starting over. "I'll take that back about my great-uncles not being worth killing. One fellow evidently thought they were, 'cause he killed two of 'em when he caught 'em butchering his milk cow.

"Anyway, I've always been told that a strain of bad blood shows up every four generations. Now, it don't affect every member of a fourth-generation family. According what I've heard, folks say it usually just hits the oldest two or three in the bunch. In our case, that would be the twins.

"And since we know it didn't hit Rachel, and since the

rest of the boys ain't got it, I believe the Copeland Curse, as some of the old folks used to call it, is alive and well in Mark and Matthew's veins." He turned his face to avoid Seth's piercing eyes. "I expect it to be the death of 'em, too, son," he added.

"You mean you think they'll turn out to be criminals?"

Dan nodded. "As soon as their luck runs out at the card tables," he said. "You mark my words." He turned and limped toward the house. "I'm not gonna tell the women about this," he said over his shoulder.

"They've got a right to know, Pa. If you don't tell 'em, I'll do it myself."

Dan came to a halt, but did not turn around. "All right!" he shouted. "I'll tell 'em! I'll tell Elsie first, then walk over and talk to Emerald!"

Seth fed and curried the mare, then left the stable door open so she could walk into the corral whenever she chose. With half an hour of daylight left, he returned to the shed and greased the last of the wagon wheels, then ran the jack down and took a seat on an upended water barrel. A few minutes later, he saw his father step through the back door of his house and head across the hill, no doubt on his way to tell his daughter-in-law about the Copeland Curse.

Seth absentmindedly picked up a pebble and threw it at a bucket several yards away. Copeland Curse, my ass, he was thinking. The twins didn't have no damned curse. What the twins did have was the attitude that the world owed them a living, and what they needed most was a good ass-kicking. He had no way of knowing whether or not he could handle that job himself nowadays, for they had outgrown him, and both were exceptionally strong.

He was confident that the ass-kicking would be forth-coming, however, for smart-alecky young men, be they large or small, seldom insulted a whole lot of people before getting a boot in the mouth. That was surely going to happen to the twins sooner or later, and Seth was hoping it would happen early on. He would hunt them up tomorrow and see if they talked to him any more respectfully than they had their grandfather. If not, he would leave them to their new pastime. The hard lessons to be learned at the poker table were many, and the sooner the better.

Seth saddled the big gray shortly after sunup next morning, then headed for town to look for his sons. Neither he nor his wife had had enough sleep, for they had talked about Mark's mistreatment of his grandfather till late in the night. They agreed that the twins' recent behavior was completely unacceptable, but neither could think of a solution. "We've both done everything we possibly could to raise them boys right," Emerald said, "so let's don't go blaming ourselves. Ain't nothing either one of us could have done no better'n we did. Mark's had a smart mouth for most of his life, and here lately Matthew's been taking it up, too.

"As for that so-called Copeland Curse, ain't nothing to that, Seth. Aunt Nora Cain told me about it back when she was trying to talk me outta marrying you. I didn't put no stock in it then, and neither do I now. What's wrong with them boys is just what you said it was: they've always had it too easy." She brushed his lips with her fingers. "I'll live with whatever decision you make, just like always."

But Seth had made no decision. Even after thinking on the matter all night and a few hours this morning, he still had no idea how he was going to handle it. By the time he got to town he had decided that he would simply open a normal conversation with his sons, then see what developed from there.

In Gatesville, Josh Ransom, the daytime bartender at the Branding Iron, informed Seth that he had not seen either of the twins today, and that they usually waited till later in the afternoon to come in. He pointed to the gaming area, where two card games were already in full swing. "You never can tell for sure, though. They played poker just about all day yesterday, and the night man said they came back later on and played till he closed at midnight." He shrugged. "Like I say, you never can tell."

Seth nodded. "Did you hear 'em say whether they had a room at the hotel or not?"

Ransom, a tall, dark-haired man who was about Seth's own age, smiled with one corner of his mouth. "Heard 'em say they didn't," he said. "Mark said they got a good deal on a tent, two bedrolls, and some cooking and eating utensils, then set up camp on the south bank of the river about two miles east of town. Said there wasn't no way in the world that they were gonna pay the high cost of restaurants and hotels at this time of year."

"I see," Seth said. "The south bank, you say? About two miles east of town?"

Ransom nodded. "That's what Mark said."

"Thank you, Josh," Seth said, then spun on his heel. "I'll stop in and have a drink with you when I've got more time." He pushed his way through the batwing doors, then walked to the hitching rail and untied the gray. He mounted and rode to the corner, then cut through an alley to the center of town, for the Branding Iron was well off the beaten path.

Five minutes later, he was riding east on the south bank of the Leon. He lost sight of the river itself a few times, for he occasionally had to ride around clusters of brush, briers, and thorns so thick that they were impenetrable. There was always a clearing beyond such an obstruction, however, and most times a treeless plain that ran right down to the water.

Seth saw the smoke first; then, once he had ridden around a thick clump of brush, he saw the tent. Unlike most campers, who usually selected a site well hidden from probing eyes, the twins had set up their tent in the middle of a clearing that was at least fifty yards wide. Even though their horses were grazing in plain view, and anybody seeing them would know that someone was sleeping close by, Seth considered the location of the camp a dumb idea. Had they pitched their tent out of sight in a thick cluster of bushes, any intruder with malice on his mind would have to do a whole lot of searching to find them, and would stand a very good chance of calling attention to himself in the process.

Seth halted the gray thirty yards away and sat looking at the tent, which was pegged to the ground only a few feet from the water's edge. Both boys lay beside the fire leaning on their elbows, their eyes glued to something on the opposite side of the river. "Company's coming!" Seth said loudly, then kneed the gray toward the fire.

The twins were on their feet instantly, but neither spoke right away. Nor did their father. He sat his saddle for several seconds without a word. He had never seen Matthew with a six-gun on his hip before, but there he stood with a Colt Peacemaker tied to his right leg with rawhide. Mark, who also wore a Colt and had a Winchester rifle leaning against his saddle, finally broke the silence. "Did you come over here to preach to us?" he asked.

Seth took his time about answering. "I don't know much about preaching," he said after a while. "The reason I'm here is to try to find out what's come over you boys lately."

"Ain't nothing come over us, Pa!" Matthew said, speaking much louder than was necessary. "We just decided to go our own way and start making our own decisions." He pointed to his brother, then to himself. "We're grown now. Ain't you noticed?"

Seth did not answer the question. Of course he had noticed that the boys were grown, but to have Matthew, who had always had such a meek and gentle disposition, suddenly begin speaking to him in a disrespectful manner was almost more than he could bear. He sat looking between his horse's ears for a while, then spoke to Mark. "Pa sure is hurt about the way you talked to him yesterday. Don't you think you owe him an apology?"

Mark exploded. "Hell, no, I don't owe him no apology! Tell him to just keep sitting around counting all that money." He shrugged, turning his palms upward. "What have me and Matthew got, huh? Nothing, that's what! Tell the old codger I think he got just what he deserved for sticking his nose into our business."

Seth sat staring at the ground for a long time, reminiscing

about his family's early days back in Kentucky. In his mind he could see the twins on their second Christmas, giggling innocently as they ran around the room or played their childish games in front of the fireplace. And Rachel, who had been three months old at the time, lying in her homemade crib a few feet away with a fuzzy blanket tucked under her chin. Seth had been a doting father, and even now could remember bragging that his sons were the prettiest babies he had ever seen. After all these years, the image was still as clear as if it had happened only yesterday.

The picture he saw when he raised his eyes, however, was considerably different. What he saw now was a pair of smirking two-hundred-pound strangers with insolence written all over their faces. He sat quietly for a few more moments, then nodded to Mark. "I'll give Pa your message," he said. He turned his horse around and headed back the way he had come. After only a few steps, he stopped and twisted his body in the saddle. "You oughtta move that tent up there in that thick brush," he said, pointing. "Sleeping in this clearing every night is just asking for trouble." He kicked the gray in the ribs and rode off at a canter.

A few minutes later, he rode through town like a statue, showing no signs of recognition even when passing people he knew well. The only stop he made was at a small grocery store on the north edge of town, where he bought cookies and rock candy for Abel and smoking tobacco for the cook. Then he rode home at a walk, thankful that he met no traffic on the road.

There was still an hour of daylight left when he reached the ranch, and even as he rode up the hill, he could see his father waiting for him at the corral. Dan had little to do nowadays except sit on the porch with his eyes on the road, and no doubt he had been watching his son's progress for the last mile or so.

"Did you find 'em?" Dan asked as Seth pulled up and dismounted.

Seth nodded. "I found 'em," he answered. "They've set

up camp on the river two miles east of town." He laid a stirrup across the saddle to get it out of his way, then loosened the girth. He said nothing else until after he had stripped the saddle and the blanket. He put them on a sawhorse under the shed, then picked the gray's reins up from the ground. "The twins talked to me the same way they talked to you, Pa." He stood staring off into space for a moment, then added, "I kind of expected it from Mark, but it cut me mighty deep when Matthew started mouthing off to me.

"I can't think of a single thing we could have done better, but there ain't no doubt in my mind that we've lost em." He led the gray to the stable and poured a bucket of oats in the trough.

Finding his father gone when he returned to the shed, Seth climbed the hill to his own house. Emerald saw him coming and stepped onto the porch to meet him. He took her in his arms and pulled her head against his chest tightly. "We've lost the twins, Em," he said softly. "It's just like you said last night. It ain't nothing we've done or not done, but we've lost 'em anyhow."

22

★

During the month of June, Jake Barry was taking his turn as line rider on the west boundary. A twenty-three-year-old man of short stature, the dark-haired, blue-eyed Barry had originally come from the Houston area, and had been on the 2C Ranch for about a year. And although he lived in the southwest line shack, there was no evidence that two former line riders had died there, for both the floor and the north wall had been replaced.

This morning Barry was riding north about three miles from his cabin when he saw a 2C cow a hundred yards across the property line to the west, eating grass that belonged to Lester Burbank's Lazy Bee Ranch. When he headed in her direction, she broke into a hard run, and he chased her at least a quarter mile before finally turning her back toward her own range.

With the cow now headed east at a fast trot and well ahead of him, Barry slowed his horse to a walk. It was then that he noticed the tracks. He leaned over in the saddle to study them for a while, then dismounted for a closer inspection. After only a few moments he decided that the tracks were several days old, and that the cattle making them had numbered at least twenty. Leading his animal while stooped over reading sign, he quickly came to the conclusion that the cattle had not wandered onto Lazy Bee property. They had been driven.

Though he was still a young man, Barry was nonetheless a good tracker, and could read the situation before him with ease: three riders had driven a small herd of cattle this way since the last rain, about ten days earlier. And the men had no doubt been whipping the animals along, for they had been moving at a trot most of the time.

Barry remounted and followed the tracks west for a while, noting that the riders had quit pushing the cattle once they were well away from 2C range. He brought his animal to a halt after about a mile, then turned around and retraced his route. Knowing that he had been riding both north and south along that boundary every day, he was wondering how so many cattle could have gotten off the ranch without him noticing their tracks.

He galloped back across the line and pulled up at a strip of rocky terrain that extended several hundred yards on each side of the boundary. Even from his saddle he could see that three men, one behind and one on each side, had driven a small herd of cattle across the property line to the west. He sat staring at the tracks for a long time, then uttered a reproachful sigh. The fact that he had not been aware of the situation earlier was nobody's fault but his own, he was thinking. He had no doubt ridden right by the tracks a dozen times with his mind a thousand miles away, clearly not taking care of his job. Shaking his head in disbelief, he turned his animal around and headed east. He must report his discovery to Rusty Walker at once, and let the blame fall wherever it may.

Barry's pony was spent by the time he reached the corral, for he had made no effort to spare the animal. Rusty Walker was standing beside the gate when the little sorrel slid to a halt nearby. "We don't push our horseflesh that way around here, Jake," the foreman said. "I hope you've got a good excuse for it."

Barry lifted a leg over the saddle and jumped to the ground. "Somebody drove a bunch of cattle off this ranch, Rusty, and it ain't been but a few days ago."

Walker, ever the cool head, stepped under the shed and seated himself on a wagon tongue. "Tell me about it," he said.

Barry dropped his horse's reins to the ground and followed Walker under the shed, where he stood leaning against a post. "It looks like they got about twenty head," he began, then described the situation on the western boundary, including his own tardiness in discovering the tracks, which were obviously several days old.

When the young man finished his lengthy narration, Walker asked, "About twenty head, you say?"

Barry nodded. "Looked like it to me. Of course, it could've been twice that many—you know how it is when a whole bunch of tracks run together."

"I know," Walker said, getting to his feet. "Give me a few minutes to saddle up, then we'll go take a look at them tracks." He pointed to the corral. "Catch up that little bay mare in the corner and put your saddle on her. That horse of yours needs some rest."

Three hours later, they were on the west boundary, where Barry sat his saddle pointing to the ground. "They came around the side of that hill there and moved onto this strip of rough terrain just like they enjoyed walking on rocks. Since I know that ain't the case, I figured whoever drove 'em through here was trying to hide their trail." He waved his arm in a westerly direction. "Anyway, they stuck with that strip of brush and rocks till it played out about three hundred yards over on Burbank's property. That's where I was when I first saw the tracks."

Following Barry's point, Walker headed across the line at a fast trot, coming to a halt at the end of the rocky strip.

He sat with his eyes glued to the ground for a few moments, but did not dismount. Then, because the tracks were so numerous and easy to read, he kicked his horse to a canter and began to follow them. And just as Barry had done earlier, he brought his animal to a halt after about a mile. "It's pretty obvious where this trail leads," he said to the line rider, who sat his saddle nearby.

"That's what I was thinking this morning," Barry said. "This is about where I stopped following 'em, too—just about right here."

Walker pointed east. "Just get on back to your job and keep this under your hat, Jake. Like I said, the trail is easy to follow, but calling Lester Burbank a cattle rustler would be about like calling Abraham Lincoln a bank robber. There must be more to this than meets the eye, and I'm gonna take it up with the boss before I go any farther." He kicked the big black with his heels and headed east.

The sun was only a few minutes above the western horizon when he reached the ranch buildings. As he brought his animal to a halt at the corral gate he could see Dan Copeland sitting on his perch at the west end of the porch. Both men waved a greeting, and then Walker unsaddled and cared for his mount. After he walked back through the gate, he stopped and stood thinking for a moment, trying to figure out whether to consult the old man about the situation or wait and talk with Seth first. Finally deciding that it made little or no difference, that anything he said to one would very quickly reach the other, he walked up the hill to the big house.

Smiling, Dan got to his feet as Walker neared the porch. "Come on up and have a seat, Rusty. I've been sitting here all afternoon by myself, and I reckon I need some company."

Walked climbed the steps and walked to the table, pulling out a cane-bottomed chair with the toe of his boot. "Jake Barry rode over from the west boundary to get me this morning," he said, seating himself. "He'd found some tracks he wanted me to look at." He placed his elbows on the table and rested his chin in his hands, then continued. "Some time during the past week or so, three men drove a good-size bunch of cattle off this ranch. The trail's just as plain as the nose on your face, and I followed it myself for more'n a mile."

Dan said nothing, just sat staring into his foreman's eyes. When it became obvious that his boss was waiting for more information, Walker continued. "The riders even had the cows on the run when they left your property, so there ain't no question in my mind about what was going on. Somebody's been stealing 2C cattle, Dan, and they drove 'em right onto the Lazy Bee."

"Are you saying you think Lester Burbank has stooped to cattle rustling?" Dan asked.

"No," Walker answered quickly. "No, sir, not in a million years. The truth is, I don't know what to make of it, but there ain't no denying that the cows went across that boundary running, and they didn't come back. Burbank himself would tell you that if he saw the tracks."

Dan sat thoughtfully for a few moments, drumming his fingers on the table. "I guess you've been thinking on it for a while," he said finally. "What do you aim to do about it?"

"I ain't decided yet. I thought the first thing I oughtta do is talk to you or Seth about it."

"Well, Lester Burbank stealing cattle, or even tolerating anybody who does, is pretty much out of the question. Hell, he's president of the Central Texas Stock Growers Association, and there probably ain't nobody in this county who's helped as many people as he has. From what I hear, he even lent some of his own brood cows to Rafe Cotton, back when Cotton was trying to put his first herd together." He sat shaking his head. "No, sir. Lester Burbank don't sound like no cattle rustler to me."

"Me either," Walker said. "The man's reputation just about puts him above suspicion, but the fact remains that the damn cows were driven onto his property."

Dan rapped the table with his knuckles. "I've been

knowing Lester ever since I settled here," he said. "If you'll hitch up my buggy first thing in the morning, I'll go over and have a talk with him."

"Yes, sir," Walker said, getting to his feet. "The buggy'll be ready at sunup." He stepped off the porch and headed down the slope. Just before he entered the cookshack he glanced over his shoulder and saw Dan limping across the hill toward his son's house. A meeting of the minds would no doubt be taking place very shortly.

Moments later, Walker took his customary seat at the end of the long table, a bowl of stew and a steaming cup of coffee before him. He nodded a greeting to each of the eight men sitting on the benches, then began to shovel the hot food into his mouth with an oversized spoon. Like always, the hands ate in silence for the most part, usually speaking only if it became necessary.

Walker emptied his bowl and helped himself to a refill, then leaned over and spoke to Jud Welty, who was sitting to his left. "When I get done eating I'll walk over to the bunkhouse, Jud. Tell the men I want 'em all to meet me there; tell 'em I've got something to say." He emptied his bowl a second time, then dropped it in the dishpan and walked through the doorway.

He had been sitting on his cot for about ten minutes when the hands began to amble through the bunkhouse door one at a time. He kept his seat till he counted eight men gathered around him in a half circle, then got to his feet. "We've got a problem, men," he said, pausing to make eye contact with them all. "Somebody's been driving cattle off the 2C."

The men glanced at each other hurriedly, then back at Walker. "You mean rustlers?" one of them asked.

Rusty smiled weakly. "I hate to call it rustling at this stage of the game," he said, "but I damn sure can't think of no other word for it." He reseated himself on his cot and described the situation he had witnessed that morning, adding that under no circumstances should any 2C rider question Lester Burbank's honesty.

"Mr. Burbank ain't rustled no cows from nobody," a
hand named Harper said quickly. "I worked for him for
more'n three years, and I can tell you right now that his
outfit is just as clean as this one is. Even talking about stealing would be enough to get a man fired over there."

Simpson Bain was speaking now: "Since we know that
the cows were driven onto his property, it seems to me that
the next step oughtta be having a talk with Burbank. You
want me to go over there in the morning, Rusty?"

Walker shook his head. "Mr. Dan's gonna do that. Since
they've known each other for a while, I reckon he oughtta
be the one to do it anyhow." He got to his feet again and
stood at the foot of his cot. "Let's all use our eyes and ears
and try to keep this thing from happening again. Cows that
are being driven make noise, and so do the men driving 'em.
Keep your ears open for that sound, and keep a sharp lookout for any tracks that don't look right."

He walked to the door and put his hand on the knob.
"I want you all to start traveling in twos. If you happen to
ride up on a bunch of cattle thieves at work, one man should
hold 'em at gunpoint while the other rides after help. If they
try to make a run for it, every man here knows exactly what
he's expected to do." He stepped outside and eased the door
to, then headed for the barn.

Dan rattled off the hill in his buggy at eight o'clock next
morning, headed for the Burbank spread. He traveled toward Gatesville at a trot for more than an hour, then turned
west on the poorly maintained road that led to the Lazy Bee.
It took him another two hours to reach the ranch house, for
most of the time he was forced to hold the mare to a walking
gait.

A pack of dogs announced his arrival even before he
reached the gate, then came running down the drive to meet
him, the younger ones playfully snapping at the mare's

hooves. Summoned by the barking of the hounds, Burbank stepped into the yard and stood waiting for the approaching buggy.

Lester Burbank was a big man, standing six feet tall and weighing at least two hundred pounds. With a dark, leathery complexion, thinning gray hair, and a salt-and-pepper mustache, he stood as straight as a fence post, even though he was past the age of seventy. He smiled broadly and threw up his hand as Dan brought the mare to a halt at the hitching rail. "Well, if this ain't a surprise," he said. "I was just standing here trying to remember when I saw you last. Get down and tie up, Dan; I believe the coffeepot's still on."

Copeland stepped to the hub of the front wheel, then to the ground, his right hand extended. "Been a few years," he said, pumping Burbank's hand. "I reckon I ain't got no good excuse for it, but I don't visit nobody much these days. Maybe I'm just getting old."

"Humph," Burbank said. "You're still a youngun yet." He pointed to the wide porch. "Come on up and have a seat while I rustle up some coffee."

Dan climbed the steps and took a seat in the cushioned chair he was offered. Then Burbank stepped inside the house. He returned in less than a minute and pulled a small table up close to Dan's elbow. "Our coffee'll be served out here," he said. "I told her to bring some cream and sugar, in case you like yours that way."

Copeland shook his head. "I drink it just like it comes outta the pot."

They sat talking of grass, water, and weather for a few minutes, then accepted a tray with two cups of coffee from a Chinese girl who appeared to be in her early teens. "She's our cook's granddaughter," Burbank said, once the young lady was out of earshot. "Been here since she was three years old."

Dan nodded, then chuckled. "Probably cooks better'n a whole lot of grown women."

"Absolutely," Burbank said. "I wouldn't hesitate for a

minute to set my best friend down to one of her meals. A fellow wouldn't believe it unless he tasted it for himself, but that little girl knows how to fix any damn thing you can name."

They sat making idle conversation for another half hour, then Dan brought up the reason for his visit. "Somebody drove off some of my cows, Lester, and they pushed 'em right onto the Lazy Bee. I decided to come over and see if you know anything about it."

Burbank answered quickly. "The only 2C cows I've seen around here are the ones your grandsons brought over five days ago."

Dan sat scratching his chin as the rancher's words soaked in. "You say my grandsons drove some of my stuff over here?" he asked after a while.

Burbank nodded, then pointed east. "Mark, Matthew, and another fellow about their own age drove twenty-eight head across that creek last Monday about dinnertime." He paused for a moment, then asked, "You didn't know anything about it, huh?"

Dan shook his head. "Lord, no."

"Well, I'll be damned!" Burbank said loudly. After a moment, he softened his voice and continued: "I already knew you'd sent a herd up the trail to Kansas, but I remember thinking something didn't sound quite right when the twins came over here a week ago saying you were running short of money till the trail boss got back.

"To tell you the truth, I was a little bit surprised to hear that Dan Copeland ever ran short of anything, especially the ability to plan far enough ahead to wait out a trail drive. I decided not to question what the boys were telling me, though, and when they said you needed to sell a few head to tide you over, I told 'em to bring 'em on. I reckon the biggest surprise I got was the price they wanted for 'em after they got 'em here: only ten dollars a head."

Dan sat staring at the floor. "Ten dollars a head!" he repeated loudly. "Three-quarter-blood Herefords, too."

Burbank chuckled. "Hell, yes," he said. "I remember telling Mark that if the 2C had any more to sell at that price, I'd like to buy 'em all." He got to his feet and walked to the end of the porch, where he stood pointing across the meadow beyond the barn. "The cattle are penned up back yonder, and they're all still wearing your brand. For some reason, my crew never got around to changing it.

"I never would've dreamed that them boys would steal from you or lie to me either, but I reckon that's life. I've seen it all in my time. Anyhow, all you've got to do is send some men over here after your cows. Give me back my two hundred eighty dollars if you want to; if you don't, that'll be all right, too."

Dan nodded, and offered a parting handshake. "There'll be some men here to pick 'em up in a day or two, and I'll send the money by them. I'll add a little extra for the hay, too." He gave Burbank's hand a firm squeeze, then walked down the steps. Moments later, he untied the mare and climbed into the buggy.

Burbank had followed, and now stood beside the vehicle. "Seems like a damn shame that something like this had to happen, Dan, but at least we got to see one another again. I think we oughtta do that a little more often, so I'll make you a deal: I'll start coming over to see you about harvesttime every year if you'll repay the visit in the spring."

Dan shook the man's hand again. "I'll buy that deal," he said. He backed the mare away from the hitching rail, then headed down the drive at a trot.

23

★

Rusty Walker, Jud Welty, and Simpson Bain left for the Lazy Bee to retrieve the cattle early next morning. Ten minutes later, with two saddled horses trailing their buggy, Dan and Seth rode out of the yard toward Gatesville. After a lengthy discussion the night before, father and son had finally agreed that a firm talk with the twins was in order.

At first, Dan had been all for swearing out a warrant charging the boys with cattle rustling, then letting the law take its course. Seth had argued against that solution right from the start, saying that even though the twins might be young and foolish, he did not believe they were thieves at heart. They had simply run out of money to support their drinking and gambling habits, he reasoned, then decided that since they were the sons and grandsons of the owners, it was unlikely that they would face harsh punishment even if they were caught misappropriating 2C cattle.

This morning, Dan and Seth were on their way to point out the pitfalls of that line of thinking to the twins. Just before bedtime last night, father and son had come to an agreement: the boys would get a fair warning, then be given one last chance. If they drove off 2C cattle again, they would be treated exactly like any other cow thieves.

Dan and Seth talked little this morning, for it seemed they had said all that was necessary before going to bed the night before. Dan stopped the buggy an hour out of town and relieved himself over the sideboard, then drove on to Jesse Hunter's livery stable. He parked the vehicle off to the side, and Seth jumped to the ground and spoke to the liveryman: "We need to leave this buggy here for a while if you don't mind, Jess. We'll finish up our little trip on horseback."

Hunter nodded and waved his arm. "Leave it as long as you want," he said. "Sure won't cost me nothing."

The Copelands mounted and rode away, Seth on his big gray and Dan on a medium-sized chestnut. They rode through the alley and stopped at the Branding Iron long enough for Seth to inspect the saloon's clientele, then headed for the south bank of the river. Seth led the way, and covered the distance much quicker than he had the first time he was here.

When he came in sight of the camp, he could see that nothing had changed. The familiar horses were grazing in the same small meadow, and the tent was still in the clearing beside the river. As Seth and his father rode closer, first Mark, then Matthew emerged from the tent. Both stood watching quietly as the elder Copelands brought their horses to a halt thirty feet away.

When it became obvious that neither of the twins was going to speak, Dan kneed his chestnut forward a few steps. "Do you boys think the men we've got on the payroll are a bunch of damn fools?" he asked. "Did you think they were too dumb to figure out that you drove a bunch of cows off the ranch?"

Mark answered with what was his usual gesture when he was unconcerned about one thing or another: he shrugged and held his arms out to his sides, palms upward.

Seth had seen enough. He kneed his own mount up beside his father's, then took over the conversation. "I don't know what the hell's come over you boys, and I don't reckon I'd be able to understand it even if I did, but you'd be wise to listen to what I'm about to say. We paid back the money you got for them twenty-eight cows you stole, and—"

"Stole?" Mark interrupted indignantly. "Stole, you say? Hell, we've spent most of our lives on that ranch. Don't some of what's out there belong to us? Ain't we got nothing coming?"

Dan's face suddenly turned bloodred, with several large veins popping out on his neck. "You bet you've got something coming!" he said, almost shouting. "And you're damn sure gonna get it the next time you go driving cows off the 2C. Every man on the ranch has been instructed to treat you exactly like any other cattle rustlers if they catch you at it. That goes for that son of a bitch who helped you drive off them twenty-eight head, too, whoever he was."

Mark had stood listening with a smirk on his face that both men had seen many times during the past year. "Well, me and Matthew both figure the 2C owes us something," he said, "and all them mean old men you've got out there might be getting their chance at us before too long." He chuckled insolently, patting the Peacemaker on his hip. "Of course, they might not be quite as brave as you think they are once they find out we know how to use guns, too."

Seth was having a problem viewing the young men standing before him as his sons. He sat his saddle seething, fighting hard to control his emotions. "I reckon the time for talking is over," he said finally, first making eye contact with Mark, then Matthew. "You've both been warned; if you commit the same offense again, you'll have to pay the consequences." He refocused his eyes on Mark. "You boys can come out and pick up the rest of your belongings, but after that I don't want to see you out there again unless it's just to visit your ma."

Mark chuckled. "Visit Ma?" he asked. "Hell, we don't want to see that bitch. All she ever does is order us around, and we don't get a damn thing outta that either. She—"

Mark never finished the sentence, for he could see that Seth had suddenly thrown his leg over the saddle and jumped to the ground. Having little doubt about what was on Seth's mind, and none whatsoever that he could best his father in a hand-to-hand showdown, Mark unbuckled his gunbelt and handed it to his twin. "Hold this, Matthew," he said with a smirk. "This little operation shouldn't take no more'n a minute or two."

Overconfident and even a little eager to take his father on, Mark had been correct about only one thing: the duration of the fight. The arrogant yearling had challenged the old bull, and it quickly became obvious that he was not up to the task. When Mark walked out to meet Seth swinging with both fists, he hit nothing but air, and several times took a blow to the head for his trouble. The thirty-six-year-old Seth continued to dance around the younger man, striking him in the face repeatedly, bringing blood with every blow.

When Mark finally decided he could not stand toe-to-toe trading punches with his father, he rushed him, knocking Seth backward and landing on top of him. Although Mark was now clearly in an advantageous position, he was unable to keep it. It was man to man now, muscle against muscle. Holding on to Mark's arms and summoning the last ounce of his own reserve, Seth gradually began to push the younger man up and away, finally flipping him onto his back.

Seth was on top of him immediately, pounding him in the face with first one hand, then the other. "Your ma's a bitch?" he was asking between blows. "Your ma's a bitch, you say?"

"He can't hear you, Pa!" Matthew said loudly. "He's out cold."

As Seth got to his feet, the unmistakable sound of a shell being jacked into the barrel of a rifle came to his ears. He followed the sound with his eyes and saw a young woman standing in front of the tent with a Winchester leveled at his chest. "Don't you hit Mark again!" she commanded. "Move away from him, then both of you ride outta here before I put a bullet in you!"

Seth nodded, then headed for his horse. He stepped into the stirrup and threw his leg over the saddle, then spoke to Matthew. "I don't reckon I'd know how to stop loving you boys," he said, "but I hope I never see either one of you again."

He turned the gray and rode out of the clearing, his father following close behind. They had ridden about a thousand yards when Seth turned to Dan. "Do you think that girl would have shot us, Pa?"

"Why, certainly that whore would have pulled that trigger," Dan answered quickly. "She's in love, or thinks she is." He rode a few steps farther, then added, "Of course, she'll fall outta love as soon as the boys run outta money and whiskey, but it won't take her long to find another fellow with a few dollars to spend. Then she'll fall head over heels again."

24

★

Shortly before noon on a hot day in August, three men rode into the town of Hamilton and dismounted in front of the Texas Bank, tying their horses at the hitching rail. All three wore thick, dark beards, and the brands on their animals had deliberately been covered with mud. The trio had been in and around Hamilton for several days looking the bank over. One of them had even made two trips inside the building, then reported to the others that the establishment was practically defenseless: the money could be taken with little or no resistance. Today, the three men had decided to do exactly that.

With a final glance in every direction, the taller of the three men pushed the door open and stepped inside the building, with his cohorts quickly moving up to stand on either side of him. The instant the door closed, all three drew their guns and shouted in unison: "Hands up, everybody! This is a holdup!"

Even as the sound of their voices reverberated around the room, the robbers could see that they had made at least one miscalculation. They had mistakenly assumed that since there were no saddle horses tied at the rail and no wagons or buggies parked in the immediate area, there would be no customers inside the bank.

In reality, there were three patrons in the establishment: a young man and an old woman stood at one of the two teller windows, and a stoop-shouldered man who was obviously a farmer, at the other. As two of the robbers waved their guns around ordering the tellers to sack up the money, the third devoted his attention to the customers, ordering them to lie down on their faces and be still. The farmer did neither, however, and jerked his own gun from the back pocket of his overalls. The move cost the man his life, for each of the robbers pumped at least one shot into him the moment he drew his gun.

The farmer got off one shot of his own as he fell to the floor, and though the slug went harmlessly through the wall, his actions bought bank personnel enough time to get their hands on their own weapons. What had been intended as a simple bank robbery now turned into a shoot-out. Two tellers and a vice-president were now throwing lead at the three men, and though the bankers were hardly marksmen, their shots were coming close enough to back the would-be robbers through the front door empty-handed.

The trio had already mounted and whirled their animals down the street when the bravest of the tellers stepped from the bank and onto the boardwalk. He fired at the receding riders twice in quick succession and then, with only one live shell left in his weapon, rested his arm against an awning post and took deliberate aim. Even as the big Colt bucked in his hand, the shortest of the fleeing men fell from the saddle. With its reins now dragging the ground, his horse made only a few more leaps, then stopped and stood looking back at its fallen rider. Whipping their horses continually, the man's companions turned south at the end of the block, then disappeared quickly.

There were several men in front of the bank right away,

listening to the teller's account of the murder and attempted robbery. The listeners included Buel Streeter, who had been Hamilton's town marshal for many years. "Looks like you got one of 'em, Dooley," he said to the teller, then trotted toward the man lying facedown in the middle of the street.

At least a dozen men crowded around as Streeter turned the man over. "Ever seen 'im before, Marshal?" somebody asked.

Streeter shook his head. "Don't think so," he answered, "but he ain't dead. If we can bring him around, it could be that he'll be grateful enough to tell us who he is."

The lawman had no more than spoken when the man on the ground raised one arm above his head and moaned. "Water," he said weakly.

A man ran to a nearby hitching rail and returned with a canteen he had lifted from somebody's saddle. Streeter jerked the stopper out with his teeth, then raised the man's head and touched the canteen to his feverish lips. "Here's water," he said. "Drink slow, then tell me your name."

The brown-haired, snaggletoothed man, who had a homely face and looked to be about twenty years old, took a sip of the water, then slowly opened his eyes. "Name's . . . name's Win . . . Winston Duke," he said haltingly, then closed his eyes again.

The marshal poured a handful of water and bathed the man's face, dragging wet fingers back and forth across his lips. "Who were the men in the bank with you, Duke?" When he got no reaction, he shook the man slightly. "Tell me, Duke. I've got to know their names."

"Copelands," Duke muttered through a slight crack in his lips, sounding as if he were talking to himself.

Streeter bathed the man's face and shook him again. "Open your mouth to talk so I can understand you, Duke. Tell me the names of the men who were in the bank with you. Come on, fellow, I need names."

After an obvious struggle, Duke finally opened his mouth. "Copeland twins," he said, speaking clearly now. "Mark and

Matthew Copeland. 2C Ranch, Coryell County." He exhaled loudly, then his chin fell to his chest. Winston Duke was dead.

The marshal was on his feet quickly. "Did you hear that man say the 2C?" he asked nobody in particular. When he received no answer, he singled out a middle-aged man named Leroy Mayhew. "Ain't that Dan Copeland's spread, Leroy?"

"I believe it is," Mayhew replied. "Ain't never heard about him having no twins, though."

"The twins are Dan Copeland's grandsons," a younger man named Willis volunteered. "I worked with 'em on Goldie Cooper's outfit during roundup two years ago, and I believe they occasionally picked up a few odd jobs from Lester Burbank. They're both strong enough to pick up a three-hundred-pound calf, but what I remember most about 'em is that neither one of 'em is worth a shit for anything. All talk, especially the one named Mark."

The marshal nodded, and wiped sweat from his forehead with his shirtsleeve. He stood looking down the street for a moment, then pointed. "I believe I see Sheriff Bench coming," he said, "and I'll be very happy to turn this case over to him." He motioned to the dead man. "That body belongs to the county now, and so does the job of catching the Copeland twins."

Pat Bench was an ordinary forty-year-old man who had gained local renown as an Indian fighter several years before. The adulation of Hamilton Countians had been sorely misplaced, however, for Bench's only real connection to the fight was the fact that he had been the first man to stumble onto the scene after the battle was over: he found the hillside littered with the bodies of dead Indians, and the two white men lying in a buffalo wallow above them were also dead.

Bench concocted his own self-serving version of the battle right on the spot, claiming that it had not been fought by two white men, but three; that he himself had also been in the wallow, and had come through the fight without a scratch. Since the bodies of the two white men had not been scalped or otherwise mutilated, the story was bought by one and all, and before the day was out the word had spread that Pat Bench had not only been involved in the heroic battle, but that his own Henry rifle had accounted for fifteen of the eighteen dead Indians. Bench had basked in the unwarranted notoriety for more than a year, then run for sheriff, winning the race by the widest margin in the county's history.

The five-foot-ten, two-hundred-pound Bench soon stood beside the town marshal, pointing to the body. "You say he said his name was Duke, Buel?"

Streeter nodded. "That's what he said. He identified the two men with him, too: the Copeland twins, from the 2C Ranch."

"That's Dan Copeland's outfit," the sheriff said. "I met him a few years ago, but I don't reckon you could say that I really know him. Anyway, the 2C's out of my jurisdiction, so I'll have to ride to Gatesville and talk the matter over with Sheriff Rountree." He pointed down the street. "They killed Sid Evant inside the bank, so the charges are gonna be murder and attempted bank robbery."

"Damn," the marshal said. "I heard all that shooting, but I figured it was just the robbers trying to put a scare into the people at the bank. I didn't have any idea that the son of bitches had shot Sid."

"Dooley says all three of 'em put lead in him," the sheriff said, then turned and headed back down the street.

A few moments later, Bench was inside the bank looking down at the corpse of a man he had known very well. A lifelong farmer who had at one time or another sold hay to practically every rancher in Hamilton County, Sid Evant had been liked and well respected by all who knew him. He was leaving behind a wife he had married while still in his teens, and four children whose ages ranged from eight to fourteen years. "Sons of bitches!" Bench said loudly, then left the building.

The posse, consisting of Sheriff Bench and eleven others,

rode out of town forty minutes later. "They've got a pretty good head start, fellows," Bench said to the men just before they mounted, "but that ain't no reason for us to kill our horses trying to catch up with 'em. The truth is, they're gonna have to slow down their pace a whole lot or they'll kill their own. What we'll do is just keep moving along at a trot or a slow canter and stick with their trail. It might take a while, maybe even a few days, but we'll eventually get 'em."

They overtook their quarry much sooner than any of them had anticipated. They had just crossed the Coryell County line when the road dipped down into a wide, level valley and ran parallel to the Leon River for more than a mile. On the opposite side of the river and very close to the water was a sharp, wooded incline that was probably two hundred feet tall and littered with boulders, many of them as large as a house.

Once the posse had ridden down into the treeless valley, several hundred yards from any kind of cover and no more than two hundred yards from the rocks across the river, they ran into a hail of gunfire. As the slugs began to hit the road on all sides of the horses, the animals went crazy. One big piebald dumped its rider in the middle of the road, then headed back over the hill at a hard run.

As lead continued to whistle past their heads and hit the ground all around them, the men dismounted and jumped into the ditch on the west side of the road. There, they had protection, but they had also given up their horses, which the gunmen were now chasing up the road by continually firing close to their heels. "Them's twelve-shot Henry rifles up there, Pat!" one of the first men to hit the ditch called out to the sheriff. "I'd know the sound of 'em anywhere!"

"I know that!" Bench answered at the top of his lungs. "Just keep your head down and be still! It looks like all they wanted to do was run off our horses and put us afoot; maybe they'll let up on us now!"

Once the posse members' horses had all been chased

back over the hill, the firing had ceased. None of the shots had been answered, for the riders had leaped from their saddles and scurried to the safety of the ditch so quickly that none had taken the time to unsheath his rifle from its scabbard. The fact that each man still possessed a handgun meant little, for the effective range of pistols was woefully short, and certainly no match for the deadly Henrys.

No further sound or movement came from the hillside, and with the hot sun bearing down and little air circulating, the heat in the ditch became almost unbearable as the afternoon wore on. "Ain't a breath of air to be had nowhere," the man squatting beside Bench said, wiping sweat from his face and neck with a red kerchief. "I believe the men that done all that shooting are long gone, so I can't think of no good reason why we have to keep lying in this hot ditch."

"You may be right, Samples," a man farther down the line said. He was quiet for a moment, then added jokingly, "Why don't you jump out there and trot up and down the road a little bit so we can find out for sure. I might walk down to the river and get me a drink of water after you do that, 'cause I'm a mighty thirsty man." Samples remained in the ditch, and nothing else was heard from him.

The sheer bank on the west side of the ditch finally began to offer the posse members some protection against the sun as the big orange ball continued to sink toward the western horizon. An hour before sunset, a man yet to be heard from spoke up in a high-pitched voice. "How far is it back to town?" he asked of no one in particular.

"I've always been told that it was sixteen miles from Hamilton to the county line," Sheriff Bench replied. "We're about a half mile into Coryell County, so that oughtta tell you how far we're gonna have to walk."

"You mean you think our horses'll run all the way back to town?" Samples asked.

"I didn't say they'd run back to town," Bench answered, "but I damn sure expect 'em to end up there. Horses might be dumb, but they don't have no trouble a-tall remembering where they get fed at."

"Well, I doubt that my bay'll go very far on his own," Samples said. "I bet I can catch him, too."

"I hope so," the sheriff said. "Maybe after you get mounted you can round up the rest of 'em."

With each man palming a six-gun, the posse climbed out of the ditch after the moonless night finally closed in. They watered themselves at the river, then headed north at a fast walk. Samples rounded up none of the horses, not even his own. One of the animals was finally located, but its owner refused to mount it. Partly because he believed it was important that the county's top law official get back to Hamilton quickly in order to begin preparations for his next move, but mainly because of his great admiration for the famous "Indian fighter," the man turned the big roan over to Pat Bench, saying, "You're the most important one of us, Sheriff. Ride my horse back to town so you can get on with whatever you decide to do next." Bench accepted the reins and mounted, then disappeared into the night.

He turned the borrowed roan into the corral at the livery stable three hours later, and then, deciding that there was nothing to be accomplished tonight, walked up the street and rented a room at the hotel. He would get a good night's sleep, he was thinking, then go back to Coryell County tomorrow. He would ride on to Gatesville and talk with Sheriff Rountree, for he was going to need the man's help in locating the Copeland twins, anyway.

Bench had no intention of deputizing another group of manhunters, for by tomorrow the killers would have a twenty-four-hour head start. Besides, putting another posse together might not be so easy after word of today's degrading, ignominious failure got around. Once in his hotel room he stood looking through the window into the pitch-black night for a few moments, then undressed and blew out the lamp. The last thought he had before going to sleep was that he might be the laughingstock of the town when he woke up tomorrow.

The posse members reached town at two o'clock in the morning, all footsore and some walking barefoot on blistered feet. And just as Bench had predicted, the horses had beaten their masters to the livery stable by several hours. The animals stood outside the corral with their heads hung low and their reins touching the ground. A quick count showed that none was missing. "I don't know about the rest of you fellows," Samples said, "but I'm just glad to get my bay back. He's always stayed close and minded what I said before, and I'm mighty surprised that he ran off and left me stranded like he did. I don't believe he would have done it if it hadn't been for all them other horses running, neither."

"Aw, hell, Samples," a man named Turk said quickly. "That horse don't give a shit about you or anybody else. The only thing he's thinking about is his next bucket of oats."

"Humph," Samples said, reaching for the bay's reins. "You can say what you want to, but I believe this horse understands about half of the stuff I say to him." He stepped into the saddle and headed home to his rented farm a few miles north of town.

The sun was already shining around the edges of the window shade when Sheriff Bench opened his eyes next morning. He sat on the bed thinking for a while, then walked to the window. Pushing the shade aside, he had a good view of the street below, and could even see his deputy, Clay Hemphill, standing in front of the sheriff's office blowing a cloud of cigarette smoke into the morning breeze.

Even as the sheriff stood watching, two men stopped to talk with the deputy, no doubt asking questions about yesterday's fiasco. The continued shrugging and waving of his arms suggested that the deputy was giving them the only answer he could: he had not yet talked with the sheriff this morning, and like they, knew nothing more than what he had heard along the street.

Bench turned back to the small table and poured water in the washpan. He washed his face and hands, then dressed and headed for the stairway. A short time later, he was seated against the wall in the hotel restaurant, washing scrambled eggs and pork sausage down with strong coffee. Though several of the customers had politely nodded to him as he entered the establishment, none had spoken to him, correctly assuming that he was probably not in a talkative mood at the moment. Even the waiter had taken his order and served his breakfast without comment.

When the sheriff left the restaurant, he could see that a small crowd had now gathered in front of his office, no doubt hammering the deputy with questions he could not answer. Bench walked down the street hurriedly, for only he could stop the wild speculations before they got out of hand. Although he preferred speaking to larger audiences, he was also politician enough to know that whatever he said to these few men would eventually reach the ears of every voter in the county. When he reached the office he elbowed his way through the crowd and stepped up on a bench beside the doorway. "Listen up, men! I've got a few words to say!"

The crowd grew quiet instantly, and Bench continued. "Of course, you all know about the problem at the bank yesterday, and that a dozen of us rode out of town to try to apprehend the killers. I'm sure you've all heard a lot of other stuff on the street this morning, but I'd be willing to bet that ninety percent of it was bullshit. I'm here to tell you the straight of it. No more, no less."

"That's whatcha always do, Pat!" a man standing in the street yelled. "Ya always did tell ever'thang jist like it was!"

Bench nodded to the man, then continued. "Anyway, the killers rode right down the middle of the road all the way to the county line, so there wasn't no reason for us to do otherwise." He made a sweeping motion with his arm to indicate the entire crowd. "I'm sure every man here knows where the road drops down into that mile-long valley right after it crosses the county line. Well, right there where the road begins to run alongside the river is where the killers opened up on us.

"Now, I'm sure you all remember that there ain't no cover a-tall on that stretch, not even a damn sapling, so we didn't have no choice but to hit the ditch. Of course, them bastards firing on us from that hillside across the river had all kinds of cover, boulders nearly as big as that hotel up yonder. Wasn't a thing in the world any of us could do but lie there and wait for dark. Of course, even then we didn't have no horses; the killers had done chased 'em all over the hill with their rifles.

"The only sensible thing to do in a situation like we were in is exactly what we did, and I don't believe there's a man here who would have acted otherwise. So don't go looking down your noses at the men who were in that posse. Hell, I'm gonna be calling 'em heroes, myself." He waited for a smattering of applause to die down, then added, "Later on this morning I'm gonna take Deputy Hemphill with me and head for Gatesville. Coryell County's where the killers live, anyway." He threw both hands in the air and stepped down from the bench. "That's all I've got to say at this time, men."

The small crowd of Hamilton County voters, who had to the last man bought Bench's lengthy explanation, dispersed quickly, eager to repeat the great Indian fighter's words to their friends and neighbors.

Deputy Hemphill followed the sheriff into the office. "I heard you say that I'm going to Gatesville with you," he said. "We're leaving in one hour, you say?"

Bench was busy unlocking a gun cabinet. "We'll leave as soon as you can saddle two good horses and get 'em up here." He handed the deputy a Winchester rifle and leaned one against the wall for himself. "You had breakfast yet?"

Hemphill nodded. "I ate enough for two men before I left the house." He was two inches taller, twenty pounds heavier, and twelve years younger than the sheriff, and was now serving his third year as Bench's deputy. Unmarried with no dependents, the brown-haired, gray-eyed young man had his own private quarters at Kate Livingston's boarding-house. Bench had hired him as his deputy partly because he was honest and sober, but mainly because he was exception-ally fast with a six-gun, and was not afraid of the devil him-self.

Hemphill stood patting his midsection. "Right now, I don't feel like I'll ever need to eat again." He laid the Win-chester on the desk. "I'll pick up the rifle when I get back with the horses." He stepped through the doorway and headed for the livery stable.

Sheriff Bench and his deputy rode out of town a half hour later. With each man carrying a Colt Peacemaker on his hip, a Winchester in his saddle scabbard, and a supply of extra ammunition in his saddlebag, they were loaded for bear.

They held their horses to a trot for most of the morning, then an hour or so before noon, arrived at the scene of yes-terday's embarrassing debacle. "Right over there is where they hid out to ambush us," the sheriff was saying, pointing to the hillside across the river. "Best I could tell, all the shooting was coming from that big boulder just below that old dead oak."

Hemphill followed Bench's point with his eyes. "I guess we'd better find a place to ford the river so we can take a closer look at it, then," he said, turning his horse toward the water's edge.

Bench continued to sit his horse in the middle of the road. "You . . . really think we oughtta do that, Clay?" he asked.

Believing that he had detected fear in Bench's voice, Hemphill halted momentarily. This was not the first time he had known the sheriff to get shaky after imagining that a particular situation might be dangerous. Had all the death he witnessed and the tremendous odds he had faced during the Battle of the Buffalo Wallow taken its toll on the great Indian fighter's nerves? Had he lost confidence in his own ability? Hemphill suspected that to be the case. "Just wait for me, Sheriff," he said. "I'll take a look behind them boulders, then be right back."

"No, no," Bench said, turning his horse toward the river. "We'll go together. Now that I've had second thoughts about it, I'd sorta like to see what's over there myself."

"All right," Hemphill said, reining his horse dowriver in search of shallower water. "No chance in the world that the killers are still on that hillside," he added, hoping his words would help settle his boss's nerves.

The sign behind the largest of the boulders was so simple it could have been read by a child: two men had spent a good deal of time here, maybe as long as three hours, judging from the animal droppings, and had even left an empty whiskey bottle. Hemphill picked it up and sniffed it, then stood shaking his head.

"They sure weren't drunk," Bench said quickly, as if reading his deputy's mind. "Ain't no drunk man alive that can shoot as straight as they did."

"Maybe not," Hemphill said. "I was just standing here wondering what kind of man would drink whiskey while he was trying to rob a bank." He put the bottle in his saddlebag, then began to crawl around on his knees picking up spent shell casings. "Thirty-three of 'em," he said when he was done. "All forty-four caliber. They had Henrys, all right."

"I knowed that right from the start," Bench said. "Don't nothing else sound exactly like a Henry."

Hemphill dropped the shell casings in his saddlebag with the bottle, then pointed down the opposite side of the hill. "They headed that way when they left here. Let's follow their tracks till we can figure out which general direction they ended up taking." He remounted and led the way.

They had followed the trail for less than a mile when it gradually began to circle back toward the river. After another mile, it crossed the river and ended up in the main road, where the tracks became intermingled with so many others that they were impossible to read. "I believe they headed right back to Gatesville, Clay," the sheriff said. "Do you reckon they'd actually be dumb enough to go home?"

The deputy shook his head and smiled. "It's hard to tell," he said. "Looks like they were dumb enough to try to mix whiskey drinking with bank robbing."

25

★

Darkness was closing in fast when Sheriff Bench and his deputy rode into Gatesville. Bench rattled the door of Sheriff Rountree's office, found it locked, then led the way to the Durant Hotel. With his saddlebags over his shoulder and his rifle in the crook of his arm, he dismounted at the hitching rail and handed his reins to Hemphill. "Take the horses down to the livery stable while I make arrangements for our lodging, Clay. I'll get a room with two beds if they've got one."

The deputy nodded, then headed for Jesse Hunter's stable at a trot. When he returned to the hotel twenty minutes later, the desk clerk, noting the badge on his chest, pointed down the hall. "The sheriff is in room number ten," he said. "It's the best thing we have."

Moments later, Hemphill knocked on the door, then let himself in. He stepped inside the carpeted room and stood looking it over for a few moments. No question about it, he was thinking, this was far and away the fanciest sleeping quarters he had ever been in. He walked past the bed the sheriff had staked out, then laid his rifle and his saddlebags on the other. Then he seated himself in one of the cushioned chairs in front of the window, tilting his head backward in order to get a better view of the fancy floral designs on the ceiling. "Did you insist on a place like this, Sheriff, or did the desk clerk just take a liking to you?"

"I told him I was the sheriff of Hamilton County, and that I wanted a decent room for my deputy and myself. The only thing I insisted on was two beds."

Hemphill stepped to his bed and bounced his fist on the mattress a few times. "Well, by God you got 'em. I don't know whether I can sleep on something this fancy or not. Never had a chance to find out before."

Bench poured himself a drink of water, then took a seat at the window. "You'll sleep like a baby," he said. "Anyway, you're supposed to have a good bed. You're a deputy sheriff on official duty, and I can guarantee you that the people of Hamilton County don't mind paying for a first-class hotel room while you're out chasing them killers."

"I guess you're right," Hemphill said. He leaned his rifle against the wall and laid his saddlebags on the floor, then pulled off his boots and stretched out on top of the covers. "First bed I ever laid down on that was longer than I am."

A short while later, the sheriff took his shaving gear out of his saddlebag, then stripped to the waist and lathered his face. He adjusted the mirror hanging on the wall behind the table, then began to scrape off his wiry beard with a dull razor. Hemphill lay on his bed watching. "I don't think I'll shave till in the morning," he said. "My beard just about grows back overnight."

"I'd wait till morning, too," Bench said, "except that I don't want to visit Sheriff Rountree wearing a two-day growth of beard." He rinsed his face and reached for the towel. "I don't know why I didn't mention this to you before, but the desk clerk says the sheriff's got a room upstairs." He dried his face, then threw the towel at a hook on the wall. "Since that's the case, I reckon I'll talk with him tonight instead of waiting till his office opens tomorrow. Want to come with me?"

The deputy raised up and sat on the bed shaking his head. "Sheriff Rountree don't want to see me, don't really even know me. You and him have been knowing each other for a while, so all you've gotta do is tell him what happened. Sure ain't nothing I can add to it."

Sheriff Bench slipped back into his shirt and combed his hair, then wiped the dust from his hat. He stepped into the hall and closed the door noisily.

Clay Hemphill lay on his bed thinking. He was finding it difficult to believe that the Copeland twins would remain in or anywhere near Coryell County, for it was a well-known fact that outlaws seldom hung their hats in the same area in which they committed their crimes. Common sense dictated that murderers and robbers put some distance between themselves and their dastardly deeds.

After a few minutes he came to the conclusion that there was no telling what the Copeland twins might do. It could be that neither of them even had common sense, for their attempt at robbing the bank had been haphazard at best. They had been shorthanded right from the start. Not having somebody to watch their behinds and stand guard over the front door while they were in the bank, and at least one man outside to hold the horses and protect them during their exit, bordered on stupidity. The second or two they had lost untying their horses was most likely the reason one of them had been killed trying to make his getaway.

The fact that they had been half-drunk when they entered the bank marked them as amateurs, for only fools and novices would attempt to mix alcohol with such activities. And the deputy had no doubt whatsoever that the killers had drunk most of the whiskey before they walked into the bank. The empty container they left behind the boulder had been a quart bottle, much more than they would have drunk during the short time they spent behind the big rock. Hemphill did not believe that they had stayed behind the boulder for more than an hour, for once they had chased off the posse's horses, they would have had no reason to remain. Yep, the killers had been close to the bottom of the bottle before the robbery was even attempted.

The deputy had a reason other than the fact that he was a lawman for wanting to bring the Copeland twins to bay. They had killed a man that he'd known well and had considered a friend for most of his life. Sid Evant had owned a farm less than three miles from where Hemphill had grown up, and had given him his first job while he was still a schoolboy. Young Clay had worked in the gardens and fields harvesting both truck and hay, and had later driven double and even triple rigs delivering the cured hay throughout the county.

Sid Evant had been a man without enemies, and no less could be said of his wife, Sadie. A kindly woman who had been the childhood sweetheart of the man she would eventually marry while still in her teens, she had been the perfect helpmate for her farmer husband, and had joined him in the fields two days after the wedding.

Hemphill had visited the couple often over the years, and could call all of their children by name. Even now he could close his eyes and see them sitting around the fireplace laughing and eating hot popcorn.

Though he was at the moment lying on the best bed he had ever seen, Hemphill could not go to sleep, for the unfairness of it all continued to race through his mind. Having started out with little money and only a small parcel of land, Sid Evant had finally enlarged his holdings and begun to prosper; then, just as he reached the point that he could hire enough field hands to take some of the drudgery out of making a living, three drunks had walked into the bank and gunned him down while he was trying to deposit his hardearned money. Someday soon they were going to pay for that act with their own lives. Deputy Sheriff Clay Hemphill had already made up his mind to that.

When Sheriff Bench returned to the room almost three

hours later, he found his deputy sound asleep. Hemphill had left the lamp burning, however, so that his boss would not have to fumble around in the dark. Bench eased out of his boots and his clothing as quietly as he could, then blew out the lamp and crawled under the covers.

He began to relive his visit with the Coryell County sheriff. He had stayed in Rountree's room much longer than he had planned, but it had certainly been time well spent. His counterpart had been the congenial host, and while he expressed a certain amount of shock that the Copeland twins were being sought for murder and attempted bank robbery, he volunteered to help any way he could in bringing them to account. When Bench stepped out into the hall at the conclusion of his visit, Rountree stood in the doorway. "It was nice seeing you again, Pat," he said. "I'll be expecting you and your deputy in my office tomorrow morning at eight."

Both Bench and Hemphill were up earlier than usual next morning. They ate breakfast in the hotel restaurant at sunup, then walked to the sheriff's office at half past seven. They were standing at the hitching rail in front of the building when Deputy Jeff Winters walked down the street and stopped at the door. He was about to turn his key in the lock when a look of recognition suddenly crossed his face. "Sheriff Bench!" he said loudly, then stepped to the rail with his right hand extended. "My mind must have been a thousand miles from here, 'cause I didn't even notice you standing there. You been doing all right?"

"Don't reckon I can complain," Bench said, pumping the man's hand a few times. He motioned toward Hemphill, then made the introductions: "Deputy Jeff Winters, meet Deputy Clay Hemphill."

The deputies shook hands. Then Winters unlocked the door and ushered the men into the office. "Have a seat," he said, pointing to the cushioned chairs on the near side of the big oak desk. "The sheriff usually gets here about eight."

After Bench and Hemphill seated themselves, Deputy

Winters moved behind the desk and started pulling out drawers and looking through one folder after another, obviously in search of one particular piece of paper. It appeared that he had just given up the hunt when Sheriff Rountree walked through the front door. Winters got to his feet quickly, saying, "I've been looking for that letter we got from Bo Nixon, Sheriff. You know where it is?"

"Aw, I can probably find it later," Rountree said. "Just forget about it for the time being, though. We've got more important things to worry about." He turned to Sheriff Bench with raised eyebrows. "Did you tell Jeff why you're here, Pat?"

Bench shook his head. "I thought I'd let you do that."

Winters moved around the desk quickly, then stood before the others with a questioning look on his face. "Tell me what?" he asked, thrusting his arms out to his sides with his palms turned upward.

Slowly and deliberately, Rountree laid out the story as it had been told to him by Sheriff Bench, then added, "The descriptions match Mark and Matthew perfectly, right down to the two-inch difference in their height. They were already growing them beards the last time I saw 'em, and I know for sure that Winston Duke's been running around with 'em for the past two or three months. Duke got shot trying to rob the bank, and he used his dying words to identify the Copeland twins as his partners. There ain't much doubt about their guilt, Jeff."

Winters sat down on the corner of the desk with an audible sigh. "Well, I'll be damned," he said. He stared at the floor for a few moments, then added, "I always doubted that either one of them boys would turn out to be worth a shit, but I sure never thought they'd pull something like this." He shrugged. "What the hell did they need to rob a bank for? Their folks are well-off."

Sheriff Rountree was busy unlocking a gun cabinet. "That book I brought back from the sheriffs' convention says that lots of times money ain't what makes young men turn to crime. They do it for excitement, and 'cause it gives 'em some kind of thrill." He handed his deputy a rifle, then took one for himself. "I suppose we'd better take a ride downriver. The twins were living in a tent down there two weeks ago. Of course, I don't expect 'em to still be there, but we won't know for sure till after we take a look."

Rountree's assumption proved to be correct. Less than an hour later, the four lawmen sat their saddles near a pile of ashes at the abandoned campsite. Deputy Hemphill dismounted and stood looking the area over for a few moments, then began to walk up and down the riverbank with his eyes on the ground. That done, he remounted, then stated with authority: "That freshest bunch of tracks are seven or eight days old, ten days at the most. Same two big horses made all of 'em."

The four men sat quietly for several seconds. Then, deciding that he might add a measure of credence to his deputy's opinion, Sheriff Bench broke the silence. "I sure don't know nobody that would argue with Clay about hoofprints," he said. "He's the best tracker in Hamilton County."

Rountree stood in his stirrups and took one last look around, then turned his horse back toward town. "There was a young woman staying out here with 'em for a while. She works at the Branding Iron Saloon, so I'll stop by there and have a talk with her. Could be that she can tell us something we need to know."

"If she will," Winters said.

Rountree nodded. "Yes," he said. "If she will."

When they reached the Branding Iron, Sheriff Bench and the two deputies remained in their saddles at the hitching rail while Sheriff Rountree went into the saloon to talk with the woman. Winters, who was holding the reins of his boss's horse, was the first to speak. "I guess she either sleeps upstairs or in one of them cabins out back," he said. "Most of them women get drunk every night and fuck till daylight, so it's probably gonna take the sheriff a half hour to even wake her up."

Rountree had been gone for more than an hour when he finally walked out of the alley and down the side of the building. He remounted, then pointed around the corner. "That whore sleeps in one of them cabins behind the saloon, and she answers to the name of Candy. I finally got her awake enough to talk, but she claims she don't have no idea where them boys went. She said she just stayed down there on the river with 'em for a while 'cause they treated her so good.

"Fed her and furnished her with good whiskey, is what she said." He shook his head a few times, then added, "I got the feeling that she knows a hell of a lot more'n she was telling me. I don't know of anything I can do about it, though; I damn sure can't make her talk." He sat nibbling at his lower lip for a while, then changed the subject, addressing his words to Sheriff Bench. "Did you fellows stop by the 2C Ranch on the way in, Pat?"

Bench shook his head. "Rode right on by," he said. "To tell you the truth, I didn't want to do much of anything till after I talked with you, Will."

Rountree raised his voice a little and began to speak much faster than usual. "There ain't a hell of a lot that I can do for you, Pat; the killing didn't take place in my county. The Copeland men and their wives are some of the finest people on earth, and they deserve an explanation as to why their sons are in trouble with the law. As the top lawman from your county, that's your job. I'd suggest that you get on with it."

Bench was quiet for a while. "I've been intending to do that all along," he said finally, sounding somewhat like a child who had been scolded. "I'd . . . take it as a favor if you'd ride out there with me, Will."

"I'll be happy to do that," Rountree said quickly. He reined his horse around. "Let's head out right now. We can eat dinner in the cookshack out at the ranch."

They rode out of town immediately. Alternating between a slow canter and a ground-eating trot, they arrived at the

2C just as the cook was ringing the dinner bell. "Let's tie up at that first hitching rail," Rountree said as they rode up the hill toward the buildings. "Then we'll walk on over to the cookshack unless we see one of the Copeland men somewhere."

They had just dismounted and tied their animals when Seth Copeland called to them from the corral. He stepped out of the enclosure and hooked a wire over the post to keep the gate closed, then walked to the hitching rail. "Hello, Sheriff," he said to Rountree, then offered Deputy Winters a nod that was intended to take the place of a handshake. Taking in the badges on the chests of the other two men, he added, "I don't believe I know these fellows, Will."

Rountree made the introductions, and when the handshaking was done, Seth pointed to the cookshack and spoke again: "The cook just now rang the dinner bell, so let's go over and see what he's got today."

He walked a few steps; then, when he realized that nobody was following, he stopped and turned around to face the lawmen, who quickly stepped forward to meet him. "I reckon dinner'll have to wait, Seth," Rountree said. "Fact is, you might not even want to feed us after you hear what Sheriff Bench has got to say."

Seth shrugged. "Whatever he's gonna say ain't gonna change the fact that a man's gotta eat." He pointed to the shed. "Let's get under that roof so he can say it in the shade. I reckon I already know about what to expect. There ain't never been four lawmen on this hill at the same time before, so that means that my wayward sons are in some kind of trouble. Right?"

The question went unanswered as the four men followed the rancher under the shed, seating themselves on upended nail kegs or wooden buckets that had been placed there for that purpose. Seth took a seat on a wagon tongue and turned to face them. "I'm listening," he said.

After a lengthy silence, Rountree nodded to Bench. "He's listening, Sheriff."

Bench related the story exactly as it had been told to him by bank personnel and the two surviving patrons, ending the long narration by saying, "I don't reckon I've ever seen either one of your sons, Mr. Copeland, but Sheriff Rountree knows 'em both, and he says the bank people's descriptions of the killers don't leave much doubt. Besides, Winston Duke, the man who was shot trying to make his getaway, identified them as his partners and told the town marshal that they lived on the 2C Ranch in Coryell County. Duke called them by name in front of a dozen witnesses. He knew he was dying when he done it, too."

Seth had listened to the story attentively and had never interrupted. He got to his feet and stood leaning against a post as the seriousness of it all soaked in. "You got any ideas about where the boys might be now?" he asked, then turned back to face Sheriff Bench.

"None whatsoever," Bench answered. "Truth is, I wouldn't even know 'em if I met 'em on the street. I expect the county commissioners to call a special grand jury in the next few days, though. The grand jury'll most likely indict 'em, then the commissioners'll post a reward for their capture. I suppose there'll be quite a few men hunting 'em after that happens."

Seth stood staring over the hillside. "You're right about that," he said finally. "And bounty hunters don't never run out of excuses for bringing their quarries in cold." He stood looking at his boots in deep thought for several seconds, then pointed to the cookshack. "You men go on and eat while the food's hot. I'll go up to the house for a few minutes, then meet you back here after you finish eating."

The lawmen headed for the cookshack while Seth made his way up the hill with unusually long strides. He waved to his wife and his mother, who were busy working in the garden, then continued on to the house. Once inside, he prowled through a box of pictures under his wife's side of the bed till he found what he was looking for: a picture of the twins taken at the county fair last year. Shoving the picture into his pocket and the box back under the bed, he left the house and walked back down the hill to the shed, reseating himself on the wagon tongue.

Ten minutes later, the lawmen returned from the cookshack. "That cook of yours sure ain't lost his touch," Sheriff Rountree said. "I don't get fed like that very often." When Seth said nothing, Rountree added with solemnity, "I can't tell you how sorry I am to bring you such bad news, Seth. I don't know what'll happen from here on, but I do know that it's pretty much out of our hands now."

"You did what you had to do, Will," Seth said. Then he took the picture from his pocket and handed it to Sheriff Bench. "This thing's about a year old," he said. "As you can see, it was taken before they grew their beards. If you'll show that picture to every lawman you know, it could be that some of them'll find the twins before the bounty hunters do. I ain't never seen a bounty hunter bring a man back alive."

Bench slid the picture into his vest pocket. "I'll do that, Mr. Copeland, and I want you to know that I'm mighty sorry all this had to happen."

Seth shook his head. "Nothing none of us could have done to change it." He indicated his father's house with a jerk of his thumb. "Their grandpa expected something like this, even predicted it, but I don't know how in the hell I'm ever gonna explain it to their ma and their grandma." He turned his back to the lawmen and began to walk very slowly up the hill toward the garden.

26

★

Two young men pistol-whipped and robbed Delbert and Molly Goforth in their own home two weeks after the foiled bank robbery, and the lady's ten-year-old nephew brought the news to Sheriff Bench. Since this crime had also been committed in Hamilton County, Bench and his deputy followed the youngster to the middle-aged couple's home, which was located in the southwest corner of the county.

The Goforths took only one glance at the picture the sheriff produced, then declared that the Copeland twins had been their assailants. The young outlaws had both been clean-shaven, the couple said, and neither the man nor his wife had any doubt that the men pictured were the same ones who had kicked in their front door with drawn guns.

"They didn't have no reason to hit neither one of us," Molly Goforth said. "All the money we had in the world was sixteen dollars, and Delbert handed that to 'em right away. The tallest one claimed we had more, and started beating on Delbert with his pistol barrel. When I started screaming, the other one punched me in the face with his fist and knocked me down. I don't remember much about it after that."

The battered condition of Goforth's face and his wife's swollen jaw clearly showed that they had been badly beaten. The lawmen spent more than an hour in the couple's home, with Deputy Hemphill writing down every word they said in a notebook. "We've gotta be getting on back to town," Sheriff Bench finally said to the couple. "I can promise you that we'll be looking into this matter, though, and I'll even send a report to the federal marshal's office."

On a bright morning in early October, a month after the Goforth robbery and six weeks after Sid Evant had been gunned down in the bank, Deputy Sheriff Clay Hemphill arrived at the sheriff's office an hour later than usual. Seeing that Bench was already there, Hemphill walked across the room and handed him a single sheet of paper. "This is my resignation, Sheriff," he said, "and it's effective as of today.

"The federal marshals ain't gonna do a damn thing about them Copeland boys, and since we ain't got the proper jurisdiction, there ain't much we can do." He laid his badge on the desk. "If you want me back after I get done with this manhunt, I'll be more'n glad to put that badge on again."

Bench laid the resignation down unread, then got to his feet quickly. "You mean you're gonna try to bring the Copeland twins in?"

Hemphill bit his lip. "I reckon that all depends on how they act when I catch up to 'em," he said. "I might have to leave 'em lying right where I find 'em. Either way, Sid's killers have gone unpunished long enough."

"Well, the reward's up to two thousand dollars now. The county already had a thousand on their heads, then last week an anonymous donor pledged another thousand. Two thousand bucks, dead or alive."

"Dead or alive," Hemphill repeated. "It don't make a

shit to me which, either. I'll accept that reward, too, and give the biggest part of it to Sid's wife and kids."

"It's nice of you to be thinking that way," Bench said. "I'm sure they're gonna need all the help they can get." He reseated himself and dropped the badge in a desk drawer. "This thing'll be right here for you to pin back on when all this is over with, Clay. I'll deputize a man to help me on a part-time basis if it turns out that I need somebody. When do you plan on leaving town?"

"I expect to be on the road within the hour," Hemphill answered. "Should have already been gone." He opened the gun cabinet and extracted his Henry, then turned back to the desk. "I'd like to take that picture of the Copeland twins along with me, Sheriff."

"Certainly," Bench said. He rummaged through the drawer for a moment, then handed it over, adding, "I don't know that their pa would appreciate this, but he ain't here."

Hemphill nodded, then shoved the picture in his vest pocket. "I don't know how long I'll be gone," he said, offering a parting handshake. "But I intend to stay on the job till it's done." Moments later, he walked down the street to the livery stable, his saddlebags lying across his shoulder and the Henry cradled in the crook of his arm.

At midmorning, Hemphill rode past the sheriff's office and took the road to Gatesville. Aboard a big piebald, and leading a packhorse loaded with everything necessary for outdoor living, the ex-deputy was armed to the teeth, and had as much money in his pocket as he was likely to need. When he had approached Sid Evant's widow for the loan of a packhorse, the lady had insisted that he also needed a strong saddler with lots of bottom, and assured him that the tall, broad-chested piebald had been thoroughly tested on several occasions. Consequently, neither the horse Hemphill was riding nor the one he was leading was his own.

He watered the animals from the river at noon, then kept on the move till he reached Gatesville, two hours before dark. He stopped at the Durant Hotel and rented the cheapest room in the house, then rode on to the livery stable and put up his horses. That done, he had supper in the hotel restaurant, then retired to his second-story room. He would take a nap, he had decided, or maybe even sleep for a few hours, for his business at the Branding Iron could best be conducted during the late hours of night. He pulled off his boots and stretched out on top of the covers. Moments later, he was snoring softly.

When he next opened his eyes the room was dark as pitch, and he felt as if he had been asleep for several hours. He struck a match and lit the lamp, then glanced at his watch to see that it was a few minutes past ten. Supposing that the Branding Iron closed at midnight, he took his soap and razor out of his saddlebag and shaved his face. Three minutes later, he headed for the stairway.

There were fewer than a dozen men in the saloon when he arrived. He seated himself on a barstool and bought a beer, then began to sip slowly as he sat looking around the room. Noticing that all three of the women in the building continued to dance with first one man, then another, and that none appeared to be attached to any particular fellow, Hemphill finally spoke to the bartender. "Which one of them girls is named Candy?"

The man smiled, then motioned to a pretty young woman with several swirls of dark hair piled high on her head, no doubt held there by a series of pins and combs. "That's her sitting over there by herself," he said. "Just walk on over to the table if you wanna talk to her."

Hemphill leaned halfway across the bar, speaking softly. "Is she . . . I mean, I might want to do a little business. Is she—"

"Like I was saying," the bartender interrupted. "Just walk on over to the table if you wanna talk to her."

Hemphill emptied his mug and headed for the girl's table. He was greeted with a beautiful smile and the fluttering of long eyelashes. "Have a seat and let's talk about it," the girl said, pointing to the chair nearest her elbow.

Removing his hat, Hemphill did as he was told.

"My name is Candy," the girl said, "and you can talk to me about anything you want to."

After deciding that he was tongue-tied, she continued: "You see something you want? You want to play?"

"Yes," he said quickly. "I want to play all night."

The girl giggled. "Do you really think you can?"

"No," he said. "But I'd like to give it a try."

She squeezed his hand. "Talk to the bartender. His name is Kip."

Hemphill walked to the bar and, after a certain amount of haggling, handed over some money and belted down a straight shot of whiskey. When he turned to look back at the table, the girl was gone. "She's done gone out back," the bartender said. "If you'll walk out the front door and around the east side of the building, you'll find her waiting for you. It's the first cabin after you walk into the alley. The lamp'll be burning."

After inhaling another shot of whiskey, Hemphill was on his way. He was out of the building and around to the alley quickly, and when he knocked at the cabin door, it opened instantly. Standing before him stark naked, and with her hair now unpinned and hanging loosely about her shoulders and her bosom, was the beautiful little brunette named Candy. "I'm waiting for you," she said.

The time for talking had passed for the moment, Hemphill quickly decided. Although he had a multitude of questions to ask this young woman, and was very eager to hear her answers, he intended to first see if he could get his money's worth. He sat down on the bed and pulled off his boots, then began to fumble with his belt buckle. "Let me do that," the girl said. She got on her knees and loosened his belt, then pulled off his pants. "I like helping a big ol' man out of his britches."

It was past sunup next morning when Hemphill finally dressed and pulled on his boots. Seating himself in the room's only chair, he took the picture out of his vest pocket and passed it to the girl, who was now sitting up in bed. "I happen to know that you're acquainted with these two men, Candy, and I need to know where they are." He put his finger to his lips to suggest that she remain silent, then continued to talk. "First, let me tell you why I'm hunting 'em." He recounted the attempted bank robbery and the murder of Sid Evant, then the details of the Goforth robbery, ending with a description of the middle-aged man's battered face and his wife's swollen jaw.

"I think Mark likes to do that," the girl said, slowly turning the picture in her hand and studying it from different angles. "He beat the hell out of me twice while I was down there on the river with them. Matthew slapped me once, too."

"Well, that alone oughtta be enough to make you help me find 'em," he said. The girl was already beginning to shake her head, signaling Hemphill that he was a long way from pay dirt. He switched to a different strategy instantly: "I'm not exactly asking you to help me, Candy, I'm offering you a chance to help yourself. If you give me information that leads me to the Copeland twins, I'll give you ten percent of the reward. Two hundred dollars."

"Two hundred dollars," she repeated softly, then handed the picture back. She folded her arms over her naked breasts and sat thinking for a few moments, then asked, "All at once?"

"All at once," Hemphill answered. "On the very same day they pay me the reward, I'll count you out two hundred dollars right here on this bed."

She sat quietly for a while, staring at the patches of dust motes illuminated by the sunlight shining around the window shade. "Two hundred dollars would be enough to get me to San Francisco," she said finally.

Hemphill nodded. "More'n enough," he said. "It'll get you there and pay your rent for several months."

She slid off the bed and began to dress. "San Francisco," she repeated as she slipped into her underwear. "I've been wanting to go there ever since I was ten years old."

"Well, this is your chance," Hemphill said. "You can go out—" He halted in midsentence, suddenly deciding to shut up and leave well enough alone.

The young woman finished dressing, then seated herself on the side of the bed. "The only thing I'm gonna have is your word that I'll get that money. Right?"

He nodded. "That's right, Candy, but you can trust me. My name is Clay Hemphill, and up till yesterday morning I was a Hamilton County deputy sheriff. I resigned so I'd be free to cross county and state lines while I'm looking for the Copelands. The sheriff has asked me to pin the badge back on after the hunt's over, and I expect to do that."

She brushed his cheek with her lips. "You're a good man, Clay Hemphill, and you certainly know how to please a woman in bed." She pulled his head against her bosom and held him tightly. "I believe I can tell you where to find Mark and Matthew Copeland, and I'm gonna trust you to bring me the money you promised. It's the only hope I've got of ever getting to California, 'cause I'd never be able to save up enough hanging around this place."

Sensing that the information was forthcoming, Hemphill kissed her cleavage and remained quiet.

"I spent three weeks in that tent with them," she continued, "and all I heard, morning, noon, and night, was Corpus Christi. I mean, neither one of them has ever seen the ocean, and that's all they talk about. Matthew wants a job on a fishing boat, but Mark always talks about getting a ride on a freighter to some other country. They discuss it every day, and both of them told me that's where they were going just as soon as they got their hands on a little traveling money."

Hemphill was on his feet now. "You mentioned trust,

Candy. Ain't that about all you're giving me to go on? It's gonna cost me both time and money, 'cause Corpus Christi's more'n three hundred miles from here."

She put her hand over his mouth. "Hush," she said. "We'll just have to trust each other, but I know they went to Corpus Christi just like I know I'm standing here."

"All right," he said. "I'm convinced that you know what you're talking about. Did either of the twins ever say anything about where they intended to stay once they got down there? Anything that might tell me where I should go looking for 'em?"

"No. They don't know anything about the town, 'cause they never have been there. Mark did ask me once if I had ever seen a lighthouse. I told him I had, and he never mentioned it again."

Hemphill combed his hair with his fingers, then put on his hat. "I'll be leaving for Corpus right after breakfast, Candy. Will you scratch your head and think real hard for me? It would be mighty nice if you could remember some little something to make my job easier."

She shook her head. "Once you get to Corpus Christi, your job couldn't be easier. All you've got to do is show that picture around and ask questions. The twins are bigger and better-looking than most men. They both stand out from the crowd, and somebody's gonna point you in their direction real quick."

Hemphill was suddenly rethinking his long-held view that all whores were stupid. This young woman seemed to be intelligent enough, at least as smart as anyone else he knew. He stood in the room for only a few moments longer. "I'll eat breakfast at the hotel," he said, "then head south. Don't worry none about the money I promised you. When I get the Copelands, you'll get your reward." He patted her on the head, then stepped through the doorway and into the alley.

After a breakfast of flapjacks and sausage, he retrieved his saddlebags and his rifle from the hotel room, then headed for Jesse Hunter's livery stable. Though Hunter recognized Hemphill as a Hamilton County deputy sheriff, and no doubt noticed the absence of the badge on his chest, he did not mention it. He simply took a coil of rope from a peg and headed toward the corral when Hemphill called for his horses.

Twenty minutes later, as Hemphill shoved his rifle in the boot and mounted the piebald, the liveryman spoke. "I sure like the looks of that horse," he said, pocketing the money for the animals' lodging.

Hemphill nodded. "I've just got him on loan, so I don't really know much about him. He seems to be about like he looks, though, and his owner claims he can carry the mail with the best of 'em." He reined the big animal around toward the road. "Good day to you," he said, then rode through the tall doorway with his packhorse trotting along behind.

Never a man to push his animals, Hemphill left town at a walking gait. It should take him somewhere between ten and twelve days to make the trip, he was thinking, for he expected to cover twenty-five and sometimes thirty miles a day. Corpus Christi lay almost due south of Gatesville, with Round Rock, Austin, and a few other towns in between. His map showed the relatively new settlement of Luling to be about the halfway point.

He had everything on the packhorse that he was likely to need during his journey, and since there was still plenty of grass for his animals, he had no real reason to pass directly through any town. Nor was it imperative that he stick with the established roads. The roads were often just as crooked as the rivers, and a man could sometimes save hours or even days by traveling as the crow flies. By occasionally consulting his pocket compass to maintain his bearings, Hemphill could ignore the roads and ride cross-country anytime it was to his advantage.

He stayed with the walking gait all morning and, at noon, watered himself and his horses at a roadside spring.

He ate a hard biscuit and a sizable chunk of Bologna sausage, then continued on his way. About midafternoon the road curved back toward the east, and Hemphill could see that it maintained the same course for the next several miles. He took a quick look at his compass, then turned south and headed cross-country.

An hour before sunset, he dismounted on the bank of a creek that was a foot deep and less than ten feet wide. He unburdened his animals and picketed them on good grass, then gathered up a few handfuls of kindling and an armload of deadwood. As soon as he had a fire going and the coffee-pot on, he spread his bedroll in a nearby cluster of bushes, then dug his supper out of his pack.

A short time later, having finished his meal of Bologna sausage, biscuits, and cheese, he sat sipping coffee and eating oatmeal cookies as he watched the sun drop out of sight behind the distant treetops. When darkness finally closed in, he extinguished the fire and set the coffeepot aside. It was still half-full of coffee, and all he would have to do in the morning was reheat it.

He dragged his saddle and his packsaddle closer to his sleeping place, then crawled into the bushes and stretched out on his bedroll, his Colt and his Henry both close to hand. He pulled the extra blanket over his body right away, for the October nights were already beginning to get chilly. Using his folded coat for a pillow, he lay listening to the stillness of the night for a while, then drifted into a dreamless sleep.

27

★

Knowing that her oldest sons were the objects of a dead-or-alive manhunt, Emerald had summoned Rachel, Paul, and Joseph home from college, saying she believed the family should be together at a time like this. Seth had picked his daughter up in a covered wagon at the women's school in Dallas, and the boys had ridden home from Waco on rented mules.

Despite the solemnity of the occasion, the get-together eventually turned into a joyous reunion, for both of the boys, and to a certain extent their sister Rachel, considered the twins' problem to be a mess of their own making. "Mark's always had a mean streak, Ma," Rachel said the same day she returned to the ranch. "I've been hearing him talk about how he'd like to rob somebody for years, and he sat right down yonder at that shed one day and told me that he thought the best feeling in the world would be to rape some uppity young girl who thought she was too good to talk to a rancher's son. He was always trying to put Matthew up to some kind of meanness, and it looks like he finally managed to do it."

"There wasn't any reason in the world for them trying to rob that bank, Ma," Paul added. "I don't recall ever asking Pa or Grandpa for money that I didn't get, and it was the same way with Mark and Matthew. They didn't pull their guns in that bank because they were truly in need. They did it hoping to get more gambling and whiskey money.

"Mark never has cared about anybody but himself, and now it looks like Matthew's turned out the same way." He stood shaking his head for a moment, then added, "It's just like the old saying goes, Ma: You dance, you pay the fiddler. Their problems are their own now, and the rest of us have got to get on with our own lives." He leaned over the porch railing and spat into the yard, for he had recently taken up the habit of chewing tobacco.

With tears rolling down both cheeks, the long-suffering Emerald Copeland stood quietly for a while. Finally, she put one arm around Paul's shoulder and the other around her daughter. "I know you kids are right about the twins, but it hurts so much. I just can't help thinking that maybe there was something else I could have done, that maybe there's more to it than we know about."

The names of Mark and Matthew were seldom mentioned in either of the Copeland households during the next several days, for all had tacitly agreed that the less said about them, the easier it would be for all.

At the end of the first week, Emerald followed her daughter out on the porch at midmorning. "Halloween's gonna be on us before you know it, Rachel. You remember how we used to walk to the field and pull punkins when you were a little girl?"

Rachel nodded. "Yes, ma'am. Seems like a hundred years ago."

Emerald pointed to a pole enclosure on the west side of the house. "Well, the punkin patch is right out yonder, and I want us to pick 'em out just like old times."

Rachel, who had grown into a beautiful young woman that any man would give a second and most likely a third look, smiled broadly. "I'd love that," she said, then followed her mother down the steps. They walked the hundred yards to the fenced-in pumpkin patch without speaking.

Once there, Emerald lowered one end of the poles that served as a gate, then pointed down the rows. "Enough punkins there to feed an army," she said. "We'll make up a bunch of pies, then put the rest of 'em up in jars for next winter. Right now, though, I want us to pick out some of the biggest and roundest ones for your grandpa to make jack-o'-lanterns out of. All my life I've had jack-o'-lanterns on Halloween, and Pa carves out the prettiest ones I ever saw."

Rachel stepped over the poles and into the field. This was by no means the first pumpkin patch she had ever seen, but the unsurpassed beauty of a productive field lying in wait for the harvest had over the years escaped her memory. She smiled as she looked down the straight rows at the large orange-yellow balls, most of which were now lying apart from the coarse, decumbent vines that had produced them. "This is beautiful, Ma," she said. "I don't know how we'll ever pick out the biggest ones, though. They all look the same size to me."

"They won't when you get closer," Emerald said. "We'll look 'em all over, then pull six of the biggest ones and roll 'em into the middles so the boys can find 'em easy. Paul and Joseph don't know it yet, but they're the ones who are gonna be lugging 'em across the hill to their grandpa."

"Knowing Paul, I'd say he'll want to hitch up a wagon to haul them over there," Rachel said.

"I don't care how he does it," Emerald said, leading the way down the rows. "Just as long as he gets it done."

It turned out that Rachel was only half-right in her prediction, for when the women had selected their pumpkins and walked back across the hill to inform the boys of their part in the process, it was Joseph who suggested that they hitch up a wagon. When Paul agreed that his brother had an excellent idea, they immediately headed for the corral. They roped the mare named Bess and hitched her to their grandfather's buggy, then headed to the pumpkin patch. "Don't forget to put the poles back up after you get done!" Emerald called as they passed the house.

When the fall roundup was over, the record showed that the 2C crew had branded more than a thousand calves. Most had been borne by first-time heifers, and all had the appearance of purebred Herefords. "These little bulls we've been turning into steers are gonna bring top dollar two years from now," Seth Copeland said proudly as the last of the animals was branded and castrated. "If there's a drop of longhorn blood in 'em it sure don't show."

"They'll pass for pure-blood anywhere," Rusty Walker agreed. "All of 'em."

Bill Penny and his crew had returned from the trail drive in early September, and the Copelands had been well pleased with the price they had received for their cattle. Though there had been ninety-three head of longhorn cows in the bunch, the remainder had been three-quarter-blood Herefords, and the first Kansas cattle buyer who looked at the herd had bought it on the spot.

Although his glance at the cattle was quick, and appeared to be very casual, that had hardly been the case. "Looks like about a hundred head of old longhorns mixed in with 'em," the buyer had said. "Now, I'm gonna accept these few head this time, but don't bring me no more of 'em. I'm trying my damnedest to get out of the longhorn business. People want better beef."

And better beef was what the 2C Ranch would produce, the Copelands had long since decided. Both Dan and Seth had recently attended a meeting of the stock breeders' association where the main topic of conversation had concerned the crossbreeding of Herefords and English shorthorns. One man after another had taken the floor extolling the many favorable characteristics of the shorthorn breed, with most occasionally referring to a large chart that had been tacked on the wall.

When the meeting adjourned, pamphlets pertaining to the crossbreeding process were handed out at the door. Both Dan and Seth Copeland had been taken with the idea, and had decided to discuss it with some well-known breeders at the winter stock show in Fort Worth. "I'll be checking on the dates between now and then," Dan said as they rode back home in the buggy, "but I believe the show runs for three days during the first week of February. No matter when it takes place, I expect to be there."

"Me, too," Seth said.

28

★

Clay Hemphill reached Luling at midafternoon of the sixth day. Riding in from the north, he halted at the first hitching rail, then continued to sit his saddle as he looked up and down both sides of the street. The town was no more than three years old, and few of the buildings had a look of permanence. Most had been hastily thrown together out of whatever material was available when Luling became the terminus of a branch of the Southern Pacific Railroad.

The crossroads settlement had quickly become a cattle center and shipping point, as well as the end-of-freight trail from Chihuahua, Mexico. It had early on come to be known as the "toughest town in Texas," and the nickname had not been misplaced. The cemetery that the townspeople called the "Hill" had claimed its first occupant, the loser of a noonday gunfight, before the last railroad spike had even been driven, and the bodies of more than a dozen other rowdies had been hauled up the slope since.

Only hell-raisers were buried on the Hill. Many of the area's so-called upstanding citizens were interred on their own ranches or homesteads, while the majority of the "ordinary" people chose the big cemetery south of town as a final resting place for their departed kin.

Hemphill dismounted and tied his horses to the hitching rail, then stepped up on the boardwalk in front of the nearest building. A sign in the window identified the establishment as Windy Joe's, and advertised the fact that whiskey, food, and billiard tables could be found inside. After living out of his pack and drinking warmed-over coffee for a week, Hemphill was more than ready for something different. He pushed the door open and stepped inside, then stood looking the place over for a few moments.

The front section of the large room was split by a thirty-foot bar, with the kitchen and dining area on one side, and several poker tables on the other. Farther toward the rear, on the same side of the room as the card tables, were the billiard tables. And although no horses except Hemphill's own were tied at the hitching rail at the moment, four men stood at one of the tables taking turns knocking the balls around with a cue. There was also one man sitting at the bar, sipping a drink while he carried on an animated conversation with the fat bartender.

Hemphill walked to the bar and seated himself on a stool. "I'll have a beer," he said.

The bartender, who stood several inches less than six feet tall and appeared to weigh more than three hundred pounds, slid off his own stool and waddled down the bar. "Howdy," he said. "My name's Joe Butcher, but most folks around here call me Windy. You just passing through? Working for the railroad? I'll tell you right now, the Southern Pacific's the best thing that ever happened to us. I mean, they brought employment to Caldwell County, and they brought money to this town. Why, I'll bet you that the Southern Pacific—"

"I don't work for the railroad," Hemphill interrupted when the reason behind the man's nickname became obvious. "Is your beer cold?"

"Cold as ice can make it," the bartender said. He drew

a mugful of the foamy brew and slid it along the bar. "The beer comes out of San Antonio, but we make our own ice." When Hemphill began to sip at his brew with no comment, Butcher joined his friend at the opposite end of the bar.

A few men came and went during the next hour, but eventually Hemphill was the only drinker in the building. The bartender refilled his lone patron's mug, then moved his own stool down the bar to make conversation easier. "I reckon you'll finally tell me where you came from if you want me to know," he said.

Hemphill wiped the foam from his lips with the heel of his hand. "No reason not to," he said. "My name's Clay Hemphill, and I live in Hamilton. I'm headed south hoping I'll run into my cousins." He snapped his fingers as if a particular thought had suddenly occurred to him. "Come to think of it, you might have seen 'em yourself." He pulled the picture from his pocket and handed it across the bar. "They're twins, just turned twenty years old."

The instantaneous look of recognition on the face of the bartender supplied the answer. "Why, that's the Mayfield twins," he said, handing the picture back. "The one named Mark spent several hours on that same stool you're sitting on about three weeks ago. I'd say you've got some riding to do if you're gonna catch up with them, though. They said they were going to Corpus Christi, and they've had more'n enough time to be there. Probably got there about two weeks ago."

"Probably," Hemphill said. He pointed to the dining area and changed the subject. "How's the food over there?"

Butcher laughed, then jiggled his ample midsection up and down with his hands. "I do all my eating over there, and you can see that I ain't lost no weight. I don't reckon it's ever made anybody sick, either."

Hemphill drained his mug and got to his feet. "I'm gonna have a go at it," he said. "I saw the livery stable at the end of the street, and I've decided to spend the night in Luling. Is that hotel across the tracks all right?"

The fat man shrugged. "I reckon so," he said. "The Adobe House a block south of it is good enough, though, and they only charge about half as much."

"The Adobe House it is," Hemphill said, then walked across the room to the dining area. He selected a table and had scarcely seated himself when a waiter appeared at his elbow. "Thank you for comin' in, sir," the gangling youth said as he placed a cup of steaming coffee on the table and handed over the bill of fare.

"I'll have the roast beef, beans, and potatoes," Hemphill said after a quick glance at the menu. The waiter nodded, then headed for the kitchen.

A few minutes later, Hemphill sat enjoying the best food he had come across in quite some time. The potatoes had been whipped and creamed, the beef was tender and flavorful, and the light, fluffy biscuits were right from the oven. A large slice of raisin custard rounded out the meal. Even after he was done eating, he was in no hurry to leave the table, for the coffee was just as good as the food. He sat enjoying a third cup long after the waiter had picked up the empty plates.

When Hemphill arrived at the livery stable a few minutes later, the farrier, who was also the liveryman, was busy shoeing a large draft horse. The muscular young fellow, who was obviously of Mexican descent, spoke without looking up from his work. "I'm sorry," he said, "but I can't stop what I'm doing right now. I've got to get this shoe shaped up while it's hot." Holding the red-hot horseshoe with metal tongs, he laid it on his anvil and pounded it with a large hammer for a while, then poked it into a barrel of water, bringing forth a hissing sound and an accompanying cloud of steam. "Now," he said as he laid his tools on a cluttered table. "What can I do for you?"

Hemphill patted the big draft horse on the rump, then pointed to his own. "I want to leave my saddler and my packhorse with you overnight," he said.

The big hostler accepted the reins of both animals and

led them through the wide doorway. "I've sure got plenty of room for 'em," he said. "Business ain't been too good lately." He stopped in front of a cubbyhole and began to unbuckle the packsaddle. "I'll lock your pack up in the office. Ain't nobody gonna mess with it."

Hemphill smiled. "There's probably not much in there that anybody'd want," he said. "It all comes in mighty handy when a fellow's out on the trail needing to throw a meal together, though." He unsheathed his Henry and laid his saddlebags across his shoulder, then headed for the doorway. "I'll be back about sunup."

He turned south and walked to the Adobe House at a fast clip. Three old men sat on a bench in front of the building, and though all nodded a greeting, none of them spoke. Hemphill returned their nods, then opened the door and stepped into the lobby. "Good afternoon!" a lantern-jawed, white-haired man called from the opposite corner of the large room. "Welcome to the Adobe!" He had been sitting on a stool behind the counter, but got to his feet as Hemphill drew near. "What can I do for you, young feller?" he asked with a scratchy voice.

"I need a room for the night."

The old man nodded. "Well, I've certainly got it," he said. "The price is right, too. You can have your pick of any room on the second floor for sixty-five cents, and I'll guarantee you that there ain't a louse in the house."

"That's nice to know," Hemphill said. He laid the money on the counter, then added, "Just give me the key to any old room you want to."

A few moments later, he leaned his rifle against the wall and raised the window, then took a seat on the side of the bed in room 210. He bounced his fist on the mattress. Not as good as the one in his room at the boardinghouse, he decided, but like Windy Joe had said, it was good enough, and he was looking forward to a good night's sleep.

Hemphill detested sleeping on the ground, and other than the one time he had traveled to Kansas on a trail drive, his nights had almost always been spent in a decent bed. Sleeping outside was a necessity when a man had to travel, but he certainly intended to put the bedroll aside when his manhunt was over.

He did not bother to light the lamp when darkness closed in, for he had no need for it. He pulled off his boots and dropped them to the floor, then undressed and crawled under the covers. While waiting for sleep to come, he lay thinking of the Copelands, and wondering exactly what would happen when he finally met them face-to-face.

Would the twins admit their crimes in Hamilton County? Or would they deny their guilt and go for their guns? Though Hemphill did not know the young men, he strongly suspected that it would be the latter, for the girl named Candy had told him that both Mark and Matthew practiced the fast draw several times a day. Mark had even boasted that he himself was most likely the fastest gun alive, she had said.

Though Hemphill knew that some man somewhere was the fastest gun alive, he seriously doubted that Mark Copeland was that man. While it was true that the twins were only twenty years old and that speed was universally associated with youth, the act of merely getting a pistol out of its holster in a hurry hardly made a man a gunfighter. Gunfighters were a breed apart, and while none of them were actually slow, it was not always the fastest man who lived to walk away from a dispute.

Though speed was certainly important, marksmanship was doubly so, for the man who could empty his holster in record time but could not hit the broad side of a barn was unlikely to survive. Of the thousands of young men throughout the West who took up the fast draw every year, many became breathtakingly fast. Few of them would ever be known as gunfighters, however, for it seemed that such men had ice water in their veins. Indeed, the man who could maintain his composure well enough to target and bring down an opponent after hearing a bullet pass within an inch of his own ear was rare. Clay Hemphill was such a man, but he doubted that either of the Copeland twins was.

He awoke an hour before daybreak next morning. He shaved his face by the light of the coal-oil lamp, then dressed and took a seat at the small table to await the light of day. He held the picture of the Copelands up to the lamp and studied it for a few moments, then slid it back into his pocket. The picture was a good one, and he would recognize the twins anywhere.

He also carried a dodger in one of his saddlebags. The handbill had been printed by the Hamilton newspaper, and informed one and all that Mark and Matthew Copeland were wanted for murder and attempted bank robbery, and that a two-thousand-dollar reward would be paid for their capture, dead or alive. Full descriptions of both men accompanied the proclamation.

Daylight found him sitting in a small restaurant two doors down from the hotel. The same three old men he had seen on the bench the day before were also in the restaurant, and once again they nodded without speaking. A waiter was there to take his order quickly, for most of the breakfast crowd was probably still sleeping. Hemphill ordered ham, eggs, and a tall stack of flapjacks.

He did not linger at his table after eating this morning, but returned to the hotel for his rifle and his saddlebags, then walked to the livery stable. When he stepped through the doorway he saw that the hostler had seen him coming, and had already taken his pack out of the office. "Good morning," the man said. "You told me you'd be back at sunup, and you're right on time." He picked up a pair of bridles. "I reckon you're ready for your horses."

Hemphill nodded. "I planned on getting an early start."

"I stabled 'em at daylight," the liveryman said as he headed down the hall. "I fed 'em both a bucket of oats nearly an hour ago, so they oughtta be done eating by now."

Twenty minutes later, Hemphill shoved his rifle in the boot and mounted the piebald, then took the slack out of his packhorse's lead rope. "Good day to you," he said to the hostler, then rode through the doorway.

He crossed the San Marcos River into Gonzales County, skirting the town of Gonzales on the west. He maintained a steady pace all day long, and at sunset camped at a spring just across the De Witt County line. He had covered at least forty miles this day, and knew that in the future he would show more concern for his horses.

Hemphill had a long-held belief that a man should not push his animals more than thirty miles a day, and he was not about to change his policy now. Tomorrow, he would get a later start than usual and make camp earlier in the day. The Copeland twins would keep. Corpus Christi had been their destination, and that's where they would be.

The settlement of Corpus Christi began as a frontier trading post founded by Colonel Henry Lawrence Kinney in 1839. Though the settlement languished in obscurity for many years, the population accelerated after statehood in 1845, and by the 1870s, the deepwater port had become the state's most popular seacoast playground.

Clay Hemphill arrived in Corpus Christi ten days after leaving Gatesville. He rode through the town at a slow pace, and though he met several men on the street, none of them spoke or even nodded a greeting. Dark shadows were already beginning to appear between the buildings, for the sun had dropped below the horizon half an hour before. His main concern at the moment was finding lodging for his animals before dark, for he knew that many liverymen felt independent enough to close up shop and go home to their families when the day was done.

He continued to ride south, and he was almost to the water when he halted at an intersection and looked to his left. There, about one block to the east, stood the big red barn and pole corral. He kneed the piebald to a trot. A few moments later, he dismounted in front of the barn and stood holding his horses' reins. So far, he had seen no one, but the large sign above the open door identified the place as a commercial operation.

Though the fading light made it somewhat difficult, he could also read the smaller sign warning patrons of the exorbitant rates charged by the establishment. Though the prices were ridiculous, Hemphill knew that he had no other choice, for he could hardly take his animals to the hotel with him. He called out, then stood shifting his weight from one leg to the other while he waited for someone to acknowledge his presence.

"Just lead your horses on into the barn, mister!" an unseen youthful voice shouted.

Hemphill did as he was told, and was met just inside the doorway by a red-haired boy who appeared to be no more than fourteen years old. "Pa's been out of town for the past three days," the young man said, striking a match to the wick of a lantern he held in his hand. "I've just about been busy around the clock, too. We stay open twenty-four hours a day, you know."

"No," Hemphill said. "I didn't know. I have noticed an awful lot of horses around this town, though." He pulled his Henry out of the scabbard, and handed over the piebald's reins.

The kid dropped the reins to the ground and loosened the cinch. "Three more stables besides us in town, and they're all just as busy as we are." He stripped the saddle and the blanket and laid them across a rack, then led the animal down the hallway. He was back a short time later, reaching for the packhorse's reins. He led the bay forward a few steps, then began to unbuckle the packsaddle. "I've heard people complain about our prices," he said, "but they're exactly the same as every other stable in town. Only difference between us and them is that we feed people's animals a whole lot better. If you don't believe me, just ask anybody."

"I believe you," Hemphill said. He pointed toward the office. "Will you lock my stuff up in there?"

"Always," the boy answered, then dropped the packsaddle to the ground and led the bay down the hallway.

A short time later, Hemphill stood at the counter inside the Pelican Hotel, a change of clean clothing under his arm and the Henry in his hand. "I'll be needing a room," he said to the bearded middle-aged clerk.

The man nodded. "Be two-fifty a night," he said. "Three dollars if you want a tub of bathwater."

Hemphill was slow to speak, for never in his life had he paid more than a dollar twenty for a hotel room. "What the heck," he said finally, then laid three dollars on the counter. "I reckon I need the bath, too."

The counterman fumbled around in a drawer for a moment, then produced a key. "I'll put you in number eight," he said. "It's already got a tub of clean water in it, and there's soap and a towel on the table." He pointed down the hallway. "It's about a dozen steps in that direction." He spun the hotel register around and handed over a stub of a pencil. "The town marshal says you've got to sign this."

Hemphill signed his name, then picked up his belongings and headed down the hallway. Moments later, he unlocked the door to the dark room. He laid his things on the floor and struck a match, then stepped inside and lit the coal-oil lamp. He replaced the globe, then stood looking the place over. Other than the large closet, the double windows, and the bathwater he had paid extra money for, the room was quite ordinary. He relocked the door, then laid his things on the table.

A short while later, he was in the bathtub. Although the water was at least room temperature, it felt much colder, and took some getting used to. He shivered for the first few moments, then suddenly began to feel like a new man.

Once out of the tub, he shaved his face and dressed in clean clothing: jeans, blue denim shirt, and Mexican short jacket. He brushed the dust from his hat and his boots with his dirty shirt, then put the handbill describing the wanted men in his pocket. He shoved his rifle and his saddlebags under the bed, then took one last look in the mirror. He turned the lamp down till it produced only a soft glow, then stepped into the hall and locked the door. Then, ignoring the desk clerk as he passed, he walked through the lobby and stepped out on the boardwalk.

29

★

He stood in front of the hotel for a while, then crossed the street to a well-lighted restaurant. A pretty dark-haired hostess met him at the door and escorted him to a table. "A waiter will be with you in just a moment, sir," she said, then cut a wide swath back to the front of the building.

A tall, skinny young man stood beside the table within a matter of seconds. "Good evening," he said. He laid a bill of fare at Hemphill's elbow, and continued to talk: "You might want to try our special seafood platter, sir. You get breaded shrimp, stuffed crabs, scallops—"

"I'll have a T-bone steak," Hemphill interrupted. "It might be the only thing on your menu that I understand."

Having halted in midsentence, the young man stood with his mouth open for a moment, then said, "Certainly, sir." He picked up the bill of fare and headed for the kitchen.

Though Hemphill had to wait a little longer than usual for his food, once it was on the table he very quickly decided that he had never been served a better meal. The meat was tender enough to cut with a fork, and the bread, sliced from a large, fresh-baked loaf, was still hot enough to melt the butter the waiter brought to the table. The young man also set a large clay bowl in front of Hemphill, then pointed to its steaming contents. "The chef sent you a free bowl of his seafood gumbo. He says if you like it, he hopes you don't forget where you got it."

Hemphill nodded, then emptied the bowl.

He was back on the boardwalk a short time later, strolling up one side of the street and down the other. He passed many saloons, and a few times even poked his head over the batwing doors for a quick look inside. He had been walking for almost an hour when he finally decided to check out the saloon with the most horses tied out front. He was just about to enter the Horseshoe Saloon when he suddenly stopped in his tracks.

There, standing at the hitching rail, was a big piebald much like his own. He looked in both directions very quickly, then leaned back against the wall, his eyes glued to the big animal. It was not the horse that had captured his interest, but its brand: big enough that it could even be read by someone with poor eyesight, a 2C stamp had been burned into the animal's hip.

When Hemphill moved to the hitching rail for a closer inspection, he noticed that the big bay standing beside the piebald wore the same brand. Any doubts that he might have had were gone now. These animals had definitely been raised on Dan Copeland's ranch. He moved back to the wall and stood thinking. Had he found the wanted men already? Was it going to be this easy?

He hesitated no longer. He moved his Colt up and down a few times to make sure it was riding loose in its holster, then stepped up to the batwing doors and shouldered his way through. He moved away from the door quickly, then stood leaning against a post while he waited for his eyes to adjust. He believed there were about twenty men in the room, although he could make out few faces at the moment. He was unconcerned about the twins seeing him before he saw them, for he doubted that either man even knew he existed.

When his eyes finally adjusted to the dim lighting, he saw the twins very clearly. They were seated at a poker table across the room and catercorner to his own position at the post. He moved to the opposite side of the bar and took a seat on a stool. He now had a better view of the five-handed card game, and even through the haze of tobacco smoke, he could read the expressions on the faces of the Copelands. Someone at the table had obviously just said something funny, for both of the twins were laughing loudly enough to be heard across the room.

A tall, skinny bartender suddenly appeared in front of Hemphill, blocking his view of the gamblers. "What'll it be?" he asked. "We just got in a load of the good stuff from San Antonio yesterday, if you're a whiskey drinker."

The last thing Hemphill wanted at the moment was something that might cloud his thinking. He shook his head. "No, thank you," he said. "I'll stick with beer tonight."

The bartender set the brew in front of Hemphill, then picked up his coin and shuffled off down the bar.

Hemphill wet his lips with the white foam, but did not drink. He liked a cold beer as well as the next man, but tonight was hardly the time for drinking. He was a man on a mission, and the only reason he had bought the brew was to keep from looking out of place at the bar.

He continued to watch the card game for more than an hour, noting that one or the other of the Copelands appeared to be winning most of the pots. If this was their lucky night, he hoped it ran out when they left the poker table. He wet his lips again, then set the mug down noisily, for a new idea had just occurred to him.

He slid off the stool and headed for the front door. At the doorway, he took one last look at the poker table, then stepped through the batwings. He checked the street to make sure no one was around to see his actions, then untied the 2C horses from the hitching rail. He wrapped their reins around the saddle horns, then began to fan the air with his hat. Even before the animals had disappeared into the night, Hemphill was back on the boardwalk leaning against the building—waiting.

The wait was not a long one. He heard the Copelands laughing even before they reached the doorway. When they finally stepped through the batwings they were almost shoulder to shoulder, and both were still chuckling. "I knew that old fart was bluffing right from the start," Mark was saying as they absentmindedly walked across the boardwalk toward the hitching rail. "That's why—" He suddenly halted in midsentence and stood with his mouth open. "Why, somebody stole our horses!" he said loudly.

The twins rushed to the rail as if to verify the absence of their animals, and when they did, Hemphill stepped in behind them, careful to stand at an angle where no stray bullet was likely to find a human target inside the saloon. He spread his legs and leaned forward in the well-known gunfighter's crouch, then spoke loudly: "Raise your hands, Mark and Matthew Copeland! You're wanted for murder in Hamilton County!"

The command was ignored. The Copelands whirled instantly, drawing their weapons as they did so. And though they got off a total of three shots, all went harmlessly into the ground. Neither man had been able to lift his arm for a level shot at Hemphill, for both had taken a .45 slug in the chest as they turned. After tottering for a few moments, first Matthew, then Mark fell to the ground and lay staring into the night through sightless eyes.

In response to the sound of the gunshots, a crowd of men quickly gathered in front of the saloon. "What's going on out here?" a man asked from the doorway, then stepped out on the boardwalk as if expecting an answer.

Still holding his Peacemaker in his hand, Hemphill asked a question of his own: "Will one of you fellows go get the town marshal?"

"I'll be happy to do that," the same man said. "By God, Ernie'll get to the bottom of this right quick." Moving almost at a trot, he disappeared down the street.

The town marshal, a thirty-five-year-old six-footer named Ernest Tidwell, was on the scene quickly, along with a deputy he introduced as Lonny Brown. After checking for any signs of life, Tidwell pointed to the bodies. "I reckon I'll have to listen to your side of the story," he said, "since them fellers ain't in no shape to do no talking."

Hemphill nodded. "My name is Clay Hemphill, Marshal, and I've been a Hamilton County deputy sheriff for years. I resigned two weeks ago so I'd be free to hunt these killers down." He took the handbill and the picture from his pocket and handed them over. "They're the Copeland twins, and they killed a man during a botched bank robbery in Hamilton. The handbill will tell you all about it, and the picture should be proof enough that I got the right men."

The marshal read the handbill first, then squatted beside the bodies, looking back and forth between their faces and the picture several times. "Sure ain't no question about you having the right men," he said finally. "You resigned from the sheriff's office so you could turn bounty hunter?"

"No," Hemphill said quickly. "I resigned so I could hunt down the men who killed my best friend. I intend to give the reward money to his wife and kids."

"Hmm," the deputy said. "Ain't many fellers would do that."

Marshal Tidwell held on to the picture and the handbill for a moment longer, then handed them back to Hemphill, saying, "Like I said, there ain't no identity problem here, and I think it's mighty white of you to give the money to that woman and her kids." He pointed to the bodies again, then added, "You got the money to pay for burying them rascals?"

Hemphill nodded. "Probably. How much do you think it'll cost?"

"A double funeral's gonna cost twenty dollars," Tidwell said. "My brother's the undertaker, so you can just give the money to me and I'll pass it on to him."

Hemphill handed over a double eagle. "I'll appreciate it if you and your deputy will write something saying you witnessed the dead bodies of these killers, Marshal. I'll be needing something to prove to the folks back home that the Copeland twins are out of business."

Tidwell nodded and pocketed the money, then spoke to one of the men in the crowd. "Go wake my brother up and tell him to get these bodies outta the street, Frog." The man nodded, then headed up the street.

The marshal stood watching till the man was out of sight. Then he turned back to Hemphill. "You asked us to put something in writing," he said. "If you'll follow us down to the office we'll take care of that right now." The lawmen led off, and Hemphill fell in behind. A short time later, they stepped into a small brick building two blocks away and on the opposite side of the street from the saloon.

The marshal wasted no time. He turned his desk lamp up brighter, then sat down and wrote a "to-whom-it-may-concern" letter on a small sheet of lined paper. Both he and his deputy signed the finished product, and then Tidwell handed it to Hemphill. "I guess this is the only thing you're gonna need," he said, "so I reckon you'll be getting on out of town now."

Believing that he had heard more than a suggestion in the marshal's last remark, Hemphill nodded. "I'll be gone before you know it," he said. He pocketed the letter, then stepped through the doorway. He headed for his hotel room to pick up his saddlebags and his rifle, for he had no intention of spending the remainder of the night in this town. When he reached the Pelican he took the stairsteps two at a time, and three minutes later he was back on the street with his belongings.

Recalling the young redhead telling him that the livery stable stayed open all night, he headed for the huge building immediately. He found the kid sitting on a stool just inside the doorway. "I guess you've come after your horses," the young man said.

When Hemphill nodded, the boy took a lantern and a coil of rope and walked down the hall. A few minutes later, he led both of the animals to the front of the building. With both man and boy working, they had the saddle on the piebald and the packsaddle on the bay in short order. Hemphill paid the youngster for the animals' lodging, then shoved his Henry in the boot. "Thank you, son, and good luck to you." He mounted and rode out of the barn, then headed north at a trot. He expected to be home in eight days. Nine, at the most.

COPELAND TWINS DIE IN HAIL OF GUNFIRE the headlines of central Texas newspapers proclaimed a few days later, and both the Hamilton and Gatesville editors had chosen to announce that a former Hamilton County deputy sheriff named Clay Hemphill was the man who had brought them down.

A week before Christmas, the anonymous donor made an appearance in the Hamilton County sheriff's office. "Here's that thousand dollars I pledged for the reward," Dan Copeland said as he dropped a cloth bag containing fifty double eagles on the sheriff's desk. "They buried my grandsons down there at Corpus Christi, but I'm gonna have 'em dug up and brought back to the ranch." He turned and headed for the open doorway, adding over his shoulder, "The boys had the Curse, but they were blood."

"Curse?" Sheriff Bench asked loudly. He trotted across the room and poked his head through the doorway. "A curse, you say? What curse?"

He got no answer.